MEET ME AT FOUNTAIN PARK

Meet Me at Fountain Park

MINDY KILLGROVE

Contents

Chapter One

Can Moments Like These Last Forever?

I wish that sometimes I would just learn to shut my big mouth. Or perhaps it's not my mouth that keeps getting me into trouble. No, it might just be my emotions that I have to learn to check before they start running wild. Apparently, today, my sentiments are trying to get me into some kind of awful mess.

While telling someone that you love them is not a terrible thing to do, it does often produce a moment of anxiety on behalf of the speaker. I now find myself in that precarious situation. My ex-boyfriend, Nathan Hamilton, called me a few moments ago. I probably shouldn't have answered the phone, but I desperately wanted to talk to him.

Even though Nathan had initially plunged right into a story about work, I wasn't listening. My mind was embarking on its own journey elsewhere. In the wake of a tidal wave of good news poured forth by all my friends, I was feeling a bit personally underwhelmed. I was thinking that I should have something wonderful happening in my life too. Brooklyn was moving in with Duke. Adair was marrying Wesley. Oh, and Benson and Jack were going to leap across the country in search of super-stardom. With their triumphs ringing in my ears, I knew what I had to do.

I wasted no time in my own quest for happiness. As soon as I had the opportunity, I told Nathan that I loved him. Now that I have said it--now that I have put myself out there--all I can do is wait.

The most perfect moment in the world is the one that occurs directly after you have taken the leap. In love, this usually means that on impulse you've said something life-altering . . . and most often the words "love" are tangled in this act. There is a mystical time span that exists between your utterance and when other people respond to your actions. In that interim, all is right in the world. You have just done something that no one, including yourself, thought that you could (or would) ever do. In that moment, you are free to bask in your own glory and soak up the internal praise that is certainly coursing through your head. Congratulations, you have just put your heart on the line.

But, as with all moments of perfection, this good feeling will come to an end.

If your original actions were heroic, you might be greeted by applause on the other end. If your intentions were sneaky, you might be rewarded with a sly wink from a co-conspirator. But, if your moment of daring was like mine and it involved telling the former love of your life that you are still smitten by him, your moment of happiness will be shattered by laughter. And it won't be the kind of laughter that you want to be a part of. It will be the kind of laughter that echoes in your ears and comes back to haunt you later. It will be the kind of laughter that hurts and continues to penetrate your feelings even after it has died away.

A few moments ago, I got swept up in the moment, and now I am sorely regretting my actions. But really, I feel like I'm not totally to blame here.

I think that I will place the culpability on my friend, Jessica Adair. She knew that I was feeling lousy and a little worthless.

She could read it in my face. Everyone else in my life, all of my other friends, had something magnificent happening to them, and here I was, floating. I'm not trying to make the situation worse than it is here. I'm just trying to say that my life was stagnant, while they all seemed to be soaring. She picked that very moment to spring on me the most important news of her life: She was getting married.

This was no small feat; for Jessica Adair to be the first of my friends to take a trip down the altar really meant something. She had always been the loudest, wildest, most promiscuous one of the bunches, and I felt a little betrayed to learn that she was going to be getting married.

In a fit of what can only be called insanity, I told Nathan that I love him. The two of us have a very long history that is riddled with cheating and fighting. But when it comes down to it--I can't live without him. He's my air. And so it was, as I mulled over Jessica Adair's gigantic glittering engagement ring, that I decided to take matters into my own hands.

Instead of telling me that he loved me back and professing that he just couldn't live without me, he started laughing. I'm sure that he meant it in a good-natured way, but it still stung. What I wanted and what I was going to get were not meant to coincide today.

"Why aren't you laughing?" he finally asked. I wondered if he was wiping away his moistened eyes. Anytime that Nathan was in the midst of enjoying a really good joke, he would tear up. This is a strange trait that he and I shared. A long time ago, we would spend hours making each other cry and laugh at the same time just for sport.

Why wasn't I laughing? That was a pressing question. Here's the thing, girls. (Be sure that you listen closely on this one.) When it comes to matters of the heart, there are times when it's okay not to laugh. It's perfectly acceptable to stand your ground (and maybe feel a little bit saddened) even when everyone else around you is celebrating, or laughing jovially. If you have conviction and you truly believe in what you're saying, there's no need to slough it off. I loved him, and I didn't want to laugh about it--not that I could tell him any of that.

"I dunno," I said, then shrugged. I realized as I was doing it that the gesture was useless. He couldn't see me, of course.

"Missy," he said, pulling my name out long in an almost-taunt, "Is something wrong with you?" I thought about my response for a minute, and then I opted for the high road.

"Nothing's wrong, Nate. I just wanted to tell you how much I loved having you in my life again. Remember when we didn't talk for like two months last year? That was awful."

"That was awful," he agreed mechanically.

"So, what's going on with you tonight?" I asked.

"I don't plan on getting into too much trouble, if that's what you mean." I could tell that he was smiling.

"You've got a date with your video games, don't you?" I questioned.

"Yep," he replied. From the immediate contrast in his voice, I wondered if he had just started up the game console. He already had that glazed over sort of tone and I thought that I probably better get out while I could.

"Hey, listen, before you get too caught up in your games tonight, I just wanted to let you know that Jessica Adair is getting married."

I had his attention now.

"Adair? Really?" He really didn't have to sound that incredulous, I started to chide, but then caught myself—I couldn't believe it at first, either.

"Yep! She just showed me the engagement ring." I felt a little weird gushing about something like this to Nathan, but I wanted to tell someone Jessica's good news.

"Are you in the wedding?" he asked.

"Sure," I said, involuntarily shrugging again.

"That's cool. If you need a date, I'll go with you."

I couldn't believe he said the words, even as they were coming out of his mouth. Did he just volunteer to go as my date to a wedding? Unfathomable.

"Really?" My right eyebrow began to twitch. Sometimes my right eyebrow has a mind of its own. Whenever I'm slightly suspicious of someone or their motives, my face goes a little haywire.

"Sure," he replied in a nonchalant way. I could hear his fingers start to move on the game controller. I knew that I had to hurry this conversation up before he was completely gone.

But before I could chime in, he added, "Remember, Missy, I knew all of those girls in college, too. I know Jessica Adair. I wouldn't mind seeing her get married."

"Wouldn't mind seeing her get married . . ." I repeated that phrase silently to myself. This was a first for Mr. Nathan Hamilton. To my knowledge, he wasn't really a wedding kind of guy. For the first time in a long time, I began to question how much I really knew about Nathan. Maybe he'd grown up just a smidge. A girl could hope.

"That's pretty nice of you, Nathan. Thanks for the offer."

I pretended to check my watch. This didn't compute for two reasons: 1. Again, he couldn't see me and 2. I don't wear a watch. I must've been really flustered to keep making all these strange and totally unnecessary body movements.

"Well, look at the time. I better let you go," I said quietly into the phone.

"Thanks, Miss--g'night," he replied. I couldn't even bid him a good night as well, because the connection suddenly ended. I pictured him sitting on his couch, video game blaring, a bowl of Cheesy Puffs to his right, and the phone falling into his lap. Before I could get too entangled by this vision of Nathan, I decided to consider his wedding date proposition.

I would want *someone* to accompany me to the reception. Nathan did feel like the logical choice because he knew the bride. But . . . why couldn't he just say that he loved me? I couldn't help but think this over. Even if he had to qualify it in some sort of way, I'm sure that he could have said it. I mean, we have enjoyed getting to know each other again, and certainly somewhere deep inside of him, he is relieved that we are friends now. So perhaps he could have just said that he loved me but added a tag on the end like: "I love you, Missy. I'm so glad that we can be friends again." That sounds okay, right?

The truth was: I really *needed* him to say it. I really needed to hear that someone out there in the world loved and cared about me. Feeling shaken and downtrodden, I decided to continue my moping in the privacy of my own apartment.

As I trudged towards the landing that was just outside my apartment complex, I looked around. When I left the Pond earlier this evening, I had not taken much notice of the weather. I knew that it was unseasonably cold for May, and I had thought to bring a blazer with me, so I was covered. But now that I was leaving the blustery winds for the warmth of my apartment, I looked around to see that a massive storm was brewing just overhead. I sprinted up the stairs quickly, unlocked the door, and rushed around the place, closing all the windows.

When I finished my chore and finally circled back into the living room, I was stunned to see that neither of my roommates--Eve, nor my little sister, Hope--were around. It was getting to be pretty late, and I had expected them home. I didn't like the idea that they were outside right now. Judging by the wind, it would be raining here within the next few minutes. I did my best not to worry about them. They were grown adults, I told myself.

Instead of fretting about my roomies, I decided to do a few more household tasks. After I finished folding the laundry and putting it away, I found that my mind was still preoccupied by Nathan and his dismissal of my feelings. Wanting to win back some of my glorious outlook from earlier in the evening (before Nathan discharged my declaration), I changed the sheets on my bed and put on a new pair of pajamas. As I crawled into bed and turned on the television, I began to feel calm. This had been a really exciting day, and I was glad that it was coming to an end. I allowed myself to nestle down into the soft cream-colored pillowcase and for the first time in what seemed like a really long time, I had peaceful thoughts.

I was still feeling pretty spectacular and almost serene, until the next morning when my alarm started beeping. It was fairly early in the morning. For someone like me who works in television, saying that it was early means that not even the birds were up at this hour. But if I wanted to be ready by the time Autumn came pounding on my door, I had to get myself up and motivated.

Yesterday, before we met all the girls at the Pond, Autumn came across a pair of running sneakers that just ventured into "cute" territory. When she tried on the pair of shoes, she said that it felt like "coming home again." Autumn had always enjoyed working out and had even been on the cross-country team in high school, but she had not given any serious thought to running in the last few years.

Inspired by the sale price that was attached to the running shoe, and the fact that Paul--a particularly handsome previous boyfriend--had drifted back into her life, she made the purchase. Minutes later, she was telling me that the shoes were a sign from God: She was meant to run a marathon.

Some people might laugh about this, but if you knew Autumn, you wouldn't laugh. She took her shoes very seriously and if she believed that one pair of them was a signal from the universe to change her life; she was going to do it. It was funny because Autumn and I had just been teasing each other about Shoe Karma. I totally believe that shoes can make a world of difference in how you feel and how well your day will go. Autumn's skepticism is always bouncing back and forth on the topic, but after reuniting with Paul--the man with the most incredible hair I have ever seen-- and agreeing to go on a date with him, she was feeling that perhaps the theory of Shoe Karma wasn't so silly after all. (Frankly, I can't account for why she and I continue to have this argument as it is perfectly clear that Autumn believes in Shoe Karma, but we do. I think this is just one of Autumn's special quirks. She doesn't want to put her total faith in anything cosmic.)

On our way to the Pond yesterday, Autumn told me that I didn't have to run the marathon with her; at which point I was able to release a huge sigh of relief. I don't think I could pound out a half marathon, let alone a full; thankfully, she just wanted to train with me. Autumn knows--and I'm sure that most other people guess--that since I make my living by appearing on television, I have to stay fit. I work out every day and I try to run about four or five times a week. I don't do anything severe, like running marathons, but I jog anywhere from two to five miles a session. I used to try to keep up with Heidi Klum when she would blog about her running, but I found that task to be a little bit tedious. I design my own workouts, and generally I run alone. I am willing to make an exception for Autumn. Even the fact that she wanted to run really early in the morning didn't bother me. I figured that if I got my workout out of the way early, then I'd have the rest of the day to focus on other things that I enjoyed. It was sound thinking, and for the most part, I was glad to have Autumn as a new running partner. I would never recommend running through the city's morning darkness by oneself. I make it a strict priority to consider my own safety in this world. Safety first, that's the rule.

I quickly slid out of bed and pulled on a pair of jogging shorts, a sports bra, and an old t-shirt. I was just lacing up my tennis shoes when Autumn opened the door. I knew that she was on her way, so it was no surprise when she entered without knocking. I didn't want to wake my roommates, after all. During one of my nighttime treks to the bathroom, I noticed that both girls had made it home safely. I was less than exuberant to see that Eve had left her muddy shoes by the door and Hope had made messy sneaker tracks all the way to her bedroom, but I (or they) would have time to clean it all later.

After fretting over the possible carpet stains again, I turned to look at Autumn. She was electric--literally. From head-to-toe, she was clad in neon colors, except for her running shoes. She had on a blazing pink headband that matched her Adidas printed shirt. Her shorts were a kicked-up azure blue, and her socks, if you can believe this, were lime green.

"What's with this outfit?" I said, snickering simultaneously. My hand quickly flew to my mouth as I remembered that I should try to not wake my roommates.

Autumn pulled me quickly out into the hallway. She waited patiently while I locked the door and stowed the key in my shoe.

"Nothing," she said, and shrugged. She seemed to enjoy the motion, so she began rolling her shoulders back and forth. "I was just really excited about going for a run today, so I dug out all of my old favorite running clothes."

"Seriously?" I asked.

"Yep," she answered, and nodded enthusiastically.

"Well, I guess the good thing about this outfit choice is that I'll be sure not to lose you once we get started."

"Actually, that is the whole idea. Haven't you ever been told that when you run in the dark, you're supposed to wear light colors so that you can be spotted by other runners, and cars, if you go into the street?" She asked this question and began looking over my own outfit selection. My grey t-shirt and black shorts admittedly looked a little shabby next to her knockout neon attire.

"Uh-huh, I've heard that. But I wasn't under the impression that you were supposed to illuminate the night with your running clothes." I tried to joke with her.

She looked down now at her own outfit. "Is it really that bad?"

I contemplated her question before answering, "Yes," I said calmly. "It's really that bad."

We both smiled at each other and started to bounce down the staircase.

"Look," I continued, "you should wear neon colors, with this I agree. But you could tone it down a tad."

"What do you mean?" Autumn said, giving me a quizzical look.

"I mean that you could wear only one piece of neon at a time, or you could throw some white in the mix. White is considered a light color as well, and it's not nearly as blinding as this ensemble." I gestured to her wild outfit again.

"Okay, okay, I get it. You hate my outfit," she said in a resigned way.

"No, no, I love your enthusiasm, but it does feel weird for *me* to be giving *you* fashion advice. You're normally so capable. Is something else going on?" I looked her way quickly and then I nodded my head. It was time to start running.

She did one final calf stretch and then caught up with me. "Nothing's wrong," she said slowly. I could tell that she was already thinking about her breathing and wanting to make it flow naturally during this first marathon training session.

"You sure?" I asked and decided to slow my run to more like a jog. I knew that Autumn was ambitious, but I figured that I probably shouldn't start out our runs together by sprinting away from her.

She nodded gratefully at the pace decrease and took another deep breath. "Nothing's wrong, really. I just feel like so much is changing."

I laughed, which was hard to do while I was jogging. "You think?" I snorted.

"You don't think?" she asked. She hadn't picked up on my sarcasm because she had been checking her pedometer.

"No, no, I totally agree with you. Last night was amazing. I can't believe what is happening to all of our friends."

"I know," she exhaled. "I thought that my encounter with Paul was pretty great, until I heard everyone else's news."

"Yeah, and you haven't even heard the best part yet." As soon as I had the words out of my mouth, I wanted to retract them. I wasn't sure if Adair had given me permission to talk about her engagement. I tried to replay our conversation in my head, but that just brought up the echoes of Nathan's laughter. I shook my head quickly, as if I could wipe away that painful memory, but it just wouldn't work.

"What're you talking about? What's the best part?" Autumn was now right beside me. Her lengthy legs managed a slightly longer stride than mine, so I had to readjust my pacing again now so that I could run in time with her.

"Did you hear about Jack and Benson?" I thought that I might be able to throw Autumn off by bringing up something that was fairly obvious.

"Yeah, I caught it," she grunted and looked at me in a weird way.

"What?" I asked.

"Don't *what*, me. You weren't talking about Jack and Benson. Were you?" Apparently, her endorphins had started to kick in by this time. Even though her statement began a little hard-nosed, she was smiling by the end. It was lucky for me, because I didn't actually want to deceive Autumn; I wanted to tell her about Adair, but I also didn't want to spoil the surprise.

"I was totally talking about Jack and Benson. I just assumed that you missed all the excitement because you were busy gloating over Paul," I said in a teasing manner, hoping that the mention of Paul again would be enough to keep her preoccupied.

"Paul is sort of great," she sighed and luckily her breathing was relaxing now. I could tell that she was enjoying this run, almost as much as she was enjoying the memory of their impromptu rendezvous yesterday. I allowed her to wallow in that memory for a few minutes. I focused on the path ahead of us, and just sort of coasted in the morning breeze. The morning after a storm is always pleasant, I think. It's like the world has been renewed.

After a span of time, I turned my head slightly, so that I could evaluate my running companion. She seemed to be doing well, so I delved back into the conversation.

"So, when are the two of you going out? I can't remember. Too much happened yesterday," I said and checked my iPod. I realized that we had been jogging for a while now. I didn't want to exhaust Autumn on the first day, so I pointed towards a small path that would lead to a park.

We veered slightly to the left and she let the question sit for a small amount of time. She seemed to be thinking about her answer, "I think that we're going to go out next weekend. I was actually hoping that we'd see each other on Saturday night, but now, I don't know."

"What's up? Is something wrong with Saturday night?" I frowned a little.

"Well, we put together a lot of different plans before Jack and Benson are supposed to leave. I just don't want to miss out on any of those, but it seemed like a lot of obligations."

"Really?" I hadn't thought about this fact. When the girls had started to plan out the next two weeks of our lives, I hadn't been paying attention. I mean, I knew that Jack and Benson were leaving for L.A. in two weeks, but I didn't know what we had planned beforehand.

"Really," Autumn sighed heavily. "The girls want to get together and do something almost every night. You know that I love Jack and Benson, but I was feeling a bit overwhelmed."

"I get it--I do," I added quickly. I didn't want Autumn to feel guilty. I loved my friends too, but I didn't think that it would be necessary to spend every waking minute with them before they left, either. (Nor did this arrangement seem pragmatic; Benson and Jack would have a great deal to accomplish before their trek across the country.)

Suddenly, I was struck with an idea.

"Autumn, tell me what you think about this plan: What if, instead of us trying to carve out a piece of time every day to spend with the girls, we all just devote one weekend?"

Autumn looked thoughtful.

"Here's what I'm thinking: Next weekend, we'll all meet at your house for a slumber party. We'll do it up old-school style. We can watch girly movies, read fashion magazines, paint our nails, and whatever else. Then, in the morning, we head to the Pond. After some brunch, we'll do a quick shopping trip, and then cap off the night with a small, but fun, going away party. What do you think?"

She didn't even have to think it over. "Yes, Missy! That would be so much better. Can we make this happen?"

"Can we make this happen?" I scoffed. "Yes, my dear, we can." With that, I took off at a sprint.

I wasn't trying to be annoying. I usually try to sprint the last two hundred meters of my run. It was about that time.

A few seconds later, Autumn caught up to me.

"Why can't moments like this last forever?" Autumn said, and the statement was spot-on. This was a wonderful moment. I felt good. My muscles felt warm. The air was luxurious. I didn't really want this moment to end, either. I fell into an easy walk and took a few moments to suck in air.

"You know," I said, "I really don't want Jack and Benson to leave."

"Me neither," she replied. "It won't be the same without them."

"*We* won't be the same without them," I amended and gave Autumn a small smile.

We continued to walk back to my apartment complex. When we reached the door, Autumn and I went our separate ways. As I was climbing the stairs back to my home, I couldn't help but be grateful for Autumn. I silently thanked my lucky stars for allowing Autumn to come into my life.

"I can't believe this is it," Adair said loudly. We were sitting at brunch on Saturday morning. Our last weekend with Benson and Jack had been priceless, so far. The sleepover last night felt reminiscent of the times that we would camp out in each other's dorm rooms in college. Waking up this morning and rolling out to the Pond also seemed like something that we used to do a long time ago. I didn't want to have that feeling just yet about the Pond, but even as it was happening, I knew that this place would never be the same for our group. This restaurant would very soon become one of the places that we *used* to go.

"Me neither," I agreed. I hugged my mug of hot chocolate to my chest. Even though it was pleasant outside today, I still felt cold.

"Stop! You guys," Benson whined a little. Tiny tears were shining in the corners of her eyes. I was fairly certain that she was rethinking her offer to join Jack. Since the school year was over, Benson didn't have any work obligations, but she was going to be forced to get a job this summer. She knew that since she was moving, she was going to be incurring all sorts of unexpected debts. To that end, she'd been searching online all week, trying to find a decent summer job. I felt sorry for her. She was leaving her friends; her boyfriend, Brian; her family; and her comfortable living, for what? A chance to hang out with Jack? Not to Jack's discredit, because I love her dearly, but it didn't sound like such a bargain for Benson. I was hoping with all my might that this would be a good decision for her.

While we all took turns soothing Benson, I allowed myself a second to check out Jack. The aura around her was shining. I don't actually believe in any of that celestial nonsense (aside from Shoe Karma, of course), but I do maintain that when people have a sunny disposition, it will shine through. Today, Jack was luminescent. She seemed much calmer than I'd expected, but she also appeared to be totally radiating energy. I wanted to scoot my chair in her direction so that I could soak up some of her good vibes. As luck would have it, she caught me staring at her. She shot a wink my way and I nodded in response.

Then, we all settled into a comfortable silence. I sipped my hot chocolate while Brooklyn poured more coffee into her cup. Autumn cut her pancake into small pieces and Benson put some Tabasco Sauce on her eggs. I noticed, while I watched everyone go about their brunching routines that we functioned like a small family unit. We knew who would need the syrup on their side of the table (Jack) and on which end the coffee pot should rest (Brooklyn). We knew when it was okay to have small side conversations and when it was appropriate to devote all ears to a particular speaker. I couldn't help but to echo Autumn's sentiments from our first running session: Why can't moments like these last forever?

I didn't want Jack to leave, but I knew that it would be best for her. Once I could accept that fact, I handled her move appropriately. But my mind floated back to Benson. What was she going to do? I couldn't let her do it. I just couldn't allow her to make this colossal mistake. My mind (and my eyes) flooded with tears. I had to stop her.

At that moment, it was as if Adair sensed that I was about to do something stupid. She put her hand in front of me, pushing me back a little way from the table. It was the same motion a parent might make when they suddenly pull to a stop in the car. She was protecting me (like a child) from making a huge blunder. She shook her head twice and I ducked mine in shame and frustration. I knew what I thought was best, and I just couldn't see the sense in concealing it any longer.

"Guess what, ladies?" Adair said loudly and all eyes swiveled in her direction. It had been a long time since Adair had shared any news with the table. Since she had been dating Wesley, her wild stories weren't quite so reckless. As a matter of fact, she hardly graced us with tales of her escapades at all any-more. I knew then that she was saving me from looking the fool by sacrificing her own very good news. I didn't actually understand why she had chosen to keep her engagement a secret from the girls, but I was relieved that she was finally deciding to tell them about it--even if she was only doing it to shut me up.

"I have big news, everyone, but I refuse to share it if..." She nodded at each one of us in turn, "any of you decide that now is the time to be hysterical." She stopped her eyes right on me and I knew what she was really threatening. *If you bother Benson and try to detract her from moving, I won't share my engagement news.*

"We'll behave ourselves; we promise," I said solemnly and realized that I actually meant it. I desperately wanted to keep Benson here, but I also knew that my opinion didn't really matter in this situation. Both Benson and Jack were grown adults. If they wanted to catapult halfway across the country, my only job was to be there when they needed someone to man the safety nets.

"What? What's going on? Just tell us already," Brooklyn said, busily buttering her bagel, so she wasn't really catching the solemn looks that passed amongst our group. As she reached for the jar of honey to add to her spread, she noticed that everyone was sitting on the edge of their seats.

"Why so tense?" Brooklyn jabbed at me with her butter knife. I nodded my head towards Adair and Brooklyn noticed for the first time that she was the only one at the table who was not staring at the massive engagement ring now covering Adair's ring finger.

"Well, hot damn," Brooklyn said under her breath. I only caught this phrase because I was sitting directly next to her.

"No way," Jack mumbled in a small voice. Even though we must have looked mighty strange, our group of girls just sat and marveled. We all looked from Adair to the ring and back, but somehow no one was able to coax real speech from their lips.

"I'm engaged," Adair whispered, with a smile gracing her lips. The Pond had never been as quiet as it was during this blessed announcement. I always hear people describing a splendid moment in time when the whole world stops and pays attention to them. This was Adair's moment. The atmosphere was saturated by her joyous news.

"Congratulations," I finally said, remembering my manners, and hoping to break the ice. Since I had known about the engagement previously, it was easier for me to snap out of the trance. But I must admit, the whole situation was a bit breathtaking. If I hadn't already been aware of Adair's new relationship status, I probably would've been awestruck for quite some time.

"The ring's beautiful," Benson said and wrapped her arms around Adair's neck. Both girls hugged and laughed. Then, I saw Adair wipe at some tears. I couldn't recall the last time that I'd seen Adair cry, but I was happy to see the tears sliding down her face now. Autumn, with her quick-thinking ways, thrust a few napkins in Adair's direction. Jess quickly dabbed at her face, trying to capture the tears before they ruined her flawlessly applied makeup.

Then, for what seemed like no reason at all, I began to cry. I wasn't sure if I was upset or happy, to be perfectly honest. I should clarify. I knew that I was ecstatic for Adair. I could feel my happiness for her (and Wesley) deep down in my bones. But I wasn't really sure if that emotion warranted the presence of tears. Just as I was about to place my finger on the source, I decided that it didn't matter. It felt good to allow the tears to flow freely. I even managed to let a laugh to escape from my quivering lips. I know that I was mixing emotions here, but I couldn't help myself. My mind was frenzied.

The finality of this moment was palpable. Perhaps that was the real reason I was crying. As we all sat around the Pond together--Brooklyn, me, Autumn, Adair, Benson, and Jack--I knew that this would be the last time we would all be together like this. There was something surreal and infinitely bitter-sweet about this moment. While I knew that the girls were moving on to bigger and better things, I didn't want to let them go. Autumn pushed napkins in my direction, and I daubed at the large tears that were cascading down my face. I looked her way and noticed that she too had grabbed a stash of paper products. Even Brooklyn, the most stoic of us all, was allowing herself to enjoy a moment of weakness. She was crying softly.

What would I ever do without these girls?

Chapter Two

Are You Sure You're Not Mad?

"I need you to meet me, stat."

I'd just answered the phone and was pleasantly surprised to hear Adair's voice coming across the other end.

"Well, hello to you, too," I said sarcastically.

"Hi, my dear," Adair said backtracking and pretending to make nice.

"Hey, what's up?" I forged ahead. I balanced my phone delicately on my hand and pressed it back up to my ear. I shifted my weight uncomfortably as I tried to decide the best way to rearrange my grocery bags and keep the phone in place. Tricky . . . very tricky.

"Well, I really need your help." Adair appeared to be moaning, but that was out of character.

"Are you alright? Are you stuck somewhere?" Her voice sounded uncomfortable, so I figured that this was a valid conclusion to draw.

"Oh yeah," she said and heaved a huge breath. "I'm definitely trapped. Meet me at 422 South Samaritan Street as soon as you can." She let out another doozy of an exhale and the call ended. I just stared at my phone for a second.

What was at 422 South Samaritan Street? I was trying to recall this bit of information, but it was lost on me. I've never been very good with geography. As a matter of fact, I have a terrible sense of direction, so my mind was whirling as I tried to remember where in the world South Samaritan Street might even be.

Just as I was about to GPS the address and point my feet the right way, my phone rang again. It was Brooklyn.

"Good morning, sunshine," she said in a breezy tone. I was happy to hear from Brooklyn. I hadn't seen her since Jack and Benson's going away bash, and even then, we really didn't get a good chance to talk to one another. I know that it had only been a week, but that honestly did seem like a long time.

"Good morning, pal. What's the story this fine day?" As I was saying it, I remembered that I couldn't get too lost in conversation, even though I wanted to. I had to focus on finding Samaritan Street and rescuing Adair from whatever situation she had gotten herself into.

"Oh, nothing much going on here," Brooklyn laughed lightly, and I heard her makeup case clang shut. I figured that she had just prepared herself to go out on the town. It seemed a little early to be heading out on a Saturday morning, but who was I to talk? Here I was, wandering the streets, picking up grocery items, when I could be snug at home in bed. Even though the prospect of lying in bed all day sounded appealing, I had errands to run and I had decided to get a move on nice and early.

"Do you know where Samaritan Street is?" I asked Brooklyn.

"Sure," she said. "It's about a block over from Duke's apartment. Are you nearby? What're you looking for over there?"

"Okay, okay, hold on a sec," I replied as I put the phone and bags down on the sidewalk. I stooped for just a minute to tie my shoe and then I turned due east. I might not know the exact location of Samaritan Street, but at least I could navigate my way to Duke's apartment.

"You still there?" I asked as I picked the phone back up. I brushed street dust off the cover and went back to the conversation. I took just a quick second to line the grocery bags up properly so that I would easily be able to transfer them into a comfortable position in my hand. I really was making progress here. Even though I sound super uncoordinated right now, this menial task was becoming a daunting challenge, so I needed to brace myself and pile my belongings up in just the right way.

"Yes, yes, still holding for Missy Lawrence here," Brooklyn replied.

"Do you know of anything or anyone important who is located over on Samaritan Street?"

"Nothing comes to mind," Brooklyn responded.

"That's what I thought," I kept talking and picked up my pace. I wasn't necessarily pleased about the area which I was entering; the buildings were constructed closely together in this part of town. That doesn't absolutely mean there is a problem or that trouble will arise here, but I always find confined spaces to be a little bit unnerving. I could never live in these houses or apartments because I wouldn't want to wake up and be able to see inside my neighbors' windows. Just as I was thinking this, a slim woman came jogging out from between one of the buildings. Even though she startled me, she clearly meant me no harm. She was just out for a morning run. I wondered why she had chosen to run between the buildings. Maybe the entrance to her particular building was on the side. I ducked my head quickly to the left to get a closer look, but then decided that I could get lost pretty quickly if I didn't keep my head in the game.

"Missy? Missy? Are you still there?" Brooklyn was now hollering into the phone, as if she thought that the connection had waned. I must have really zoned out on her. Oops.

"What's going on with you this morning? You sound so weird and you're going to some undisclosed location. Are you chasing a lead?" Brooklyn was a smart lady. She knew that sometimes my job as a reporter could send me on some crazy wild goose chases, but I was fortunate; this didn't have to do with work, and I was off duty.

"No, no, nothing like that," I said. "I just got a very cryptic phone call from Adair telling me to meet her ASAP at 422 South Samaritan Street. Do you recognize the address?"

"Naw, but I can Whatslife it for you, if you want," she offered graciously. I thought about it but declined.

"No, it's okay. I'll find the place just fine and then I'll use my superhuman powers to rescue Jess from whatever debacle she's created."

"That sounds about right. I can just picture you tying your hair into a high ponytail, and then effortlessly lifting a car off the stricken maiden." I could hear Brooklyn push her hair away from the phone earpiece. I was beginning to wonder about all the noises occurring on the other end of the line.

"Well, we know that I'm tracking down Adair, but I cannot figure out what you're doing up so bright and early this Saturday morning? It sounds like you're getting ready to go out. Oh, is Duke taking you somewhere? Brunch, perhaps?"

"Puh-leeze. I wish." She scoffed and then I heard her keys jingle. She was definitely going somewhere.

"I'm going to meet Cara this morning," she finished.

"Really? What's up with Cara?" I asked. Brooklyn had been spending an awful lot of time with Cara lately. I knew that they had always been good friends, but I couldn't really understand how that worked. Cara was a party girl, but Brooklyn preferred to stay home and hang out with Duke. I shrugged. Maybe, I didn't need to understand their relationship. Maybe I was just a little jealous that Brooklyn was hanging out with Cara instead of me.

"Nothing's up with Cara. We're just going shopping and then we'll have lunch or something,"

Brooklyn said sounding nonchalant. But I felt like something was wrong. Something was missing.

"Oh, okay," I replied. I tried to match the carefree sound in her tone, but even I thought that I sounded odd.

"Listen, I have to ask you something," she paused. This seemed to have come out of the blue, but I decided to let her go with it.

"I'm listening," I said. I really didn't like the tone of her voice. I didn't really know what was wrong with this situation, but something felt off. I knew that Brooklyn and Cara hung out on a regular basis, so I didn't think this had anything to do with their shopping trip. If my ears weren't deceiving me, I'd say Brooklyn was beating around the bush.

"Ugh, I hate getting involved in all of this mess," Brooklyn sighed heavily. "Here's the thing, Missy. Cara wants me to ask you if you're still mad at her for stealing Mitch from you."

"Seriously? Seriously!" I said incredulously. "Is she serious?" I felt a shot of laughter bubble up in my stomach but my brain was working overtime right now. Before I could laugh, my head started to make some sense out of Brooklyn's statement.

A few weeks ago, I thought that I was dating Mitch Torino, a bartender at Hunter's Saloon. We went on a couple of dates and had a good time. Even though we weren't serious, I had miscalculated something that he said and I wound up thinking that he was my boyfriend . . . until he asked me if Cara would consider going out with him. When I realized my error, I was absolutely mortified, but I didn't kick up too much of a fuss when the pair finally hooked up. In truth, I hadn't really thought about the pair since then. I guess that I'd assumed they were now dating. That was about the end of that story, as far as I was concerned.

But now, what was this question about? What exactly had Brooklyn just said? My mental tape recorder played back the inquiry: "Cara wants me to ask you if you're still mad at her for stealing Mitch from you." Now, that question wasn't exactly on the mark, was it? I didn't consider the end of my relationship with Mitch to have occurred because Cara entered the picture. I certainly didn't view her as a thief. I took a deep breath and tried to contemplate how I actually felt about the whole situation.

When I thought that my ideas were coherent, I decided to answer Brooklyn.

"Nope," I said. It was concise, but it was truthful. That's what I was going for.

"Nope, what?" Brooklyn asked.

"Nope, I'm not mad at Cara," I answered. I elected to side-step the whole "stealing" accusation. Since I didn't think of it that way, there was no reason to continue with that line of thinking.

"Are you absolutely positive?" Brooklyn pressed.

"I swear," I said solemnly, and I meant it. I really wasn't upset with Cara, whatsoever.

"Ha! Cara has been so nervous for nothing," Brooklyn said, seeming to perk up instantly. She rushed into her next sentence, "I told her that you didn't care about Mitch. I told her that the two of you only dated casually and that you really didn't like him much, so it's no big deal."

"Hey," I interrupted. "I liked Mitch."

"Okay, okay, you liked Mitch, whenever you weren't ogling his older brother."

"You know that I had a thing for Joey first!"

"Ha!" Brooklyn taunted. "I'm just teasing and besides--do you really want to get into this conversation?"

I didn't even want to think about it. A few months ago, I had major crushes on both Joey and Mitch. The bartending brothers both worked at Hunter's Saloon. Interestingly enough, they lived together too. I really had been hardcore crushing on Joey, when suddenly and most unexpectedly, I had gotten into a relationship with Mitch. It was a messy situation. Adding Cara to the mix now was a bit bizarre, I will admit. But at least with her dating Mitch, I was free to check out Joey again. I'm sick, I know it, but I just can't help myself.

"Brooklyn, we're good. I swear. Please, relay *that* information to Cara."

"Done and done," Brooklyn said and snapped her fingers on the other end of the line. I pictured the bright red nail polish glittering on her fingers. It was a weird thing to think about right now, I know, but all the same, it came to mind.

Since my mind was a mess, and I clearly was spending too much time pondering Brooklyn's nail polish choice, I nearly walked right past my destination.

"Wait a second," I said into the phone, as my feet skidded against the uneven pavement. "Did I tell you that I was going to 422 South Samaritan Street?"

"That sounds right," Brooklyn answered.

"Well, I think I'm here."

"You think?"

"Okay, okay—retract that. I know I'm here. I can see the green numbers painted on the front porch rails. But this doesn't look like anything. It's just a house."

"Is that such a bad thing?" Brooklyn asked.

"No, I guess not. I just thought, by the way Adair sounded on the phone, that I really would be rescuing her from a hostage situation or something." I tried to joke about the subject matter, but I sort of had been worried about Adair. Now, standing on Samaritan Street, I couldn't wrap my mind around this being an emergency.

The house that was located at 422 Samaritan Street was quaint. It had been painted a brilliant white, at one time. The paint was only slightly faded now. The shutters and the trim were done in a rich forest green, and there were thin white lace curtains visible in the windows. The house didn't stand out from those around it, but it didn't blend in, either. There was something special about this location, but I just couldn't put my finger on it.

"Well, don't be too disappointed if you don't get to rescue someone today, Super Girl. I'm sure there will be plenty of chances in the future."

"Something just feels different about this place. I can't quite determine what vibe I'm picking up. I'm not sure if I should be scared or captivated."

"What do you mean?" Brooklyn asked.

"I don't know," I answered. "There is something . . . something special, I think, about this place. I'm just not . . ."

Brooklyn cut me off, "Do you need backup? Do you want me to swing by there?"

I considered her offer for a minute and then shook my head. "No, no, I really do think this place is all right, but it just doesn't match up," I shared, and then described the exterior to Brooklyn.

"I just don't see the problem, Missy," she said.

"The problem is this: This place is adorable, but when Adair called, she sounded distraught. The two ideas don't align."

"Well, you know there's only one way to get to the bottom of this mystery, Miss Reporter . . ." Brooklyn allowed her voice to trail off and I knew what I had to do. It was time to hitch up my big girl pants and head inside. I needed to help Adair, one way or the other.

"All right, I'm out of here. Wish me luck?" I said.

"Luck!" Brooklyn said brightly and I quickly ended the call. I thought about stashing the phone in my purse. If something was going to pop out from around the corner, I knew that it would be wise to have both hands free to defend myself. But then I recalculated the matter. If something really was wrong, I wanted my phone handy so that I could call the authorities as soon as possible.

I readjusted my grip on the phone and the bags that I held in my hands. I thought about ways that I could use the grocery bags and their contents to defend myself. The deodorant that was inside one of the bags wouldn't do me much good, but perhaps I could swing the bag at an assailant and knock him or her off their guard.

As I was mounting the steps to the front porch, I tried to calm myself down. I usually consider myself to be a rational person, but for some reason today, I was totally on edge. As I stood on the front stoop, I took two deep breaths to calm my nerves.

"Missy, this isn't a detective show on TV, and you aren't the heroine in a mystery novel. There is nothing weird going on here." I repeated this phrase to myself twice before I pushed open the screen door that led to the porch.

As I stood in the entryway to the house, I allowed myself to absorb my surroundings. It was beautiful here. I actually felt the tension that had accumulated in my muscles ease. Even though I wasn't inside the house yet, I was shocked to see the vibrant flower arrangement placed on a small table. The table itself was covered in white lace with a plate of glass encasing the delicate surface. The flowers were a gorgeous purple and they were not a variety that I easily recognized. I leaned forward and allowed myself a quick sniff of their aroma. Beautiful. Relaxing. I felt much better as my hand reached for the door handle.

I turned the knob and stepped across the threshold into the interior room. The scent of vanilla rushed to greet me. I smiled and closed my eyes automatically. I have always thought vanilla contained soothing powers. I allowed the atmosphere to soak in around me and envelop my earlier doubts. When I opened my eyes, I very quickly realized where I was, and I suddenly felt like a fool. Why hadn't I contemplated this before? I had no idea. I was way too quick to overreact.

I swiveled my head from side to side, looking for Adair. Now that I was at the designated location and I found it to be totally harmless, I was in much less of a rush to find her. Just as I was considering checking out the place on my own before I went to find my friend, I heard a shriek. It was unmistakably Jessica Adair's voice.

I began to sprint towards the area where the sound must have been produced. There, I found Jessica Adair, staring at herself in a mirror.

"What have they done to you?" I asked, a bit of incredulity registering in my tone.

"They've made me a bride," Adair whispered as she peered at herself in the full-length mirror.

"Yes, yes, they have," I said, circling Jessica quickly and finding a spot off to the right side. I just wanted to gaze at her for a moment. She was stunning. Right here, before my very eyes, stood one of my best friends, Jessica Adair. She had ditched her trademark hot pink stilettos for a pair of soft white kitten heels. In place of her perfectly tailored pencil skirt was a full, frothy rich white skirt. On top, she was wearing a completely silver sequined bodice. The dress was so gorgeous; I felt tears spring to my eyes.

"Jessica, I don't even know what to say." This sound came from the opposite corner of the room. It was Jessica's mother. She was standing close to her daughter, but I hadn't noticed her until she spoke. My eyes had been so glued to Adair that I had ignored everyone else in the room. I watched as Jessica's mother stepped up onto the platform with her daughter. She straightened the zipper in the back of the dress and pinched pleats into the tulle of the skirt.

I decided that I probably shouldn't be intruding on this affectionate moment between Jessica and her mother. I managed to avert my eyes from the bride-to-be long enough to scan the rest of the room.

We were in the dressing room of a place that I assumed was Samantha's Bridal Store. I came to this conclusion because there was a small stack of business cards placed on a table to my left. (A genius deduction, yes, I know.) I thought that Samantha's Bridal Store on Samaritan Street was sort of cute, so I decided to continue my appraisal of the room.

The dressing room was larger than anyone that I had ever been in before. There was one sizable "viewing area." This is the spot that we currently occupied, along with one oversized platform, a smattering of Victorian-style chairs, and two petite coffee tables sporadically placed. The coffee tables featured bridal magazines, swatches of colors, and of course, business cards.

There was also an ottoman placed near the landing of the platform. I assumed that the tailor would use this cushion when she went to work fitting the gowns.

Beyond this end of the store, (I should say house, but it just didn't feel like a house anymore) there were three booths that brides or bridesmaids used as fitting rooms. The stalls were made of handcrafted wood and had little ivy leaf accents painted on them in hunter green. As I took all of this in, I began to appreciate and understand the exterior decor, as it coordinated with the inside of the store nicely.

Once I had surveyed the room, my eyes began to focus on the other occupants. Aside from Adair and her mother, Jessica's little sister, Janet, was seated in one of the tallest chairs. She was leaning forward, trying to look absorbed by the whole gown trying on process. I say "trying" because she didn't really look enthralled. In fact, she looked a little bored. I imagined that she was either really envious or she was just plain unaffected. Jessica and her sister had a decent relationship, but they weren't best friends, so maybe this whole thing wasn't her idea of a good time.

Sitting beside Janet was a familiar face. The person in the chair was so fidgety that I should've recognized her earlier, and I would have had I not been so distracted by the amazing gown and the girl wearing it. To Janet's left was Sydney, a former college pal and a sorority sister. I started to ask what she was doing there, but then I remembered: Adair, Sydney, and I had met on our first weekend at school. We'd spent the entire night talking and flirting shamelessly with the boys in our dorm. We all had an instant connection. Later in the year, we decided to join the same sorority.

Even though I had lost contact with Sydney, it was apparent that she and Adair had remained friends. I realized instantly that Adair had chosen her bridesmaids based on the building blocks of her life. She selected her sister as the maid of honor because they had grown up together, but she had asked Sydney and me to be by her side because we had also grown up together; just in a different way. I felt a little honored that I was a part of this special circle of people.

I nodded my head in Sydney's direction, and she beamed back at me. I won't pretend that her positive greeting was because she was delighted by my presence. The last time that Sydney and I had interacted hadn't been pleasant, but I was glad that she was happy to let bygones be bygones. Frankly, I couldn't even recall why we loathed each other so much at the end of our undergraduate days, but our relationship had cooled significantly by the time we had graduated. I smiled in her direction again to let her know that I, too, was willing to let the past go. Just as I was about to say something, a woman from the shop--I'm guessing Samantha, herself--came around a thick velvet curtain carrying an assortment of veils.

Sydney popped up from her seat and raced to help Adair look through the selection. Between Adair, her mother, Sydney, and the salesclerk, I figured that my input wasn't necessary.

So again, I decided to settle back and absorb the scenery. This time, I focused on Sydney.

Why had I hated her in school? I just couldn't recall. I allowed my eyes to drink in her appearance. She looked pretty much the same, as we all did. After all, we weren't that far removed from the college circuit.

Sydney was a bit on the round side, except that she had very voluptuous curves. So perhaps she wasn't round at all; she was more buxom. Just as I was observing her figure, she fidgeted from side to side, and I recalled just how twitchy she could be. Sometimes, I thought that she did this to accentuate her figure, and maybe she did. But other times, like now, I believed that she was just dealing with a nervous habit.

I couldn't see her eyes quite clearly at present, but barring any decision to get colored contacts, Sydney had truly beautiful eyes. They were a sad grey color, but somehow, she made them sparkle. I think that was the part of her personality that I always liked best. Sydney wanted to be happy; she wanted to spread joy and warmth to those around her. Even when she was being a pain in the behind, she was doing it with a smile on her face. It was a lovable quality, and I must conjecture that her jovial attitude is the reason Adair kept her around.

Just as I was thinking all these things, Sydney displayed that elaborate sense of joy.

"Jessica!" she exclaimed. "This is it! This is the one!" In her hands she held a delicate white veil. From where I was sitting, it looked a little small. As a matter of fact, it didn't actually look much like a veil. It looked more like something a flower girl might wear. I was a bit confused.

I stepped forward to examine the fabric. It was awfully pretty, but as I suspected, it was slight. Jessica started to finger the fabric delicately. Her mother began to cry small tears. She patted them from her cheeks with a wadded-up piece of tissue that was resting in her fingertips.

"Jessica, I think . . ." and just as I was about to attempt to talk her out of the miniature veil, the boutique owner rounded the curtain again. This time she was carrying a small plush pillow. The deep crimson of the pillow was hardly needed to illuminate the tiara that was nestled on top. The gleaming object looked so delicate that I took a step back. I now understood what was happening. Jessica was going to attach the veil to the tiara. She wanted the jewelry to be the center of attention, and to serve that purpose her veil needed to be a bit underwhelming.

Once the crown entered the room, Janet popped up out of her chair. She was now standing by my elbow.

"Beautiful, huh?" she whispered to me.

"Yeah," I whispered back. I felt inspired at that moment. I watched, awestruck, as Samantha cradled the crown in her hands and then dexterously placed it onto Jessica's head. She secured the veil loosely beneath with a few hairpins. Taking three large steps back and a collective breath to help control our emotions, we gave Adair room to see her reflection in the full-length mirror.

I had been to weddings before, but I had never seen a bride so beautiful as Jessica Adair. She quite literally took my breath away.

"Amazing," I said in an encouraging voice. I looked to my side, to see if Janet would join in with an acknowledgment, but to my disappointment, she was texting.

Sydney noticed the pause too but picked up the slack. In her nervous way, she started blathering about. "Oh, Jessica, you are so beautiful. This dress is fantastic. Your shoes are fabulous and your tiara . . ." she trailed off for effect.

"It really is great, isn't it?" Adair looked at herself in the mirror as she said this.

"Do you think that Wesley will like it?" I said, trying to lighten up the situation.

"He better," Adair broke eye contact with the mirror and stared my way. "I can't breathe in this thing, so someone best appreciate it." She laughed quickly as her hands flew to her side. I had no idea that the dress was so confining. It looked like it was made to be worn by Ms. Jessica Adair.

An hour later, I felt exhausted. Even though I wasn't doing any work at all, my mind and my limbs were tired. I realized that I had come to Samantha's Bridal Shop expecting to fight and all I got in return was a few hours of wedding gown fittings. I wanted to ask Adair why she had demanded my presence, but just as I was about to ask this question, she provided some answers.

Adair shook out her long blonde hair. She ran her fingers through it, seemingly thankful that the tiara and veil had finally been removed. As she was stepping out of the skirt, she addressed the room.

"Okay, ladies, now it's your turn."

"Excuse me?" Janet said.

"Not to try on wedding gowns, silly," Adair said and gave her sister a playful smile. "Now it's your turn to try on your bridesmaid dresses." She motioned for Samantha to join us again, and the eager attendant disappeared into a back room. She emerged seconds later pulling a rack of gowns behind her. I was quite shocked to see that the dresses assembled on the line were all sorts of colors. There didn't seem to be a theme here.

"Ah, Jess," I asked, "are you going with a rainbow theme, or what?"

She laughed lightly. "No, no." Now that she was free from her own wedding gown, she was padding around the room in a pair of leggings and her bare feet. She quickly slid a beige camisole over her head and patted it down against her sides. Scantily dressed, she sauntered over to the rack of dresses and pulled one from the order.

"Your dresses are going to be in this style." She held up the gown for our inspection. It was a sleeveless number that fell to the floor. The material was a little heavy, but I assumed that it was going to be a winter wedding, so I didn't bother to ask questions. The bodice was intricate, and it wrapped across one side of the stomach. There was a small rhinestone clip located at one side that nicely secured the wrap feature. I thought the rhinestone was a lovely touch. It reminded me a bit of her tiara.

Sydney stepped forward to take the dress from Adair's hands. Adair gave her a charming smile and looked grateful to Sydney for coming into assist. She quickly turned to pluck another gown off the rack.

"And this," she announced, "will be the color of your gowns. It's called 'pool,' I think. Right, Samantha?" She looked in the shop owner's direction and the woman nodded her head.

"This is really such a gorgeous color," the woman said in a voice that was almost inaudible. I guessed that she was trying to appear a delicate individual. (I guess I can't be really certain that this was an act, but I couldn't explain the soft quality in her tone otherwise. She did want us to hear her, right?) She took the gown Jessica was holding and held it across both of her arms. "Many of our summer brides select 'Pool' for their bridesmaids because the shimmering blue offsets the tan skin tones of the attendants."

"Hmm . . ." Sydney nodded in a thoughtful manner.

"Wait a sec," I began, "did you say 'summer' brides?"

"Yes," Samantha stared at me with large purple eyes. That's right. She had purple eyes. It was a bit of a shock to absorb her eye color, but I chalked the colored contacts up to her desire to appear pleasing and attractive to her clients. I have to admit: even though I wasn't a huge fan of the tiny little voice or the bizarre eye color, I liked Samantha. She gave off a very soothing vibe. Also, her store was genuinely gorgeous. She seemed to have a knack for being pleasing overall.

"I'm sorry, I don't understand," I said, looking at Adair for help, but she wasn't paying attention. She was sorting through the clothing rack with Sydney. I turned to Janet.

"Janet, when's the wedding?" I asked.

"A couple of months," she shrugged.

"A couple of months," I echoed. "Why?" I hadn't meant to be rude, really, I hadn't, but I couldn't understand the rush. Adair had concealed her true feelings for Wesley for so long that I just imagined that they would enjoy a nice long engagement to get accustomed to their new status being made public.

"Because I want to marry Wesley *now*." Even though I hadn't thought that Adair was listening to my conversation with Janet, she was quick to answer this question. When she turned to look at me, I could see hurt reflecting in her eyes. She appeared to be furious. At her side, Sydney was also giving me a death stare.

"I'm sorry, I'm sorry. I really am. I didn't mean to make waves. You just hadn't told me when you were getting married." I was speaking in my most pitiful voice, and truth be told--I actually felt wretched. I honestly had not meant to cause a fuss in the middle of a bridal store.

There was a long awkward pause and in those few moments, I contemplated leaving the store. I could follow through with my fitting on another day. I adjusted my purse on my shoulder and bent down to retrieve my shopping bags from earlier in the morning.

When I did this, Jessica laughed, and Sydney joined in. I just stared at them with a mixture of sadness, relief, and if I'm going to be really honest--loathing.

"Put your bags down," Sydney said.

"We're just messing with you," Adair agreed and motioned for me to drop my things.

"Huh?" I asked, definitely feeling bewildered.

"Missy," Adair came over to stand next to me. She threw her arm around my shoulder. "Of course you didn't know the wedding date. I know that I never told you the date. I'm just screwing around." She pinched the side of my arm and continued. "Things were getting way too serious in here, so I just thought that I would mix it up a bit. And besides, I don't really care if you think I'm getting married on the fly. Wesley and I are in love. We want to be married in the summer. Boom! End of story." She made a motion like she was wiping the subject from her hands and she went back to the dress rack.

I kind of just stood there for a minute, feeling out of place. My instincts were telling me to check my cell phone and pretend that I had missed an important phone call. I could be out of the store in the next five minutes and I could feel embarrassed somewhere else.

I don't really know why I felt this way; it's just a part of who I am. I have a tough time taking a joke. More specifically, I have a tough time being the butt of a joke. I know that Adair was trying to be fun, or whatever, but why did she have to make me feel bad? I was truly humiliated. I think what made the whole scene feel worse to me was that Sydney and Adair were now yucking it up at my expense. Just as I decided to shrug off the situation, Janet sidled up behind me.

"You look like garbage, you know. Your whole face just slid to the floor."

"Thanks," I said, with as much sarcasm as I could muster.

"Don't take it personally." She nodded towards her older sister and her gal pal. "They've been like that since we got here."

"Like what?" I asked, faking nonchalance.

"They've been all giggly and obnoxious and even though it seems totally out of character for Jess, she's been extremely rude." She raised her left eyebrow in my direction. "They actually pulled the same stunt on me just a few minutes before you arrived." Now it was my turn to raise my eyebrow back at her.

"Yeah," she whistled under her breath. "A couple of real jokesters, those two. Jessica hadn't told anyone the wedding date but came in here expecting us to know all of her plans. Just so you know: She was a total bitch when she confronted me about it."

"I don't understand. Why is she acting like this?" I felt my hands self-consciously wipe the hair away from my face. I tucked a few strands behind my ear.

"You don't spend a lot of time with Jessica *and* Sydney, do you?"

I looked at Janet in a bewildered sort of way. Until a few hours ago, I hadn't really known that the two girls still hung out.

"I'll take that as a 'no,'" Janet said, grabbing the underside of my arm. She pulled me close to her, whispering in my ear. "Jessica's a great sister, but she's awful when she gets together with Sydney. I can't stand to be around the two of them." I moved back an inch from Janet's face so that I could inspect her eyes. She believed what she just said. She pulled me close, and began murmuring again,

"Jessica is making other people feel bad about her abrupt wedding announcement because she doesn't want it to be awkward for herself. Don't you see? She made *you* feel bad so that *she* didn't have to feel that way." This time I eased my way slowly out of Janet's grip. I focused for a minute on Jessica and Sydney as they pawed through the clothing rack. This wasn't the Jessica Adair that I knew.

My Jessica was comfortable in her own skin and she made choices that she knew she could stand behind. I was sure that if she wanted to marry Wesley tomorrow, she would have a good reason for it. My mind couldn't compute the things that Janet had so liberally shared.

Even though my brain was struggling to unscramble the information, my eyes were not to be deceived. I watched as Sydney and Adair laughed and grabbed dress after dress. I couldn't really comprehend why they were scouting through the clothes, since Jessica had already picked our style for us, but they were sorting as if looking for a real treasure.

"This one's hideous," Sydney giggled as she pulled a brilliant orange number from the rows.

"Those long sleeves would look awful on anyone," Adair agreed with a snide chuckle.

"Are the dresses ready?" I asked just to bring things back to reality. I stepped towards Samantha, and she actually looked at me now with a grateful expression. She seemed to be relieved that the process was going to keep moving. I wondered briefly if she had another bridal appointment set for this afternoon.

"Right this way," she said in her small voice and gestured with her hands toward one of the ornate dressing rooms. I followed her to the first room on the left and ducked inside.

"Thank you," I murmured.

"You are quite welcome, dear." Her voice was still very soft. As she closed the door behind me, she whispered, "The wedding is scheduled for August 27th."

"Thank you, again," I replied, lowering my voice as well. It felt improper to speak loudly in front of this woman.

"I'll bring a couple of sizes for you, if you wish." She looked at me for a brief second, contemplating my measurements.

"That would be fine," I said and bowed my head in her direction. She shut the door softly behind her and I collapsed onto the soft cushion situated in the corner of my dressing room. I took off my shoes and squeezed the thick carpet through the spaces between my toes.

"That's better," I said allowing my head to tip back against the wall mirror. I closed my eyes and took a deep breath.

A quiet knock on my door brought me out of my reverie. I opened it a crack and saw that Jessica was standing outside. As the room was a bit confined, I didn't invite her in, but I did perk up to show her that I was listening. She poked her little head inside the room.

"Are you okay? I was just joshing you. Are you sure you're not mad?" She looked genuinely remorseful, so I shook my head.

"It's cool, buddy. But if it's okay with you, I'll just get fit and then I'll head home. I have been running around all morning long, and I really need to vacuum the apartment." I wasn't sure if my story about vacuuming was a sound enough excuse, but Jessica nodded her head anyway.

"Okay, I'll call you later then?" she asked.

"Sure," I replied and tried to give her a warm smile.

Because Samantha was a professional, she pulled my correct dress size off the rack immediately. It would be perfect, after a few minor tweaks. Since I have no chest to speak of, that part of the dress would need to be downsized, but that all seemed pretty typical. She wrote down my measurements and my preferred dress size, and then I was on my way.

As I exited the exquisite little house, I took a moment to collect my thoughts. It wasn't even noon yet and twice -- count it, twice—I'd been asked if I was mad about something. Had I done something lately that would make people think that I was an angry person? I tried to pull my thoughts together, but I couldn't recollect anything out of the ordinary.

As I walked down the steps, I continued to contemplate my behavior. Was I doing something wrong? Was I making inappropriate jokes or were my comments dripping with sarcasm? I just couldn't think of the last time I felt this . . . bombarded. It was difficult to label the emotion.

I picked up my pace to that of a brisk walk, and before I knew it, I was jogging. Even though I had a purse slung over my arm and bags in both of my hands, I was trying to run through my feelings. I was suddenly grateful that I had worn tennis shoes this morning. The heels that Samantha had loaned me at the bridal store had put a little sore spot on my tiny toe, but I decided to coast through the pain.

After a few minutes of serious sprinting, and some deep contemplation, I still had no clue what was going on. Then, it hit me: Was I positive that I *wasn't* mad?

I inhaled deeply as I came to a stop in front of Fountain Park Apartments. I retrieved my key from my purse and held it firmly in my right hand. Did I have something to be mad about? I flexed my fingers around the sharp edges of the key. Was I really mad and just pretending to be okay? I didn't know. With a jerk, I thrust the key into the exterior door, then, I pounded my way up the stairs and decided to put this topic on the shelf to be contemplated another day. After all, anger, if it even exists, doesn't just disappear.

Chapter Three

Are You Sure I Did This Properly?

"What's with all the rage?" Autumn took a step back as quickly as possible. It was a Wednesday night and I had talked her into taking a cardio kickboxing class with me. At this point in the hour-long sweat session, the instructor had partnered us up. We were currently practicing our roundhouse kicks, and my most recent attempt had nearly knocked Autumn's block off. Luckily, she had danced away just in time.

"What rage?" I asked. I repositioned myself and struck out at Autumn again. She danced back again. I was glad that Autumn and I had been partnered together. Even though she had never really been into kickboxing, she was quick on her feet. She knew when to move and when to strike. I hated it when I came to this class and got stuck with partners who were fearful, or worse, uncoordinated.

"What rage," she scoffed, this time blocking my next kick with a gloved left hand. She brushed my leg to the side, and then attempted to throw a jab in my direction, but she couldn't catch me unprepared today. I caught her wrist quickly and pushed it away from the target.

"And stop!" The instructor called through the room amplification system. "All right class--let's take a minute to break. Catch your breath and grab some water. Don't forget to keep those feet moving and your chests lifted." Autumn and I quickly nodded at the instructor in acknowledgment, and we broke towards the outsides of the room, in search of our water bottles.

I grabbed my purple container and pulled the plastic straw to my teeth. Gratefully, I took a large gulp. Maybe I was going a little hard today. I took a minute to inspect my appearance in the mirrors that surrounded the small exercise arena. I was sweating like a pig. If my sister Hope had been here, she would have said that I was glowing like a pig--same difference.

I balled the edge of my blue cotton shirt up in my hand and used it to wipe the sheen of sweat from my forehead. I was seriously dripping buckets here.

"You're gross," Autumn pointed out as she set her aqua water bottle back on the ground next to our feet.

"Thanks," I said and gulped down another swallow of re-freshment.

"I'm kidding," Autumn clarified.

"I know," I nodded in her direction.

"Good, I just wanted to be sure that you knew I was joking, because I'm hoping that you don't try to kick my head off any more tonight," she said and gave me a playful swat. She circled around so that she could get back to her workout position.

"Was I really being that brutal?" I asked and positioned my-self back into my fighter's stance.

"Yeah, you're a little scary." Just as Autumn said this, the instructor began speaking to the class again.

"Scary," I thought. That was a new way to describe me.

I took a small step towards myself in the mirror, smiled in my most menacing way, and completed a perfect jab- jab- round-house combination. Maybe I was a little scary, and maybe, just maybe, I even liked it a little.

After the class was over and I had congratulated the in-structor on a job well done, I headed towards the benches to change shoes. Autumn was already sitting in the area, unlacing her Nikes.

"So, do you want to talk about it?"

"Not really," I replied.

"So, there *is* something bothering you?" she pushed.

"Actually, I didn't think that there was anything wrong, but people--you included," I poked my finger in her direction, "just keep asking me if I'm mad. I really didn't think I was, but maybe I am."

"That's ridiculous, Missy." Autumn had now pulled out her bright orange gym bag. She still had a major thing for neon colors, and she insisted on splashing as many vivid colors into her workout wardrobe as possible. I assumed that she got so bored wearing neutrals to work all day that she truly reveled in the fact that her fitness attire was bright and sunny.

She continued, "You know if you're upset or not. You control your own thoughts and feelings. For example," she said, turning towards me and pointing across the room at a guy who was using the forty-five-pound dumb bells. "If I told you right now that you thought that guy over there was cute, would you automatically assume that I was right? Would you accept that as fact if I told you how to think and feel?" I thought about her question for a second, and then took a minute to actually look at the guy she was pointing towards.

He had dark curly hair, and he was lifting those dumb bells like they were play toys.

"Autumn, that guy *is* cute."

"Is he?" She wrinkled her nose. "I can't tell anymore."

"What?" I asked, suspiciously.

"I only have eyes for Paul, remember?" She said this and batted her eyelashes dramatically. I gave her a small punch on the arm.

"Now, you're the one who's gross," I said and tucked my shoes into my black shoulder bag. I stood up and slid my bare feet into the sandals that were waiting.

"Okay, okay, so that was a bad example," she said with a laugh.

"Yeah," I agreed and started to move towards the door.

Autumn was right behind me before I knew it. "Missy, I don't know what's going on with you." She paused. "What I mean is: I'm not sure if there's something wrong, and it worries me." I turned to look her full in the face.

"I appreciate the concern, dude, but I've got nothing. You know if I decide that I have anything to share that you'll be the first person I'll call."

"I know," she sighed. She was now standing right beside me, but she wouldn't look into my eyes. She was actually kicking a pebble with the toe of her shoes. My mind quickly flashed back to the horrible grimace I had given myself in the mirror. What if I had become a little intimidating? Of all the people in my life, I didn't want Autumn to find me unapproachable. I took a step backward so as to widen the space between us, and then I gave her my full attention.

"Okay, here's the thing," she said, inhaling deeply. I sort of prepared myself because I felt like a lecture was coming. "I think your problem is that you haven't had a date in a while."

I felt momentarily wounded. It was one thing for me to acknowledge my own twisted love life; it was another thing for Autumn to throw it in my face. She must have noticed the hurt look on my face because she forged ahead quickly with her thoughts.

"Missy, Missy, don't take it the wrong way. There's nothing wrong with taking a hiatus from dating. It's just that I feel like you haven't connected with a guy in a long time. After Cara stole Mitch from you . . ."

I cut her off, "She didn't steal him!" I yelled.

"Either way," Autumn went on, "after that whole fiasco, you sort of withdrew from the rest of the world. We can't tell if you're just taking a break or if you really are suffering."

"Who's 'we'?" I asked with caution. Had my friends been talking about me?

"Don't get all upset, here. The 'we' is just me and Paul. I talk to him about you and . . ."

"But Paul doesn't even know me, Autumn!" I heard a bit of fury rise in my voice. I wasn't really sure if I was insulted by this whole conversation or if I was just angry that she had discussed my issues with her boyfriend. I started to turn away.

The pleading tone in Autumn's voice brought me back abruptly, "Missy, I know, I know! I know that you don't know Paul and that he doesn't really know you; I know that you guys have only met a handful of times, so that's why I talk to him about you. He's an outside source. He doesn't judge one way or the other."

I was weighing what Autumn said. That was one good thing about having a boyfriend; they can make a very nice sounding board.

Autumn took my brief, non-violent silence as an opportunity to continue with her train of thought.

"Anyway, when Paul and I were discussing your mood shift the other night, he mentioned something that you might be interested in doing."

"No, no, no," I said, inching away from Autumn. "I am not going on any blind dates with any of Paul's available friends."

"No, no, it's nothing like that," Autumn said quickly and grabbed my shirt sleeve to physically align me with her. "Eww . . ." she commented and let go of my shirt. I had been dripping all over the place by the end of the training session. It was her mistake to try and touch me. She wiped my sweat off on her pants and tried pointing the conversation in the right direction.

"Paul's suggestion isn't exactly like a blind date. It's more like a party."

"A party? How is that supposed to make me feel better?"

"Just listen," she shushed me.

I shivered a bit. Even though it was pleasant outside, and we were in the middle of June, it was eight o'clock at night, and I had just literally drenched myself with sweat. She noticed my reaction to the chill, so she pulled me towards the building. In the glow of the gym lights, she told me what she and Paul were really planning.

"Have you ever heard of a pheromone party?"

"Nope," I said and shivered again. I started to dig around in my gym bag for a hoodie but was disappointed to realize that I hadn't come prepared. Even though I wasn't totally paying attention, she charged ahead with her story.

"Paul's friend, Kyle, is throwing a pheromone party this Saturday. You're cordially invited, but you have to come prepared."

"Prepared?" Now she had my attention. I shifted my bag to the shoulder that was opposite Autumn so that I could step closer to her.

Her own excitement level visibly picked up, due to my sudden interest. "Okay, first thing's first: A pheromone party is different than anything I've ever been to before."

"Okay," I nodded.
"And, I can't guarantee that you'll like it."

"Autumn," I groaned. "Just spit it out already."

"Okay!" She was almost giddy now. "Kyle, Paul's friend, invited everyone he knows in the city, both male and female. To prepare for the party, you need to find an old cotton T-shirt. Tomorrow morning when you go to work, you need to wear a T-shirt under your clothes, all day long. At the end of the day, you take the garment and put it in a plain brown paper bag. Since today is Wednesday, you really need to do this all day tomorrow because the shirt has to sit in the bag for three days. If you want it to be ready in time for the party, you have to do it tomorrow."

"Okay," I paused. "I don't get it."

"Well, some scientist somewhere recently conducted a study about the pheromones that humans produce and give off. He has a theory that humans are attracted to each other based on these aromas that our bodies produce. He says it has something to do with our relationship to the rest of the animal world."

"Anyway," I prompted her. It seemed like she might be about to take a detour in the explanation process. It wasn't often that Autumn began many discussions with information about humans being relatives to other animals, so I wanted to make sure that she stayed on track.

"Anyway," she proceeded, "the idea of a pheromone party is that everyone comes to the party carrying their soiled shirts. The smell, because it has been left to linger on the bag for three days, has intensified. So, if his theory and his research hold any truth at all, you should be able to take a whiff of all the other bags in the place and find your soul mate based upon which scent you prefer." She finished this sentence and gave me a very toothy grin.

"That sounds a little on the disgusting side."

"No, no way. It's not gross at all. It would just be us, returning to our baser instincts."

"Us?" I questioned.

"Sure," she shrugged. "Paul says that we should participate too."

"Paul says?" I asked. "And you don't concur?"

"Actually, since it's for the sake of science, I'm totally game. Plus," she whispered leaning close to me and then backing away when she remembered my sweat, "I knew that I could only talk you into doing it if I was on board too."

"Well, you're right about that."

"Oh, come on, Miss. It'll be fun. I promise."

"Can you promise that?" I looked at her with accusing eyes. I knew that I was being a bit ornery, because in truth--the journalist in me was intrigued--but I didn't care. "What if the party turns out to be just a bunch of uggo's smelling each other?"

"Uggo's?" Autumn raised an eyebrow.

"Ugly people," I clarified in the most obnoxious way possible.

"Missy, come on, don't try to make this into a bad thing. It's a good thing. And a fun thing." She slid in the last line for good measure, I believe.

"It does sound fun," I confessed.

"Yeah?" Autumn's voice raised an entire octave she got so excited so quickly. "You just seem so skeptical. Are you sure you really want to do this?"

"I think," I said slowly. "And besides, you want me to do it, right?"

"Right!" she cheered gratefully. She began running her fingers anxiously through her hair. I could nearly hear the nervous energy crackling through her fingertips. "That's great. Okay, I'm going to let you get on your way now, but before you go, do me one giant favor."

"Oh yeah? What's that?" I couldn't figure out what other request she might fling my way this evening.

"Promise me that you'll shower and throw this shirt out as soon as you get home."

She was laughing as she finished that sentence. She thought she was so funny.

I mustered up the smarmiest grin imaginable. "What? You mean that you don't want me to embarrass you by passing around my dirty gym laundry at your little science experiment?"

"Exactly," she said, laughing louder.

"You are incorrigible," I said, and shook my head slightly.

"That makes two of us," she replied and turned to walk away. She turned back to me once more and waved her hand politely. I stood there for a minute and watched her walk down the street. Just as her electric-colored bag started to lose its brilliance, I thought of one last question.

"Autumn!" I yelled, and quickly raced after her, covering the distance between us in a few long strides. "Autumn," I caught her by the arm. "One more thing: What happens if you sniff all the bags and don't find any of the people appealing? Or worse, what if everyone else takes a deep breath of your pheromones and finds you repulsive?"

"I don't know." Autumn looked thoughtful for a minute. "I never thought about it." She scratched her nose quickly, and then took a conspiratorial look around us before she continued. "If their noses fail, I guess people will just have to match up based on their eyes."

"Huh?" I asked.

"Dress up, girl. Even if you smell bad, someone's bound to pick you up because you'll look so good."

"Seriously?" I wrinkled my forehead a bit.

"That's *my* hypothesis: If you look amazing, people won't actually care how you smell." With that, Autumn checked the time on her phone, gave me an apologetic look, and turned off in the other direction.

"Okay then, well, I'll see you on Saturday?" I yelled after her.

"I'll call you before that!" She shouted over her shoulder, "Just be sure to follow the directions!" I only barely heard the last part. For such a slight person, she certainly allowed her long legs to stretch out quickly and cover a lot of ground.

I turned in the opposite direction and started walking briskly to my apartment. I was still a little bit chilled, but I realized my reaction was more than that. For the first time in what seemed like almost a solid month, my outlook was brightening. Even though I was pretty certain the whole pheromone party thing would be a bust, it did sound fun. Plus, my curiosity was piqued. I felt a new skip enter my step as I wound my way down the street leading to my building.

As I climbed the stairs towards my home, I began to feel giddy. I couldn't wait to tell my roommates about the pheromone party. Maybe they would want to come too.

But when I entered the apartment door, I was bummed to find that neither Hope nor Eve were there. I quickly ran to the refrigerator, and sure enough, two separate messages, one from each girl, had been posted on the outside of the freezer.

Hope's message, which was written across the back of a Lob receipt, read:

At work

Welcome to Suckville

Population: One

I shook my head and felt a little sad for Hope, but as is true with any profession, sometimes you have to work, even when you don't want to. Then I turned my attention to Eve's scrawl. While Hope wrote in a big loopy pattern that I was able to identify as letters, Eve's words were deep black and rigid. They were always legible, but for some reason, it took longer for me to decipher Eve's messages because the writing was so severe. Eve's message was just as concise:

Flew to Portland with Savanna

Big Game

Need $

Wish me luck?

"Luck!" I said aloud to the vacant air surrounding me. I shrugged, and as my shoulders moved, I felt the sweat creases on my clothing deepen into my skin. Remembering that I had a shower to take, I raced towards the bathroom. I was actually excited to slip into a new shirt and let my pheromones sink in. Call me crazy, but I was ready to stink it up.

"What if no one likes me? What if I smell funny? What if I don't like anyone else? What if I think that everyone stinks? What if I'm the only person in the room without a match?" I was calling these questions out in rapid fire. My brown paper bag was sitting beside me on the seat. I was being so neurotic about this little get together that I had nearly seat belted the bag into place. Instead of doing that, I kept reaching over and fiddling with the darn thing. I was taking the top ends of the bag and pinching them between my spider-like fingers. I was making small folds in my bag, but I didn't care. I was a nervous wreck and I needed to do something to try to calm my nerves.

I was seated in the back of Autumn's cobalt blue Honda Civic. She was letting Paul drive, even though it was her car. Twilight was just starting to settle on the city, and I was actually glad to be moving away from the bright lights. Even though she had failed to mention this fact earlier, the pheromone party that we were attending tonight was not exactly located within the city limits. It had been such a long time since I had left the city that I was a little surprised to find out that I couldn't just walk to the host's apartment.

We were heading to a house somewhere out in the country, and even though I tried really hard not to dwell on it, my mind kept thinking about the last "country" party that I had attended. It was at this fiesta that Mitch and I parted ways, and he and Cara became an item. I tried to convince myself that this instance had been an isolated incident. This time, I had nothing to lose. I was just going to the party to meet some new people and smell some shirts; no big deal.

The problem was that I had been really embarrassed at the past party. Even though I had tried to deny it, I was so humiliated by the incident that an onlooker might argue it was my reason for staying out of the dating scene. While I don't want to give credit to that theory, I can't exactly deny it either. So, here I am, feeling insecure, tucked into the backseat of

Autumn's car. I was not anxious for history to repeat itself, so I tried to fill the time by peppering Autumn and Paul with questions.

"First of all, Missy, slow down," Autumn said, turning in her seat to give me a genuine smile. I tried to smile at her in return, but my grin just came out lopsided.

She gave a lighthearted chuckle and reached over to the side of the seat to grab my hands. She placed her hand steadily on top of my left one and pulled it off the mutilated paper bag.

"Secondly, you have to calm yourself."

I nodded and tried to breathe deeply in and out. Paul shot me a look in the rearview mirror.

"Missy, everything's going to be fine. You know that Autumn would never lead you astray. And besides, this party's supposed to be fun. If we all decide that it blows, we'll just leave."

I nodded again, but this time with more conviction. That sounded agreeable. I removed the paper bag from the seat and nestled it on the ground next to Autumn's and Paul's bags. Now, with my hands free to fidget all over the place, I looked around the car for something to do. My eyes stopped on the back of Paul's head, and for a brief second, I considered running my fingers through his hair.

Paul had the most amazing head of hair. It was luxurious and thick and was an interesting mix of chestnut brown with blond highlights. I convinced myself when I first met him that the highlights were natural. I figured that since he was a soccer player, he probably spent a lot of time outside. That would give the rays of the sun a chance to kiss his hair. The front part of his scalp was really the most amazing part. It wasn't exactly curly, but it had a wave to it. I must admit that the thing I found most attractive about Paul was his hair. I realize that information does not come as a shock here, but I almost found that fact to be a little sad. Even though I had originally been gung-ho about Paul and Autumn getting back together, glossing over my strange obsession with his hair, I couldn't say a kind word about him. He definitely wasn't earning any brownie points by forcing my pal to go to this pheromone party. I realized now that Autumn had been urged by Paul to attend this event, and that she brought me with her as a human airbag. I reflected on the "excitement" that she had feigned during the invitation and felt a little saddened for my friend. Since I had the time, I continued to evaluate Paul, in search of some finer points.

Even though, by conventional standards, Paul was considered good-looking, there was something about him that I found a bit odd. Aside from his sweeping locks, he had green eyes, a small dusting of freckles across his tanned face, and an athletic build. I think that on a normal day, I would have thought that Paul was the cat's meow, but something about him just didn't sit right. I was always thinking that I would take the time to mull this fact over, but I never made any spare time for my investigation into Paul's looks. Now that I had all the time in the world, I could finally feel free to examine Paul.

I settled back against the cloth seats and started to dissect what I could see of Paul's physique. From this angle, I decided to start by examining his arms. But before I could even decide whether I felt that he was hiding tattoos underneath his shirtsleeves, my phone began to ring.

It was Nathan. Hmmm . . . perhaps he could sense that I was about to meet someone new, so he just thought that he would pop back up again. Nathan and I had not spoken in a few weeks. We regularly sent each other text messages and emails, but I hadn't really wanted to say anything to him in a while, so I'd refrained from calling. Even now, I thought momentarily about silencing the ringer and allowing my voicemail to pick up. My thumb moved over the silence control button, but I quickly changed my mind. Talking to Nathan would be a fine distraction--far preferable to checking out Autumn's boy-friend.

"Hello," I said softly into the phone. Autumn turned to give me a quizzical look. "Nathan," I mouthed in her direction. She rolled her eyes and forced herself to turn back towards the front of the vehicle. I was relieved that her eyes weren't on me, but I knew that Autumn, and maybe Paul, would be listening to this phone conversation. I decided that it would be best to can the flirting before it even started and keep the call breezy and non-committal.

"Hello, sunshine," Nathan laughed easily into the phone. He continued, "Literally—hello, sunshine—where have you been? It has rained here for the past three days. Please tell me that you're having better weather than we are."

"Of course, we're having better weather than you are. You live in Pittsburgh. I live in Charlotte--as if there is any true comparison." I figured that some light teasing was harmless, es-pecially since it was about the weather. And luckily, I stopped myself before I began chiding him about moving back to N.C. That would've been a topic that Autumn wouldn't have been happy to hear me discussing with my ex-boyfriend.

"Agreed." Nathan's voice brought me back to reality. "Char-lotte is so much better than Pittsburgh. Sometimes I feel like I live in a black hole. And the Steelers fans are relentless. Even though it's the offseason, football is all anyone *still* wants to talk about. Whenever I mention the Pirates or the Penguins, the conversation somehow gets steered back to football and the Steelers. It's exhausting, really."

"It sounds like it." I tried to sound sympathetic.

"So, whatcha up to tonight?" Nathan asked casually.

"Actually, I'm getting ready to do something that might interest you, since you're a scientist."

"You're preparing to expose some scoundrel for dumping toxic waste into the area river?" Nathan said this in a mocking way, but I got the feeling that he was hoping my plans had something to do with work.

"No, not today. Perhaps that will be my lead story for Monday. Do you have anything that you would like to share?" I like turning the tables on Nathan. He would usually talk about his job endlessly, but there were some parts of it that he was obligated to keep undisclosed. If he let the wrong information leak, he could be in major trouble. As a reporter, it was my job to dig, but I generally gave my friends a free pass on some of their work-related secrets.

"Nathan, I'm just kidding," I said gently.

"Right," he joked, coyly.

"No really, we're talking about my Saturday night here, and it doesn't actually have anything to do with work."

"Really?" he asked. "Do you have a date?"

"Not exactly," I said. Then I plunged right into telling him about the pheromone party. He was really intrigued. Because he is a scientist, he thought that it sounded like a sound theory, but he also conceded that it seemed like a good reason for a really nerdy guy to hit on lots of hot girls.

"I hadn't thought of it that way," I said, and for the first time, began to picture the type of people who would be showing up to this bash. Would it be just a room full of geeks?

"Well, who do you know that's going to be there? You aren't going by yourself, are you?"

"Nathan, is that concern I hear in your voice?" I was flirting again, and the second the words came out of my mouth, I regretted them. Autumn swiveled in her seat and raised her eyebrow in an all-knowing motion. She seemed to be telegraphing her distaste for my behavior.

I plunged right ahead. "I'm actually going to the party with Autumn and Paul."

"Who's Paul?" Nathan asked on the other line.

"Paul's Autumn's boyfriend," I said clearly.

"If Autumn has a boyfriend, why's she going to the party? Isn't the whole point to find someone as a potential date?" Nathan sounded confused on the other end, and I couldn't blame him. This had been my original question too. I tried to think of the best way to answer this query without offending Autumn or Paul. I decided to stick with Autumn's cover story.

"Autumn and Paul are going to the party because Paul's friend is the guy throwing it. They thought that it sounded like fun, and they knew that I'd never go to the thing if they didn't come with me."

"Is that all true?" Nathan asked.

"Probably," I confessed.

"Okay then," he said, and I imagined him shrugging his shoulders as he accepted my version, or should I say Autumn's version, of the truth.

"So, what are you doing tonight?" I asked, trying not to allow any flirtatious vibes to seep through my question.

"Well, my evening's not quite as exciting as yours, but I do have a date."

"Oh yeah?" I felt my face flush red. It was totally uncontrollable. Even though I was going out and trying to find someone to date, I didn't want Nathan doing the same thing. Even though I knew that I was being a hypocrite here, the whole situation just felt wrong.

"Who's the lucky lady?" I tried to cover quickly.

"She's just a girl," he said lightly. His casual tone reminded me that I had sought to keep this entire conversation on the breezy side. I readjusted the phone in my hand and forced myself to stick to my earlier resolution.

"Well, I hope that you have a good time," I said with as much cheer as I could muster. Autumn swiveled her head towards me momentarily and rolled her eyes quickly towards the heavens. She turned back in her seat, shaking her head slightly.

"I will," he said confidently. Ugh--I hated the implications that came with that statement. My mind started trying to quickly erase the images that had popped into my brain.

"I've got to go, Nate. Really, have a good time tonight and be careful!"

"I could say the same thing to you," he drawled.

I hung up the phone before he could say anything else. I didn't want to think about Nathan out on a date; I had much bigger things to consider. The foremost thought in my mind right now should have to do with preparing my nose for some proper sniffing. Just as I was thinking of a polite way to approach someone after I had determined that I liked their smell, Paul pulled off the county highway and onto a long gravel driveway. Cautiously, he eased his foot off the pedal and gripped the steering wheel tightly. I tried to look out the side windows so that I could get a glimpse of the house, but the backseat did not afford a very generous view.

I drummed my fingers nervously along the back of Autumn's headrest. When the car finally settled to a stop and Paul removed the keys from the ignition, Autumn turned to talk to me. She was unbuckling her seat belt and playing with a few stray pieces of hair.

"Now, Missy, there is absolutely no reason that you need to be nervous." She nodded to Paul, and he exited the car. She continued to fidget with her hair, even dropping the passenger side mirror to take a peek.

"Everything's going to be fine, just fine," she whispered at her reflection. I watched her as she looked at herself. For the first time, I realized that she wasn't actually talking to me. This was a sort of affirmation for herself. It occurred to me that maybe Autumn wasn't as jazzed about this party and experiment as she had let on. Maybe she really did like Paul, and she didn't want to lose him to another girl who smelled more appealing.

Abandoning my own insecurities momentarily, I swept out of the car. I slammed my door shut and grabbed the handle to open Autumn's door for her.

"You'll be fine, girl. You look terrific," I commented, giving Autumn a reassuring smile, and she nodded before stepping out of the car. She nearly lost her footing as she emerged. Her heel got caught in a piece of the gravel driveway. I caught her hand easily and looped my arm through hers.

"Should we stick together for a while?" I asked, hoping that she would consent.

"I think that would be a good idea," Autumn said and began to lead the way towards the party.

As we were walking towards the house, I politely observed the exterior décor. Even though I had been lead to believe that a man lived here, it was pretty obvious that a female had, at least at one time, graced these premises.

There were two large flower beds directly in front of the house. Since it was June, the flowers were blooming beautifully. The grass in the front yard had been cut recently and it smelled quite refreshing. I noted little spigots emerging in spots, indicating that the owner watered his lawn on a regular basis. We were on large red, flat stones, used as a pathway for visitors leading up to the home's front patio. A white railing sectioned off the flower beds from the patio space, where a delicate white wicker set of furniture sat. I thought the overall effect was charming, and I mentioned so to Autumn.

When we finally followed Paul into the house, I was even more surprised by the elegant touches that were to be found. There were vases of fresh flowers strewn throughout the living room. A large fireplace was the centerpiece of the area, and perched over the mantel was a variety of knickknacks. This didn't exactly scream "bachelor pad" to me.

"Don't most guys put their televisions over their fireplaces nowadays?" I asked Autumn, and she shrugged politely. She continued to survey the room, but she also seemed extremely focused on keeping Paul's gorgeous hair in her sights.

We continued to pass through the living room, admiring and remarking on every little piece that we noticed.

"This place is darling," Autumn said, and I nodded to show my agreement. We were still trying to keep tabs on Paul, but since we kept getting so distracted checking out the house, he had since disappeared. I pulled Autumn towards what I thought would be the kitchen, and we nearly slammed into a couple of tall blond guys.

"Um, sorry about that," I said, feeling the heat rush through my veins. They were really cute.

Autumn reached out and touched the arm of the guy on the left. "I must apologize. We weren't watching where we were going." She relaxed her hand and the man smiled at her gently. I was glad to see that his teeth were relatively white and straight. I'd been a little worried about the kind of people who might show up tonight. Surveying the prospects now left me feeling optimistic. No one looked too scary, and everyone seemed to be properly groomed. (I say this, even though we were all carrying brown paper bags that contained our dirty laundry. I know, I know, it's conflicting, but seeing that everyone around me cleaned up nicely left my outlook just a bit sunnier.)

Just as I was about to forget the whole "scientific" purpose of the evening and allow myself to dive into a conversation with Autumn and these extremely good-looking men, I let my eyes search the crowd. Almost everyone here was on the respectable side of the ogling spectrum.

"We hope to see you guys later," I called as I began to heave Autumn towards the direction of the dining room.

"Why on Earth did you do that? One for me, one for you."

"What about Paul?" I asked quickly.

"Right," Autumn said, still holding her head high. I wondered about this uncharacteristic attitude. Normally, one of Autumn's best qualities was loyalty. But I wondered again if perhaps it wasn't Autumn being disloyal here. Maybe she was just trying to make the most of a really bad situation. I knew that she liked Paul, but if he was forcing her to try and find a new guy to date, who could begrudge her seizing the opportunity? I most certainly did not expect Autumn to remain entangled with a man who seemed ready to ditch her.

Before I could dwell too much on this idea, Autumn flicked her hand in the air. She was gesturing towards the dining room, so I led on.

In the dining room, we found the rest of the brown bags. We also met the moderator, who I quickly deduced was also the host. He was dressed in a white lab coat, and I thought it was quite a cheeky statement. For tonight, at least, he was conducting a science experiment. I resisted the urge to go over to him immediately and instead waited patiently in the line that was forming.

We would have to wait for a few minutes to register our bags. The scientist would assign each bag, and person, a designated number. Then, once someone sniffed a bag that they liked, they would approach him again and ask for the name of the individual who seemed to strike their fancy.

"I like this party already," I said quietly to Autumn. As I was whispering to her, I noticed that this was the first party that I had ever been to that *didn't* require me to yell at my companions. I heard music tinkling only lightly in the background, but I was happy to find that I wouldn't have to waste the entire evening able to only make out just snippets of conversation. The host had kept the atmosphere mellow and soothing to allow for easy chatter amongst his guests.

"I'm glad that you do. I was a little worried." The frown lines on Autumn's face deepened as she seemed to be concentrating on something just in front of us. I leaned over her slightly and found her point of focus. She was watching Paul greet the host and hand over his bag. I observed as Paul shook hands with the man and went through the polite conversation necessary to become registered for the party.

"It'll be fine, Autumn," I said, casually patting her hand and tucking her closer to my side.

"Okay," Autumn said and took a deep breath. She squared her shoulders and forcefully made the effort to avert her eyes from Paul.

"Let's just talk about something else, okay?" Autumn asked, and I was happy to tell her about my latest news story. Even though it was a bit bland, I knew that Autumn would be polite enough to listen, and then engage in questions afterwards. This would certainly take her mind off her roaming man.

"Are you sure I did this properly?" I said aloud to no one at all. It was about an hour later. Autumn had drifted away from my side, and I was currently leaning over the bags of dirty shirts. I shouldn't actually say that they were soiled, because they all appeared to be clean. Truth be told, I had sniffed about twenty bags already and I wasn't having any luck. They all smelled like brown paper bag to me. I picked up one more and held it to my face. I tried to take a big deep breath but found that I was still disappointed. I didn't detect anything out of the ordinary.

"Shoot," I said and kicked at the table leg.

"My sentiments exactly," a man across the table said and placed two of the brown baggies back onto the table.

"Are you trying to cheat?" I asked, suspiciously.

"Not exactly," he replied, with an impish grin.

"Then why are you sniffing two bags at once?" I asked, walking around the side of the table so that I wasn't being impolite, yelling across the room.

"Truth?" he asked, his eyebrows doing a funny wriggle.

"Sure," I shrugged. "Why not?"

"The truth is that I was looking for *your* bag," he said and extended his left hand in my direction as if he wanted me to place my own inside his. For the first time, I gave this stranger an appraising look. He was tall and lean. He stood extremely erect, so I was guessing that his height didn't bother him. He had light blond hair and dark brown eyes. The contrast was quite interesting. I was nearly mesmerized by the effect.

His ensemble reminded me more of business casual attire, than party wear, but I could understand how some guys just liked to look professional all the time. They had a way of dressing up, even when they didn't mean to. Briefly, a picture of Nathan crossed my mind. He was one of those type of guys. He looked great wearing anything. But before I could contemplate his image too much, I focused my attention back on this attractive stranger who was apparently looking for me.

I brought my full focus back to *this* man and *this* party. He was quite alluring. He had pink pouty lips and an extra white smile. I imagined that he never had to use those sloppy whitening strips that I was forced to apply religiously. (Gotta keep those chompers pearly for my adoring public.) No, no—instead, this man was born with great teeth. He was wearing a smoldering red polo shirt and crisp khaki pants. This ensemble might have been understated on anyone else, but the way it hung on his frame was ridiculously sexy. I felt the corners of my mouth twitch up into a smile.

Coming to my senses, I held out my hand to return the shake. "And why do I deserve the honor of being sought after?" I felt a little embarrassed about my grammar in the last sentence. I couldn't think of a good way to word it; I was aiming for coy, but also trying to sound intelligent. Perhaps I failed.

Luckily for me, he seemed undaunted. He quickly manipulated my hand so that he could flip the palm down. He bent his head in a graceful swoop and barely touched the tip of his lips to the rough side of my hands. I blushed a little bit. I also looked over my shoulder in search of Autumn. I wondered if she was seeing any of this.

"Well, Mademoiselle, if you want the truth again, I'll give it to you." He released my hand and gestured towards the living room. I led the way and I'm not ashamed to admit that I felt a little blip of happiness when he placed his hand lightly on the small of my back.

I moved to the corner of the room and settled down neatly into a kitchen chair that had been displaced earlier to accommodate those who wanted to sit down. The man found a chair for himself near the closest wall and pulled it over towards me. We were almost sitting on top of each other because the room was so crowded, but looking over his well-toned physique again bolstered my attitude. I definitely wasn't opposed to sitting this close to this man.

"Are you ready for me to tell you why I've been looking for you all night?" he said in a conspiratorial way.

"Sure," I shrugged, trying to sound unaffected by this clear flattery.

"I know who you are," he whispered excitedly.

"Oh," I groaned. "You've seen me on TV, right?" This didn't always happen to me, so I can't pretend that being recognized by a fan wasn't a big deal, but tonight was different. I didn't want some fan to approach me at the party simply because I was a TV personality. I wanted a guy to be looking for me because he was actually interested in me. I know that I sound a bit selfish and maybe even a little snobby, but I was looking to build a relationship, not become part of someone else's brag book.

"I've seen you on TV, but you are sooo much more than that." The way he drew out his "O"s sent cold chills up my spine. Maybe he wasn't just a fan. Maybe, he was a stalker.

I tried to scoot away from him. I was only about an inch removed when I ran into someone who was standing behind me. I started to feel that I was slightly trapped. I immediately scanned all possible routes that might allow me the safest exit. I know that I was overthinking this because, let's face it—I was at a crowded party. If this guy got all handsy on me (or worse) I could just bump into the person behind me and ask for a little assistance. Or, if things got really out of control, I could always try out the new roundhouse kick that I had been perfecting at class last week. I smiled internally, silent cheering myself onward.

"Okay," I said, attempting to give him a winning grin. "What did you say your name was again?" I realized full well that he had not dropped his name yet, but I figured that if someone was going to get all creepy on me, I would need to gather as much information as possible for the inevitable police report.

Am I jumping the gun here? Probably, but ladies can never be too careful when their safety is concerned. I scanned the room quickly to find Autumn. The good news was that she was staring at me. She gave the man I was sitting with the once-over and shot me a thumbs-up. I blew my hair out of my face and turned again to face this man.

"I'm Steve Martin."

I was so stunned by his answer that my manners escaped me. "No, you're not," I answered too quickly.

He laughed lightly, "Sure I am. I'm Steve Worthington Martin. My dad and brother are the lawyers who own Martin and Martin. Any chance you've heard of them?" His eyes were twinkling when he said this last line.

I didn't even have to scan my memory. Of course, I had heard of Martin and Martin. They were only the largest law firm in Charlotte. Furthermore, the Martin building was directly next door to my news station WSTA- Charlotte. I walked by Martin and Martin every day on my way to work.

"Sorry," I said instantly, trying to cover up my unforgivably rude retort.

"This might not surprise you, but I get that kind of reaction a lot. Many people think that I just made up my name or that I'm trying to copy the actor or something."

"Well, aren't you?" I asked.

"No, not at all," he replied.

I gawked at him a little. "Really? I mean, you could use your middle name, couldn't you? You do know that there is a famous man in Hollywood with the same moniker, right?"

"Yes, I'm familiar with his work." He laughed and shook his head. "And if I thought by sharing his name, I could ride his successful coattails, I most certainly would. But you can see that we suffer two very distinguishable differences . . ."

My eyebrows shot up, urging him to continue.

"Our first difference is, of course, that he is much older than I am, and the second difference is that I'm devastatingly handsome."

I laughed but couldn't find it within me to disagree. I was shocked by how my body was reacting to this man. Instead of trying to inch away from him, as I had been doing seconds ago, I was now scooting forward in my chair. The mere mention of his untarnished beauty really had my engine revving.

When I said nothing and only chuckled, he continued talking.

"You see, when I was born, obviously my last name was not negotiable, but my parents selected the name Steven because it had been my maternal grandfather's name. My mother was very fond of her father, and after his passing, she wanted to honor his memory. It just so happened that the coupling of the two names stuck me in a category of comedians."

"I'm sorry if I embarrassed you. I didn't mean to be offensive."

"No offense taken here, Missy Lawrence. I'm a huge fan of yours. Consider us even."

"Even?" I asked with an arched eyebrow.

"I think that maybe I was leading you to believe that I was some crazy celebrity stalker or something," he said with a sly wink.

I hate it when people read my mind. It reminds me of my boss, Ross Neil. Ross is always doing that sort of thing. Just as a quick question pops into my brain, he spits the answer in my direction. I hardly have time to function around Ross. But somehow, when Steve Martin was able to interpret my thoughts, I didn't mind so much.

"No harm, no foul," I said and dusted my hands against the side of my skirt.

"So," he began.

"So," I picked up the cue. "You said that you were looking for me. Is there any particular reason?" I attempted to bat my eyelashes at him, but just wound up feeling like a dork.

"Actually, there was a reason," he said, pulling his chair into a closer proximity with my own.

"And it was . . ." I ventured.

"I wanted to meet you. And before you get all huffy puffy like you did before, you should know that it's not because I'm a fan."

"Well, thank you very much, Mr. Steve Martin. That didn't sting at all." I said this in a teasing manner, but it did actually strike a very sour note with me.

"No, no--not like that. I mean that I am a fan of your work, but I didn't track you down just so I could get autographs or pictures."

"Okay," I said slowly. "What do you want then?"

"I wanted to tell you that I just recently got hired at WSTA."

"Wow! You're working at the station? What will you be doing there?" As soon as I asked this question, I felt silly; one look at this tall handsome man made it clear that he would be working on–air. He was far too good-looking to hide behind the scenes.

"Actually, I'm just going to be doing an internship for a while. I'm in law school right now . . ."

I cut him off. "Law school? How do television and law go together?"

"Actually, they don't always coincide, but lucky for me, they do this time."

"Explain, please," I said and leaned forward so that he could feel my interest.

"Well, you see, I was walking into Dad's office the other day, and this gorgeous woman, Melody Castina, you know her, right?" I nodded confirmation at him so that he could go on with his story.

He continued, "Melody saw me walking into the building. She hurried to my side and caught the door just as I was about to enter. She exclaimed that I was the most beautiful man that she'd ever seen, and she wanted to know if I was an attorney."

"Well, that's pretty sad," I said with a grumpy look crossing my face.

"Why's that sad? It sounded like a compliment to me." He looked puzzled.

"It's disappointing because Melody has a boyfriend--a very serious boyfriend--actually." My mind jumped to an image of Ethan doing Melody's make up on Thursday morning. I planned to give her a piece of my mind just as soon as I could get ahold of her.

"Oh, no, no, you misunderstood. Melody wasn't hitting on me. She was propositioning me."

My eyebrows shot up.

"Quit reading too much into what I'm saying. You're jump-ing to conclusions." Steve Martin slapped my hand like I was his best friend. I allowed my mind to relax a pinch.

"Anyway," he said, "Melody said that I was attractive to her as a guest for her show. She and Ross have been discussing bringing a lawyer onto the program who will field questions from the public and comment on special cases that are news-worthy."

"Oh," I cried, smacking my forehead. "Melody wasn't picking you up. She just wanted you to be on the show." I breathed a visible sigh of relief. I really hadn't been looking forward to breaking the news to Ethan about his girlfriend.

"Silly girl, as if Melody has the desirable equipment to keep a man like me satisfied." When he said this my eyes shot up to look him right in the face. At first, I wasn't sure if he was trying to make a pass at me, but then his true target became clear. He averted his eyes so that they were looking in the direction of a really striking blonde guy that was standing to our left.

"Oh," I said quietly. "Nice."

"Nice?" He laughed in a pert sort of way.

"Right," I said, "nice."

He patted my hand softly and pulled me closer.

"Are you sure that you're not disappointed?" I felt my blood temperature skyrocket faster than it had in a really long time.

"Ah," I tried to spew out some words that made sense, "are you sure that you're not interested in girls?"

"I'm sure," he nodded.

"Then, I'm sure that I'm not disappointed," I answered, then tried earnestly to work myself out of the awkward position that he had put me in.

"That was a very naughty trick that you just pulled," I said and laughed a little.

"Was it?" he asked and flicked his hair out of his face.

"Oh, come on, you know how good-looking you are."

"Do I?" He shot me a friendly wink.

"Obviously," I said and continued. "Here I was, thinking the best-looking guy in the place had actually come looking for my companionship, but, no, instead you just want to talk business."

"Well, that's not entirely true," he said and leaned forward again. I could see how well-toned his chest was through his red Ralph Lauren Polo shirt. "You see, I am the best-looking guy here and I did come looking for you in particular--but we don't necessarily have to talk about business, if you don't want."

"Okay," I considered this for a minute. "What do you want to talk about?"

"Let's discuss this whole pheromone party thing. Why can't we get those bags to work?" As soon as the words were out of his mouth, I started laughing.

I had come to this party tonight to start a new relationship with a man, and now I had exactly what I needed: a fine male companion. Steve Martin and I were bound to get along very well. As the night went on, he told me more about his new internship at the station, and I learned that he did kind of want to be a lawyer, so he was currently in law school. As it was summer break though, he was supposed to be working for his pops, but he was much more excited to be working with me at the television station.

As Steve Martin and I spent the next few hours together, I began to wonder if he really was a comedian at heart. He was hilarious. I don't know if he was just trying to impress me, or if he really was that funny, but multiple times I had to wipe the tears away from my eyes. I found myself feeling pretty grateful to have stumbled upon a new friend. Plus, neither of us was ever able to get the pheromone bags to work, so maybe, just maybe, we were meant to be together.

After bidding my new pal a good evening, I happily hopped into the back seat of Autumn's car. I noticed that she now had her hand laced lightly through Paul's arm, and I thought that they both looked content. I realized for the first time since I had started sniffing bags and lost track of Autumn that I had kind of left her all alone. I knew that I couldn't broach the subject now, what with Paul standing right beside her, but I was intrigued about the events of her evening.

My mind began to race just thinking about how successful my night had been. If Autumn was still hanging onto Paul did that mean that her night was equally wonderful, or that she was just settling for what was currently on the menu? I resolved to have a conversation with her at a later date.

Once I settled in for the long car ride, I fished in my purse to find my cell phone. I had two missed calls, both from Hope, and I had one new text message. It was from Eve. It read:

I won! I won! I won! Small money, but big win! Coming home tonight! Sorry about all the !

I was so excited for Eve that I let out a small whoop. Autumn turned her head abruptly, and Paul's eyes darted back and forth, but he managed to keep the wheel steady.

"Are you okay?" Autumn asked.

"I'm great," I said, and for the first time in weeks, I actually meant it.

Chapter Four

Can I Get an Update, Please?

I just finished typing the words: "Can I get an update, please?" onto my computer screen when my phone rang. I knew that it was Benson before I even checked the Caller ID. The email that I'd been about to send was meant for Jess and for Jack also, but I knew that Benson had been reading my mind. (Hmmm . . . This mind reading thing has been happening to me a lot lately. Am I that much of an open book? Maybe I should work on that.)

What with the move to L.A. and the upcoming nuptials of our shared friend, Jessica Adair, the month of June and the first part of July had practically flown away. Summer was my favorite season of the year. I loved the sunshine, and even though the sun had an edge to it now because of the excessive heat, I still felt blessed to be soaking up the rays. Plus, my new best pal, Steve Martin, and I had already made one impromptu trip down to Myrtle Beach. We decided that since we only lived four hours from the beach, we should take advantage of it. While I had been bathing away in a sea of Vitamin D bliss, my friends, Jess Benson and Jack Swammie, had been settling into their new apartment (if you could call it that), in L.A.

Jack had appeared in the New Artist Showcase that was held last spring in uptown Charlotte. Even though her performance was amazing, the whole thing had seemed to be a bust at first.

She hadn't received a recording contract until months later. Despite the delay, Jack eagerly packed up her gear and headed out for the great wide open as soon as she got the offer. Interestingly enough, she had snagged Benson to come with her on the journey.

Since Jess was a second-grade teacher, her skills were marketable anywhere in the U.S. She could easily find a job close to their very tiny apartment and she was planning to start that job hunting process very soon, as she would need to have a new job by the fall. She claimed that she would be just as happy teaching in the California sunshine as she had been in the Charlotte rays. I wasn't quite sure about that when I found out that she was going to have to take a summer job as a waitress at the bar down the street to help pay for her expensive move, but to each their own, I always say.

Jack and Benson had been in L.A. for about six weeks now, and I had not heard from them since their plane landed. I had begun to think that they were purposely ignoring me. I tried calling, texting, and emailing, but all of my efforts had gone unnoticed. I grudgingly decided to send one more email before I really started to worry about the pair.

And now, as if to assuage all my fears, Benson was giving me a ring.

I nearly burst with enthusiasm as I picked up the phone.

"Hello!" I said, feeling breathless.

"Hello!" Benson squeaked in return. She sounded happy, but Benson always sounded joyous, so I still needed to be cautious about this phone call.

"Is everything okay? Are you all right? Is Jack okay? Why haven't you called me?" The phone was silent for only a brief second before I heard Benson's girlish giggle on the other end.

"We're fine, Missy. We're just fine. I'm okay. Jack's in good health. Everyone's practically perfect."

"Okay, okay. Then, well, why haven't you called me?" I knew that I was sounding a bit matronly, but let's be serious here: if everything and everyone was fine, then why not let your best friend know about it?

"Oh, Missy, please stop being so overdramatic. You know how crazy life can get when you move to a new city." I quickly pictured my move to Charlotte, and I suddenly knew that I might be overreacting a tad.

"Oh, come on Benson, if I hadn't called *you* in six weeks, wouldn't you be sleeping by the phone, wondering if I was alright?"

"Did you really do that?" Benson asked, actually sounding touched, although I'm pretty sure that she was also mocking me.

"No, Ms. Sarcasm, I didn't sleep with the phone propped up by my head. But I'll let you know that you were one email away from being reported as a missing person." Benson seemed to consider this because her next comment was less colorful.

"I hadn't thought about it that way. I'm sorry about dropping off the face of the Earth; it's just . . ." I waited for her to flesh out the rest of the sentence, but it never came.

"Benson, are you sure that you're *perfectly* fine? Are you certain that there isn't something that you really want to talk about?"

"You always know when I have something on my mind. Yep, there's something that I need to talk about, but let's start by catching up first." I propped my feet up onto my desk and settled in for a nice long chat.

I told Benson about my job and how things were going at work. I had recently reported a story that was pretty interesting, and Benson complimented me on my hard-nosed journalistic instincts paying off. I also told her about Steve Martin, and she laughed a little when I confessed that I still sometimes struggled to be around him because he was so beautiful. It was like waving a chocolate cupcake right in front of my face before a workout. I knew I couldn't have it, even if I really wanted it.

She told me about her new school, the other teachers, and the students that she would be teaching in the fall. Even though the move had been at an inopportune time, Benson had made it work. Luckily, she found a job very quickly in a little neighborhood school. She was also happy to be at the bar because she was making some really good tips, and she knew that waitressing was only a temporary situation. She was just so relieved to have found another teaching job that she didn't care much about her other occupation.

"Kids are kids--no matter where you go," she said.

From our jobs, we moved to relationships, and in a fascinating turn of events, neither of us really had anything to report. I was currently not seeing anyone seriously, and she had just recently called it quits with Brian. While this might have usually garnered some sort of melodrama, this breakup needed to happen.

Brian was a decent guy and Benson was a good girl. While they liked each other immensely and they got along well, long distance relationships are stressful. Benson explained that most of her nighttime talking had been with Brian and that preoccupation had actually been the reason that she had neglected calling me sooner. She had logged so many hours on the phone with him over the last few weeks that she didn't have the time or the energy to call me up.

Even though most people would have been a little salty, I didn't get my undies too twisted over this fact. I actually understood where Benson was coming from. She had liked Brian. Shoot, she probably still liked the guy, but she had also made her decision to move. She had to deal with the repercussions. I was just grateful that she was calling now.

For our third order of business, we discussed Adair's upcoming wedding festivities.

"Ooohh, I got the wedding shower invitation in the mail today. It is gorgeous. Well done, Lawrence," Benson gushed.

"You know, I really like the design too, but I can't take credit for it. Adair's sister is in charge of the wedding shower, so she handled the invitations. I thought that they were very pretty, but also a little bit bold. You know, just like Adair."

"Exactly," Benson agreed. "And where is this venue? I don't recognize the address." I quickly dug around on my desk and pulled out the wedding shower invitation. The electric pink lining popped out at me once again as I pulled the textured paper from the slim envelope.

"You know, I'm not sure where it is, but I know that it's supposed to be beautiful. Apparently, Jess' sister booked a conference room at this winery that is right outside of the city. I didn't even know that it existed. But Adair's happy, so I'm happy."

"I'm so excited to come to this," Benson said with true glee.

"Really? Are you really going to be able to make it?" I knew that Benson and Jack were scraping pennies to afford their move and the apartment. Even though Adair had insisted that we send Benson and Jack invites to the shower, I was pretty sure that it was just a gesture. I had no idea how they would be able to pay for the flight back.

"I don't know," Benson said, sounding incredibly despondent. My heart hurt a little when I thought that I might've just burst her bubble. She'd been so jubilant seconds before, but now, as if the reality of the situation was just hitting her for the first time, she seemed truly sad. I began to wonder if she missed her home and her friends. "I know that I would like to be there though," she concluded, aiming to keep her tone upbeat.

"Well, if you're able to attend, you know that we'll be happy to see you; be sure that you plan to stay with me. You can borrow my bed if you want to. And now--don't let this go to your head, but I don't just give up my bed for anyone."

Benson giggled.

"I can't wait to come home and see all of you again."

There was a long pause. I had been thinking about the wedding details, and frankly I don't know what she had been thinking about. I blamed myself a little for what happened next. I should've kept the conversation moving.

Benson's voice cracked and I could hear as she burst into tears. "Missy, I never should have left."

"What?" I pretended to be shocked, but I also sort of felt like this was bound to happen.

"I never should've left Charlotte. I miss it so much," Benson moaned into the phone. I let her cry for a few seconds, and then I tried to come to the root of the problem.

"Jess, are you sad about Brian?"

"Of course, I'm sad about Brian," she sniffed.

I waited. I didn't want to pressure her. It had been six whole weeks since I'd heard word. I didn't want her to tune me out again. Plus, a million things could've happened to her in the last few weeks, and I didn't even know where to begin on that topic.

Eventually, her breathing calmed down and she was able to pick up the conversation.

"I miss Brian a lot," she said, and I could feel her sadness seeping through the phone. "But I miss the girls much more." I nodded and murmured reassuring sounds in her direction.

"Adair didn't announce her engagement until after Jack and I had decided to move. And even when I did know about the wedding, I didn't think about all of the hoopla that surrounds it. I didn't realize that I was going to miss *everything*." She said "everything" as if she were dropping the word into a large empty bucket. It sounded so heavy.

"Sweetie, you're not going to miss everything. You will be here for the wedding, right?" The wedding was scheduled for only a few short weeks away. It was to take place at the end of August.

"When does the school year begin? Will they even give you the time off?" I asked tentatively.

"Oh, that's not the problem. We don't start until after Labor Day. I'll be good to go in that department." Even though this sounded like a pinch of good news, the joy didn't reach Benson's voice. She still sounded downtrodden.

I'm not quite certain why Adair and Wesley had chosen to rush the engagement, but I wasn't arguing. I remembered how uncomfortable I had felt in the dress shop. I thought that maybe if I told Benson that story, she would lighten up and realize that she wasn't really missing anything special.

She listened patiently as I told my tale, and then she reacted in a totally unexpected way.

"I'm surprised that you forgot that, Missy."

"Forgot what?"

"How could you whitewash the whole thing?" Benson sounded a little shocked, but I still didn't know where she was taking it, so I stayed mute.

"You don't remember why you and Sydney stopped being friends, do you?"

"Nope, I can't remember a thing. I was wondering about that when I saw her in the dress store that day."

"The reason you stopped being friends with Sydney was because you didn't like hanging out with Adair when she was around. You loved Jess, but when the two of them got together, it was almost like they would pick on you."

"Huh," I grunted and began to search my memory. I wonder why I had decided to stay friends with Adair but I elected to cut Sydney out? I just couldn't recall the details. Perhaps my subconscious had a reason for all this madness, but that was beyond me as well.

"Well," Benson said.

"Well," I responded. "I got nothing. I can't remember our tension, but I know how I felt in the bridal store, and it was lousy. You know I love Adair, but planning her wedding has not been especially easy."

"I hear ya," Benson said thoughtfully. "I just hope that you realize how lucky you are that you get to be a part of it." She sniffed quietly, and I was afraid that she was going to start sobbing again.

"It's okay, sweetie. You know that we would love it if you could be here."

A full minute passed before Jess answered. "I don't know. I don't know if I'll be able to make it." Her tears pushed their way into the last statement, and I felt the sorrow wash across me, long distance.

"Benson, why don't you start at the beginning? Remember? It's me, Missy. You need to tell me the whole story--the real story. This time, start at the top and don't sugarcoat it. Okay?"

"Okay," she sighed. I heard her take a gulp of fresh air and I knew that she would feel better if she had someone on the other end who was really listening. I quickly switched off my computer screen so that my attention would not wander.

"Alright Jess, I'm ready. What is really going on?"

"Well, it all started as soon as we got out here." I realized as soon as she said this that the problem was Jack. For the first time in this present conversation, I recognized that even though we had talked about the big move and all that implied neither one of us had really discussed Jack. I braced myself for the news that was to come.

"Go on," I cheered encouragingly.

"I decided to move with Jack to L.A. because I thought that it would be a great learning experience and I really didn't want her to be all alone. While my job is relatively stable, hers is not. Being in the music business is no joke."

She didn't have to remind me of that: I was in the television industry, and I knew how fickle an audience could be.

"Anyway, I just couldn't bear the thought of her wandering the town and trying to find her way out here all alone, but that is exactly what she has done to me."

"How?" I asked.

"Well, it started innocently enough," Benson said, breathing deeply. "The first couple of days out here were a lot of fun. I found the waitressing job pretty easily and Jack went to meet her boss the same day our flight landed. We had a good time unpacking our things into our tiny apartment. We even celebrated during the first weekend by heading out to the beach."

"That sounds nice." I couldn't think of anything else to say.

"It was nice," Benson affirmed. "But then, things changed. On Sunday night, when we got back from the beach, I got a phone message from Brian, and I just had to take the call. Jack really wanted to go out and listen to some live music, but I had to pass. I had to talk to Brian."

"Uh-huh," I said. I wanted her to know that I was still paying attention.

"The next night was the same thing, pretty much. We both went to work on Monday and then had dinner together. That night, Jack wanted to go out and explore the town, but I had to stay in and talk to Brian. So, she decided to go without me."

"Okay," I murmured. I wanted to say something else so that Benson wouldn't think that I was annoyed by her story or that I wanted her to get to the point, but I couldn't come up with anything dazzling.

"I didn't really mind so much that she wanted to go out so often. I actually considered it to be pretty normal behavior. We went out on a regular basis back in Charlotte, and now that we're in a new place, it only made sense to go explore the area. But then, Jack stopped coming home altogether."

"Huh?" I felt like I had been caught a little off guard. I knew that something was coming, but I had not expected this.

"Well, she comes home, but I never see her." Benson took a pause to breathe for a minute.

"What do you mean?" I asked to fill the silence.

"I mean that I wake up every morning and she's gone. When I come home from work, there is always a note from Jack saying what she's up to, but I never actually see her. She says that she goes to work, comes home about noon, and then heads back out to work. After work, she goes out to night clubs, either to sing or watch someone else perform."

"Okay, while that sounds swell and everything, I have to ask a dumb question: Where and when does she sleep?"

"I don't know, Missy. I just don't know." Benson was not crying, but she did sound exasperated.

I swallowed the other questions that were crowding my brain in the hopes that she would continue with her own story.

"When I broke up with Brian, I really needed someone to talk to, but she wasn't here. She was at some blues club, I think."

"You could have called me," I interjected, and Benson huffed a bit.

"I know that," she said. "But I didn't want to call you. I wanted to talk to Jack. I wanted to speak to my roommate."

I tried not to be offended by her last comment, and in my silence, she was quick to apologize.

"Missy, I'm sorry I said that. I wasn't trying to hurt your feelings."

"I know--I know that you're just upset."

"I *am* upset," she said, as if she were pounding her fist at the same time. "I just don't know what to do about Jack. Every night, I tell myself that I should just go out and find her. Occasionally, in her notes, she will tell me where she's going.

I always try to psych myself up to go out and find her, but L.A. is such a big city and I really don't want to get lost on my own."

"I can understand that," I said. And I could understand; Benson probably weighed one hundred and ten pounds, soaking wet. She was a slight little thing, and I would hate to think of her roving the streets alone, trying to find Jack.

"So, what have you been doing while Jack is out?" I wanted to try and refocus on the subject at hand. I also wanted to move forward in the conversation. I didn't want Benson to dwell on her loneliness.

"Well, I go to work." I pictured Jess counting off these items on her fingers. "After work, I come home and I make dinner. Then, I used to call Brian, but I won't be doing that anymore. "

"Is that it?" I had to ask. I hated to think of her being all alone all night long like that.

"Actually, it's not," she said, much to my surprise. "As time went on, my conversations with Brian became shorter and shorter, so I had more time to do things at night. I started going out with a few other people from the bar. We don't do anything wild, but we have a few drinks or some coffee at a couple of the local dives."

"That sounds nice," I said.

"And on the weekends, we've been going into the city and dancing at a few nice places."

"Oh, that's great," I said in my cheeriest voice. I have to admit that I felt relieved.

"You know what? It is a lot of fun, but there is still a giant hole in my heart. I feel like I've lost Jack."

"I'm sorry," I whispered.

"And you know what the worst part about losing Jack has been?"

"What?" I asked.

"It is because of Jack that I lost all of you." She said that last statement like the knife was literally twisting straight into her heart.

"No, no," I said with intensity. "You didn't lose us. We're still right here and we are still going to love and support you, no matter where you decide to go."

"Thanks for saying that Missy, but I still feel the loss. Even now, when I'm on the phone with you, I can feel the gap. I want to talk to you about all the plans for Adair's wedding, but at the same time, I don't want to talk about them because I might not get to be a part of them."

"Oh, honey, don't talk like that. Of course you'll be at Adair's wedding."

"I don't know. I honestly can't think of a way to raise all the money necessary to make three separate trips this summer. I most certainly will miss the bridal shower and the bachelorette party. I'll be lucky if I have the cash to fly in for the wedding. Why did she have to schedule everything in such a short amount of time? At least if the events had been spread out over a few months, I could've found a way to pull money together slowly, but surely."

"You could just come back for a whole week at a time, you know. You could come for the shower and then stay awhile with me. Then, you would still be here for the bachelorette party."

Benson seemed to be processing what I was saying, so I decided to keep flinging out viable options.

"Or..." I charged ahead, "You could fly in for the bachelorette party, stay a week, and then go to the wedding."

"I can't do that," Benson whined. "Remember, there's a whole extra weekend between the bachelorette party and the wedding. That would mean that I'd have to try and get off work for almost two weeks. I don't think my boss would go for it."

"Okay," I said slowly, "you could just come back home permanently." I knew it was a shot in the dark, but I was really starting to feel Benson's pain. I had adopted her despair as my own.

"I thought about it. Honestly, I did. Brian and I even talked about my moving back to Charlotte. He said that I could easily come back to Charlotte and live with him. Then, next year, I could just go back to my old school, and everything would be like it used to be."

"But?" I didn't know what else to say.

"But I didn't want everything to be the same as it always had been. I wanted to do something exciting. I wanted to be someone else, even for just a little bit. So, I told him that I was going to go through with this move."

"But why, Jess? Why should you stick with something if it is hurting you so much?"

"I don't know, Missy. I just feel like there is some reason that I need to stay here. I just feel like I am needed here."

"Jack?" I questioned.

"Maybe," Benson whispered. "Maybe there will come a day when she gets tired and comes back home. Or maybe there will be a time when she's in trouble and she realizes that she needs me."

"I hope not," I said.

"I agree," she replied. "But if that day ever comes, I want to make sure that I'm here for her when she needs me."

Even though Jack had abandoned her, Benson was hanging on to the hope that she would return. I wanted to laugh a little, to make her feel better, but I couldn't do it. She was willing to turn her whole life upside down on the off chance that someday Jack would need her help. She was truly a better person than I.

During this interlude, I heard Benson sigh heavily.

"Enough about me," she said. "So, tell me what's going on with Adair's bachelorette party."

Chapter Five

What Do You Say That We Go on a Date?

"What is this supposed to be?" I lifted my fork and watched while the green sludge slid its way back towards the plate.

"Should it really look like this?" Hope was leaning into my right side and holding a forkful of the concoction at arm's length.

"Oh, get over it," Brooklyn said as she courageously stuffed a large bite into her mouth. She took a moment to chew, and I realized that she was actually enjoying the stuff. She wasn't just faking it.

Eve smiled gratefully and took her place at the head of the table. Now that Brooklyn had broken the ice by taking the first bite, we all felt obliged to join in on the fun.

It was a Thursday night--a few days after I had spoken with Benson--and Eve had convinced me and the crew to skip our Pond time and come to the apartment. She was so excited about her big win on the Poker Tour that she was feeling generous; not princely enough to buy us all dinner, but she was up for cooking. She also had a special recipe that she wanted us to try. It involved using a large amount of pesto sauce and garlic. She was sure that we would all like the dish if we gave it a try.

Even though the pasta cuisine looked like it was from another planet, I was happy to have everyone together. Normally when I went out to eat at the Pond with the girls, my roommates didn't join in. They maintained that it felt wrong to butt in on our bonding time. While I always assured them that the Pond was not a sacred place, they argued that it was "our group's place," as we had been going there to unwind since our college days. I had not been to the Pond in a very long time, but having everyone together tonight was making me feel less disheartened.

I looked around my crowded kitchen and saw all my favorite girls, with a few exceptions. Obviously, Benson and Jack were not in attendance, and Savanna was probably just pulling back into the state right now. While she and Eve normally played on the World Poker Tour together, during her downtime, Savanna would occasionally go visit her parents in Georgia. She was scheduled to be returning from that trip anytime now. And it was not a moment too soon; I had something that I wanted to ask her.

Adair, Brooklyn, and Autumn had all gratefully dug into the garlic-pesto pasta, but I noticed that Hope, like me was still a little skittish.

"Listen, Eve, I love you and all, but you know how I feel about calories."

"Missy." She looked at me in a fierce way. "Pesto has a lot less fat in it than marinara or Alfredo sauce. Just try it."

I ignored her command. "No, see, you don't quite get it. I don't mind consuming calories, but if I'm going to stuff a fork-ful in my mouth, I want it to be for the right reason." I pointed to my plate. "I'm not sure that this counts as the right reason."

For that comment, she batted at me with her napkin.

I looked over to see that Hope was still sitting with her fork poised over the plate.

"Shall we do it together?" I said, and I nudged her with my elbow. She nodded and we both piled a big helping onto our forks.

I opened my mouth wide and placed the whole scoop, fork included, inside. I chewed quickly as I watched Hope stick out her tongue and carefully lick at the corner of the sauce. She wasn't planning to take a bite after all.

The rest of the girls were deep in conversation, so luckily they were ignoring Hope and me. Finding the taste of pesto in my mouth repulsive, I quickly looked for a way to spit it out.

I ought to explain my strict policy about food. If it's not worth the calories, Don't. Eat. It. That means that you shouldn't put something in your mouth, unless you're willing to live with the fact that you just ingested needless calories. I found a paper napkin tucked under the corner of my plate, and with one furtive movement, spit the pasta into it. I wadded up the refuse and got up to quickly toss it in the trash.

"I saw that, Lawrence," Eve said as she gave me an angry stare from the other end of the table. "You didn't even try it."

"Yes, I did," I started to protest, but her icy glare had me locked down.

"Okay, okay, so I'm a picky eater," I said. "I can't help it if I eat with my eyes."

"You eat with your eyes?" Adair snorted.

"Yes," Hope sighed and put her fork down. I think she was relieved that I was the one receiving a tongue-lashing, but she was quick to come to my aid. "You know what she means: If something doesn't look appetizing, then her mind warns her not to eat it."

"I don't know what they're talking about," Autumn said. She then took a healthy bite of her pasta and used her napkin to daub at her face. "This food is delicious, Eve. It only looks weird if you aren't used to eating pesto."

"That's what I keep trying to tell them," Eve said, then gave an exasperated sigh.

"That's right--two peas in a pod: my sister and I." I put my arm across Hope's shoulder, then quickly removed it. Everyone was already sitting awfully close together to fit around our miniature kitchen table; I didn't want to sacrifice any more space.

"Well, if you don't like it, then you don't have to eat it," Eve said slowly, putting her fork down and looking at both of us seriously.

"Thanks," Hope said, happily picking up her plate and mine in one swift motion. She raced towards the garbage can, emptied both piles of food into it, and then went to the sink to rinse the dishes. She was a better waitress than she gave herself credit for.

"I'll make the pb and j," I said as I hopped up from the table. I could tell that my friends around the table were getting antsy. They were expecting Eve to explode. Eve just has one of those personalities that can sometimes be described as fiery, but tonight she just shook it off. Instead of yelling at us, she turned her attention to Adair.

"So, Adair, tell me about the wedding planning," she said and picked up her own fork again.

Adair was happy to change the subject. "I love getting married. I think that everyone should get married once a year." We all laughed. Only Adair would say something like that.

"I mean," she persisted, "planning a wedding is a lot of fun. Not only do I come home every night and see the perfect man curled up on my couch waiting for me, but I get to spend all daydreaming about the perfect day in which we will become man and wife."

"That sounds lovely," Autumn said.

"That doesn't really sound like Adair," Brooklyn countered. She put her fork down and turned just slightly in the constricted dining space to face Adair. She put her hand on Jess' shoulder. "Tell us the truth: What have you done with Jessica Adair?"

Adair laughed and looked to Eve for help. Eve shrugged. She didn't really know what to tell her. They didn't know each other that well, so I couldn't fathom why Adair was looking at Eve for assistance. This was another small hint that Jess was floundering.

Brooklyn persisted, "What's really going on, Jessica? I know you, and you don't get all googly-eyed over weddings and perfect boyfriends—fiancés--whatever. You just don't. You tell me the truth right now or I'll . . ."

"You'll what?" Now that I was back in my seat, I was intrigued.

"I don't know what I'll do, but I'll come up with something," Brooklyn finished.

Even though Brooklyn's threat had been empty, Jessica looked defeated.

"All right, you caught me," she said softly and looked up at Brooklyn with pleading eyes. "I keep telling myself that this *is* fun, but I'm not sure that I'm doing it right."

"What does that mean?" Eve was now poking at her pasta. I wondered if perhaps she had decided that her own dish wasn't as edible as she wanted everyone to agree.

"It means that I'm scared. For so long, it's been me: Jessica Adair against the world. And now, all of that is changing. I'm afraid that I'm going to say something inappropriate or that I'm going to embarrass Wesley in front of his family. You know that we're meeting with them all more often now, right?"

We were aware of how much time Jessica had been forced to spend with Wesley's family lately. Wesley's mother seemed like she would be a nice lady, but she had really been giving Adair a hard time. One would think that having a woman like Jessica Adair become part of the family would be like winning a prize. Jessica was beautiful. She had a very successful and lucrative career. And, above all, she loved Wesley. But none of that was sufficient for Wesley's mother. No one would ever be good enough for Wes.

Adair continued, "Anyway, even though they're not adding too many stipulations about the wedding, they are commenting on everything that we pick."

She let her eyes scan all of ours at the table before she continued. She leaned forward in a secretive manner before she continued with her story.

"For example, the other day, Wesley and I were telling his mother and sister about the flowers that we'd picked for the ceremony. They both looked at the sample photos and then exchanged the oddest looks." She mimicked what I assumed to be their facial expressions.

"Then, Wesley's mother looks at me and says, 'Is this what you really want? Those flowers are nice, but they are so ordinary. I think that you could pick something that would be a little more extravagant.'"

We all just looked at Adair. I frankly didn't know what to say. I don't think that anyone had ever questioned Jessica's taste before.

"What did she mean by that?" Brooklyn asked for us all.

"I don't know. But you see, that is the sort of thing that I have been spending all day puzzling over. What did she mean 'ordinary'? Or what about 'extravagant'? Was that her way of saying that the flower arrangements look cheap?"

"Well," Autumn said, tossing her napkin onto the side of her plate, "what does Wes say when you ask him about his mom's comments?"

"He's no help," Adair sighed, clearly flustered. "He just says that she didn't mean anything by it and that she always feels like she has to put her two cents in, even when she doesn't have anything helpful to say."

"Geez," Brooklyn groaned, and scooted back from the table. We all followed her with our eyes, and she began emptying her plate into the garbage, then rinsing it at the sink. I assumed--and I am guessing that everyone else did too--that Brooklyn was about to say something, but she refrained.

Taking advantage of the silent moment, Eve went around the table collecting everyone's plates and one-by-one, dumping their remaining contents into the trash can. No one had finished the meal, and everyone still looked pretty hungry.

"Why don't you all go into the living room and talk?" I motioned for my friends to take the sofas, and then I walked back to the kitchen counter to help Eve clean up.

"You okay?" I asked while she started scrubbing one of the plates. She moved the dish cloth back and forth methodically and never looked me full in my face.

"That was one of Rich's favorite meals," she finally said. Rich's smiling face flashed before my eyes. Rich had very nearly been the world's most perfect guy. He played guitar. He bought special presents. He actually listened when his girlfriend talked. Above all, Rich had loved Eve with all his heart. But when Eve elected to join the World Poker Tour, she and Rich had been forced to break up. We didn't talk about him often because the subject was a little painful.

"Really?" I looked at her with my eyebrow arched. She bobbed her head in response.

"I'm sorry," I said. "I didn't mean to sound surprised, but . . . I am. Did he really like it?"

"I don't know," Eve said and continued washing. "Now I'm starting to wonder." A small smile crept onto her face, and she placed the spotless dish onto the drying rack.

"Do you think that he just pretended to like my cooking?" Eve stopped washing for a moment and looked at me with a hopeful gaze.

I thought it over. "That *does* seem like something he would do," I finally conceded.

"Yes, it does." She shook her head slightly and went back to washing. I walked away from her and circled the table, picking up forks and leftover napkins. When I returned the forks to the sink, I decided to ask the forbidden question.

"So," I said, "have you heard from Rich lately?" To my delight, and surprise, she smiled again.

"Yeah," she breathed, and couldn't stop the smile from creeping into her voice. "He called me last night. He actually mentioned this pasta dish and that's what inspired me to make it tonight. I never imagined that he was only trying to be nice when he said that he liked it." This time, she put her dishware down and produced one of her full-out, wholehearted laughs. When Eve does this, her whole body shakes, and most people start laughing with her. I patted her on the back and joined in what felt like a small celebration.

She wiped the tears from her eyes and went back to washing dishes. "Rich is a good guy."

"Rich is the best guy," I offered.

"It's too bad that he's too good for me," Eve finished.

"Yeah, well, he's too good for me, too, if that makes you feel any better." As I said this, Eve stopped washing again and let out another round of belly shaking laughter.

"Yeah, yeah," she finally squeaked out once she caught her breath. "Rich was far too good for us all. You know, Missy, we really should stop using him as the standard by which we judge other guys. We're not going to find anyone quite so perfect. And even if we do, they'll be too good for us, too."

I stood there for a moment and let that sink in. She was right, of course. To find the right guy, I had to find a perfect balance between what I knew to be perfect and what I knew to be sufferable. I thought briefly of Nathan, but dismissed the thought as quickly as it came.

Eve did something unexpected then--she ushered me out of the kitchen.

"Get out of here," she coaxed. "You're being a terrible hostess. Your friends are sitting out there gossiping without you, while you're in here yucking it up with me. Scoot!" She shooed me with the back of her hand. I was glad that she had come to her senses and asked me to vacate the kitchen area. Things were getting way too serious in there. I needed a little relief. I was hoping that in my absence, the girls would work out a solution to Adair's mother-in-law issues.

"And that's about all he had to say about that," Brooklyn finished her sentence as I walked into the room.

"Who had to say about what?" I asked, as I crossed my ankles and sat down on the floor.

"Boo!" Hope yelled and tossed a pillow in my direction.

"What? What did I do?" I looked around to make sure that I hadn't sat on something or walked on someone's toes.

"You can't just come in during a conversation and start asking questions," Hope said and peered at me with an annoyed but mischievous look in her eye. I knew that she hated it when I interrupted like this, but I had to know what was going on. Like it or not, that was one of my vices. I had to be included in all conversations.

Autumn tucked her legs up underneath her on the couch and looked in my direction, "Okay, Missy, here's the quick rundown: Brooklyn is happy living with Duke. She doesn't even mind the fact that their dog, Mr. Nasty, decides that he has to sleep with them every night. But this morning at breakfast, Duke dropped a bomb on Brooklyn."

"What? What did he say?" I had to know.

"He said that if she ever wanted to get married, she would have to get a job," Autumn said quickly.

"Huh?" I looked at Autumn, and then my eyes shifted back to Brooklyn. She only raised her eyebrows in response.

"But, Brooklyn," I said, "you already have a job. I don't get it."

Adair now took her turn rolling her eyes. "Well, you see, I offered to give Brooklyn a job, but apparently what I have to offer is not good enough for Duke."

I looked at Adair, stunned for two reasons: 1. Brooklyn really did already have a job. She worked at the local bookstore, and 2. If Adair had just given Jack a job, then she and Benson would never have had to move to L.A. I vowed right then that someday I would confront Adair about the whole Jack issue, but I knew that now wasn't the appropriate time.

Before I could stammer out a coherent thought, Brooklyn finally took the storytelling reins.

"You see, Miss, the short story is this: I do have a job at the bookstore, but that's not enough for Duke. As you know, his job is very dangerous, so he wants to make sure that if something were to happen to him that I would be able to take care of myself."

"Okay," I drew the word out long, still trying to process the situation.

"He says that I need to not just get a new job, but also . . ." she gave both Autumn and Adair mocking looks. "Duke says that I need to find a *career* so that I'll always be able to support myself, even if he's not around."

"That sounds weird," I replied.

"It *is* weird," Brooklyn answered back.

"No, seriously," I said and gave her a long look. "Even when I keep trying to get the idea straight in my head, it still sounds off. Let me break it down and see if I have it right." I looked at Brooklyn for permission, and even though she looked a little annoyed by my calculating, she nodded graciously.

"Okay," I said, as I tried to tick ideas off using my fingers, "Duke has a dangerous job. Someday, he would like to marry you. He wants you to have a career so that when you get married, you'll have something that will sustain you if he gets injured on the job."

"Yes!" Brooklyn answered enthusiastically.

"Yes?" I said, emphasizing the fact that I was asking a question and not joining in the cheer.

"What's the problem?" She looked at me with slit eyes.

"I don't get it," I said.

"What don't you get?" she asked.

"Why are you excited? It doesn't sound like a very good thing to me."

"He is thinking about the future, silly girl," Adair chimed in.

"And that, is a very good thing," Autumn finished for her. I let that marinate for a minute, before I continued.

"But..." I said, "the future that he's contemplating involves one where he's hurt, or dead, or just plain not in your life." Everyone became really silent; maybe too silent. I was suddenly sorry that I said anything.

"Oh well," Brooklyn dusted off her own shoulders. "This glass is half-full. Duke is thinking about our future together and he wants to marry me. Good enough for me."

"Really?" I probed. I probably shouldn't have pushed my luck. I felt like I was doing this a lot lately, but I just wanted to be sure that I was hearing all of this correctly.

"Really, really," Brooklyn replied while she checked out her nails. "I can't believe that Duke came up with all of these ideas on his own. I can't believe that he was really sitting back and thinking about our future together."

"He probably wasn't," Adair said off-hand. "His mother probably gave him the idea."

Brooklyn's face changed for about a millisecond and then she seemed to discard the idea again.

"Well, Jess, as we have previously discussed, mothers can have plenty of sway in the minds of their sons. But overall, they are only doing what they think is best. So, we let them have their moments and then we go about our day, right?"

"Right," Adair said and nodded her head in a curt way. It was like she was memorizing this advice, one more time, just to be sure.

"So, how do I look?" We all whipped around to see Hope emerging from her bedroom. During the new career conversation, I hadn't realized that Hope had slipped out of sight. Apparently, she had gone into her room to change her clothes. Now she was standing here in a very cute sundress. It had small flowers all over it and she had completed the look with a beautiful pair of lilac-colored sandals. I thought that it might be a little late in the evening for a sun dress, but I didn't want to rain on her parade.

At that moment, Eve came out of the kitchen. "Where are you going?" she asked as she threw a dish towel back onto the counter behind her.

Hope blushed. I don't remember the last time that I saw my little sister blush and it was a welcome surprise now.

"I have a date tonight," she said as a huge grin spread from ear to ear.

"Really?" Autumn asked. "Are you going out with anyone we know?" Even though this was a polite question to ask, it didn't really make sense. Hope usually didn't go out with us, so she didn't know many of the people that we did. Her crowd was generally a bit younger.

As I started to say this, I decided that it was not my place to go pouncing on everyone else's ideas tonight, so I just sat in chill-mode.

"Actually," Hope replied as she started to load her purse with goodies, "I don't think that any of you would know him. He works at the Lob with me. "

"Oh," I said, and everyone else nodded in acknowledgment Hope was still working at the Lob as a waitress until she could finish getting her Fine Arts degree. She was going to be a professional photographer someday; I just knew it.

"Anyway," she said as she slipped the big purse onto her forearm, "his name is Dan, and he has been hounding me for a long time to go on a date with him, but I kept refusing."

"Why?" Brooklyn asked. She was now sitting forward in her seat. "Why didn't you want to go out with him?"

"I don't know," Hope shrugged. "I just didn't." We all looked back and forth, but she didn't offer any more information. Sometimes, the answer was really just that simple.

"Anyway . . ." Eve said sarcastically.

"Anyway, when he asked me out the other day, I decided to go for it, so we're going to the movies tonight." She quickly glanced at the clock on the wall. "I really have to go. Do I look okay?" She asked the question of the whole room but looked at me for approval.

"You look great," I said automatically. But at least it was honest; she really did look nice.

"I'm going to be late," she called and quickly pulled the handle to the exterior door. She swiftly moved out into the hallway. We all laughed. Anyone who knew Hope knew that she was always late.

"Wish me luck," she shouted as she began to race down the apartment stairs.

"Luck," we all yelled after her. After Hope's impromptu exit, it seemed like the energy had been drained from the room. We all just sort of looked around at each other.

Eve was the first to speak up. "Does anyone want to go get a drink?"

"God yes," was Adair's reply.

We all dutifully put our jackets on. The evening had become quite nippy, and I had to loan a sweater to Brooklyn, as she had not thought to bring one with her. Usually, she didn't stay through dinner and drinks, but I had the feeling that even though she wanted to act as though things were on the up and up with Duke, she really had some issues that she needed to work through.

As we walked into Calamity Jim's, we were greeted by a squeal of delight. Savanna was perched on a nearby barstool, and she was evidently very happy to see us. Eve practically ran to her side, as it was clear that she was just as excited to see her friend and partner in crime again.

We all exchanged hellos and decided to try to find a place at one of the booths so that we could all sit together. Minutes later, we were relaxing in the familiar surroundings and trying to catch Savanna up on what she had missed.

When our server, Carly, arrived, Savanna ordered a round of shots for everyone and a beer each.

She looked around to see just how grateful and excited we were, but she was instead greeted by defeated faces.

"Savanna," I said softly, "even though we appreciate your generosity, we all have to go to work tomorrow. It's only Thursday night, dude."

Savanna laughed her sweet southern chuckle. "Ladies, ladies, I almost forgot. How silly a me." We all laughed weakly too but realized that the damage had been done. She had already placed the order.

"It's cool," Adair said resolutely and put her hand in the center of the table. "We'll all just drink our shots and our beers and that will be it, right?" We all placed our hands on top of hers and agreed that we would only drink what had already been ordered. In true team fashion, we then sent our hands into the air and started laughing.

Three hours later, our promise had been broken. We started out with good intentions, really. I, in particular, had truly meant to keep my oath and drink what was already provided. But then, before I knew it, I realized that I missed going out on Thursday nights. Thursday nights were fun. I hadn't gone out during the week like this since I'd dated Cowboy. And then, when I thought about the whole Cowboy fiasco, that made me want to drink even more.

About a half-hour before Calamity Jim's was set to close its doors, the girls started to disperse. Each girl thanked Savanna profusely, as she had insisted that she pay for all our drinks. So technically, it was indeed her fault that we got intoxicated that night.

Adair and Brooklyn elected to share a cab and Autumn grudgingly decided that she would probably just crash on our couch and go back to her own home tomorrow morning before work. Since Savanna didn't seem like she was ready to leave the bar just yet, I decided to hang out with her a little longer. Plus, I still had something that I wanted to ask her.

"So, Savanna, what are you doing a week from Saturday?" I asked as soon as all our friends had cleared out.

"I don't know . . ." Her words were no longer crisp, and her accent was muddling everything even further. Savanna did not get drunk that often, but when she did, it was usually a major deal.

"You have a birthday coming up, you know." I said this in a teasing tone, but it was lost on Savanna. She just shrugged.

"I know, I know, I have anotha birthday right around the corna," she sighed and twirled her finger in the air.

"Are you alright?" I said, taking a hold of her hand.

"I'm gonna be so old, Missy," she said in her overdramatic fashion.

"No, you're not," I replied.

"Yes, yes, I am," she shook her head furiously and took a sip from her Bud Light. "I'm gon' be so old," she repeated.

"Listen," I said, trying to calm her down. "I have a surprise for your birthday, but since you know that I am not very good at surprises, I wanted to tell you about it now. Can you handle it?"

"Yeah," she said, and I could see the attention coming back into her eyes.

"Okay," I leaned in. "For your birthday, I got you tickets to see *Little Women* at the Square House Theatre."

"Oh Missy, tha's so thoughtful. I love it." Her cheeks were stained pink from her happiness. "Are ya goin' with me?" She could hardly contain her enthusiasm.

"I did better than that: I got four tickets!" I said this with pride.

She held up her fingers and counted four: one-two-three-four. But then, she still looked confused. "I don't get it."

"I got four tickets," I said gently, "so that you and I could take dates." My eyebrows went up on that last part. I had not been on a really good date in a long time, and I knew that it had been even longer for Savanna. Since she was on tour so many days out of the year, she didn't often have a chance to find a guy and start dating him before she had to move on again.

"So, your present to me is really just a chance to go on a double-date?" She looked even happier now that she had figured out my little plot.

"Exactly," I said. Then I swept my hand across the barroom. There were about twenty men left. "Take your pick. Who do you want to ask out?"

She blushed. The southern belle was coming out in her again. "Actually," she pointed across the room at our friend, Stephen. "I'ma thinking I'll ask Stephen to go with me."

"But he's just a friend," I began, and then I noticed the look on her face. Maybe he was just a friend to me, but Savanna seemed to think differently.

"Oh," I said, drawing the word out in a long fashion. "Okay, well, hop on over there and ask him out. It's next Saturday at 7 p.m. Tell him to meet us here at six."

"Will do," Savanna said, and she nearly jumped out of the seat. I wasn't sure if it was a good idea to start asking out guys on a day when we were so intoxicated, but then again, I figured that it couldn't hurt. Alcohol equals liquid courage, or so I've been told.

While she was on her mission, I began to scan the bar. My choices were limited. I knew that I could wait and ask someone to go with me later, but I kind of liked the idea of doing it right now. I wanted Savanna and I both to have dates ready to roll at the same time. I was fairly certain that Stephen would say yes.

So, I continued to inspect the bar, trying to gather and then narrow my options. There were a few guys that I didn't know. They were sitting at the other end of the bar, and they were pretty cute. But I wasn't really sure if attending a play was the sort of thing you asked someone to do if you didn't know them. That eliminated one cross section of gentlemen.

I then turned my attention to the table of guys that I did know. There was a whole poker crew sitting a couple of tables over. I realized, now that I was looking in that direction, that I knew every guy at the table because we all had played poker together at some time or another. I decided that I would ask one of those guys to be my date because at least I knew that they were decent people.

I decided that random selection would probably be best. I focused my complete attention on the table of guys and the first one to turn around was Jonathon. He was a nice guy with dark thinning hair and big eyes. He was cute enough that I would be happy to ask him out. I waved my hand in his direction, beckoning for him to join me.

He nudged the guy next to him, Cary, to let him know that he would be vacating the table for a while. Cary looked in my direction and gave me a long and total once over. He smiled slightly, and I felt gratified knowing that if he were going to eyeball me like that, he would at least appreciate what he saw.

Jonathon sat his beer down first and then took a seat on the other side of the booth from me.

"How's it going?" I asked casually.

"Were you waving to me just now?" He replied.

"Yes," I said patiently.

"Cool," he replied and took a drink of his beer.

"Last call!" One of the bartenders yelled. This announcement made me uneasy. I thought that I would talk to Jonathon for a few minutes before springing the question on him. But apparently, the bar had decided that it needed to close whether my mojo was working or not. I threw caution to the wind.

"Hey," I said, "what do you say that we go on a date?"

Chapter Six

How Much Do You Owe a Guy After One Date?

"There is nothing like the feeling of a first date," I said dreamily.

"There is nothing like the feeling of a first kiss," Adair said, making a goofy face. She shoved half of her banana in her mouth. We were seated around the Pond. Even though the sun was shining beautifully, it was a breezy day, and Charlotte was being plagued by high winds. I don't know what I expected, but the wacky weather was killing me. On this particular Saturday, the girls had decided to meet at the Pond for brunch. Every single girl had a date scheduled for that evening, and we were gathering together to celebrate the unprecedented event.

With the absence of Jack and Benson still creating a hole in our universe, Brooklyn had thought to invite Cara for the occasion. While Cara was not my favorite person in the world, she wasn't so bad to have around.

"Oh Jess, you're too twisted for words," Autumn laughed and nudged her elbow into Adair's ribs.

"Yes," she sighed and paused to wipe the corners of her mouth. "I am." She winked at the table of women. We all laughed at Adair's antics. The further she sank into happiness with Wesley, the more good-natured she appeared at our weekly get-togethers. She was absolutely glowing twenty-four hours a day and we had Wesley to thank for taming the wild beast. Appropriately enough, Adair and Wesley were actually going on a date tonight. They wanted to take a mini break from all of the wedding hoopla and just do something normal. Frankly, I didn't blame them.

"Back to first dates," Brooklyn said and brought the laughter to a conclusion. "Explain to me what's happening this weekend."

"Okay," Adair took the reins. "My fiancé, Wesley," she held her head high as she said his name, "has this really great friend, Curtis. I told Curtis so much about Autumn that he is dying to meet her. I really think that they'll hit it off. We're going on a group date tonight."

"Ahk!" I nearly choked on my glass of water. "What about Paul?"

"What about him?" Adair asked, seeming to be a bit confused, too.

"Paul," Autumn said calmly, placing her napkin delicately onto her lap, "Paul knows all about this date tonight. We both are experimenting right now."

"Did you break up?" Brooklyn asked.

"Not officially," Autumn answered. Her nonchalance was uncharacteristic. I began to think about Autumn's actions over the last few weeks. I wouldn't really say that she was different, but I would say that Paul had changed something about her.

"What does that mean?" I asked.

"It means that we're still together." Autumn's hands were wrestling with each other inside her napkin. "But, it also means that we are willing to go on dates with other people."

"So, you have an *open relationship*?" Adair asked. I was a little surprised that Adair didn't actually have this information. Since she had set up the date with Curtis, I just assumed that she knew the details about Autumn's relationship status.

"Not exactly," Autumn said, and the wave of pink that rushed into her cheeks was noticeable.

"Tell me about this Curtis," Cara said as she dipped her sausage in syrup. Even though it seemed out of place for Cara to interject in such a fashion, I was grateful to her. Autumn really seemed to be struggling here and the grand inquisition probably wasn't making the situation any better.

"Curtis," Jess said excitedly, "is drop dead gorgeous. He is just amazing." She licked her lips. "I call him Hot Curtis," she giggled. "Anyway, he is a college friend of Wesley's. They were fraternity brothers."

"I just love frat boys," Cara interrupted. "There is just something so alluring about eight boys living in a house together."

"Really?" Brooklyn raised her eyebrows.

"You remember the boys that lived in the EX house, don't you?" Autumn looked at Cara in shock. The EX boys were our sorority's brothers. We loved those guys more than anything, but living in the frat house was never considered glamorous or seductive by any means. It was deemed disgusting. Cara never answered; she just kept staring off into space. Chances are that she was remembering some college escapade.

"Anyway," Adair continued with her profile of Curtis, "Curtis and Wesley were fraternity brothers and now they hang out about once a week. Curtis teaches special education, and he coaches football."

"That's hot," Brooklyn said between sips of her cranberry juice.

"I think so, too," Adair snickered. Maybe Brooklyn had been joking, but Jess didn't seem to notice.

Calmly, Autumn joined the conversation. "Well, if this Curtis guy is even half as wonderful as he seems to be on the phone, then I'm certain we'll hit it off just fine."

"Oh, so you've already spoken to each other?" Cara raised her eyebrow.

"Did someone say phone sex?" Adair was back in on the conversation.

"No," Autumn giggled, "Curtis and I have already spoken twice this week. We seem to be hitting it off, but don't jinx it, you guys."

"All right," Brooklyn said thoughtfully. She seemed to be calculating, "So, Autumn is meeting Curtis for the first time this evening and Missy is going out with Jonathon tonight . . ."

"Jonathon?" Adair interrupted, "Poker Jonathon?"

I laughed, "Yes, well, Poker Jonathon *is* his real name." Jonathon and his friend Tony owned the poker company, so he was at almost all the games. Jonathon and I would hang out on occasion, but tonight was the first night we had planned to do something exclusively together. I had tickets to the theatre and was taking him to see *Little Women*. It was the musical adaptation, and I wasn't quite certain how the whole affair was going to turn out. I had asked Savanna to bring a date, and she selected our friend Stephen. I thought that if nothing else, I would have two very good buddies who could help buoy the evening.

"Okay," I continued, getting back on topic. I didn't really want that much attention concerning the Jonathon date. I didn't even know if I liked the guy; I was just testing the waters. "I'm taking Jonathon to the theatre tonight, and Autumn is going to a football game with Curtis. Cara, who is on your agenda for the evening?"

"His name is Dustin," Cara began as she licked the back of her fork.

"Yes," I prompted. "And where did you meet Dustin?" In my mind, I was silently thanking my lucky stars that Cara wasn't still dating Mitch. I didn't think that their relationship would last very long, but I had to admit that I was a little bit delighted to hear that they had broken up. I still maintain that I wasn't upset that they became a couple, but I will concede that I wouldn't have been able to sit through listening to all the gory details of their relationship. I liked Mitch. It wouldn't have been fair to listen to someone else talk about being with him.

Brooklyn became all excited, "She met him last Thursday at Buffalo's. We went out for wings, and she picked herself up a man!" Adair and Brooklyn began making catcalls and I joined in on the fun.

"Stop it," Cara laughed through our annoying ruckus. "Stop teasing me. I really need your opinions, girls." We all came to an immediate silence. It was as if the court was now in session.

"All right," she continued, "I met Dustin last Thursday and he called me the next day. He said he'd really enjoyed my company the night before."

Adair interjected, "I don't see the problem. Sounds wing-a-riffic so far."

"Let her finish," Brooklyn said and rolled her eyes. I had a feeling she already knew the story but was stumped by the ending. I leaned forward and listened more intently.

"Anyway," Cara laughed, "he asked me to go out with him tonight but wondered if it'd be okay if he sent me something at work first. I'd told him about my job," she explained.

"Actually," Brooklyn laughed, "she doesn't remember telling him about her job. She doesn't even remember what he looks like," she concluded in an almost singsong manner.

"Oh, that's priceless," I snickered.

"Well, you can't go out with him if you don't remember him," Autumn said in her pragmatic manner.

"Why not?" Cara scoffed, "You're going out on a date tonight with someone you've never even laid eyes on. I at least met this guy." She looked a bit offended by Autumn's announcement.

"Yeah," Adair said, "but you don't remember him."

"That's beside the point," Brooklyn was still laughing. "Tell them the rest of the story!" She nearly fell over her chair because she was laughing so hard. It was sort of weird to see Brooklyn acting in this manner; I wondered if spending so much time with Cara had rubbed off on her. Maybe she was getting to be a bit silly now, too.

"Well," Cara sighed, "the thing he wanted to send to my work was a dozen pink roses. I was visiting with a colleague today at lunch and they announced over the loudspeaker that I was needed in the central office. Apparently, Dustin had dropped off the heaping vase himself." We all began to burst into laughter.

"Besides the fact that you can't remember his face, I really don't see the problem here," Autumn offered.

"What do you mean you don't see the problem?" Brooklyn blurted. "She meets this guy that she doesn't recall. He calls her the next day, delivers a dozen roses to her office, and . . ." Brooklyn stopped short and looked in Cara's direction.

Cara finished the sentence, "And today when I got home from work, I found a note slipped under my door." I felt my eyes bug out. I couldn't decide if things were romantic here or just plain creepy.

"What did the note say?" I wondered aloud.

"It said that he had stopped by to see where I lived so that he wouldn't get lost when he returned that evening," she said. I had a feeling she was keeping something from us. There had to be more to the story.

"Tell them the other part," Brooklyn pumped her for more information.

"The card on the flowers said that he hoped the roses made this day very special for me because he planned to make every one of the rest of our days together just as special."

"Gross," Adair said and nearly choked on the last portion of her banana. "That is so syrupy sweet that I want to puke."

"Even worse is that he doesn't even know her," Autumn whispered. She was now focusing all her practicality on this observation of Dustin's character. "How can he say that he's going to make all your days just as special? This is your first date, right?" She was nearly hysterical with fear by the time she finished her last thought.

"Quit haranguing the witness, prosecutor," Brooklyn joked. "This is serious business."

Cara joined in, "What should I do?"

"Well, you can't cancel the date," I said.

"She most certainly can," Brooklyn announced. "This man doesn't even know her, and he has appeared at her place of business, sent her a dozen roses, and turned up at her house knowing full well that she wasn't even there. That's bizarre. I don't care what anybody says."

"I agree with Missy and Autumn," Adair finally said.

"You cannot honestly tell me that Cara should go out with some wacko just because she doesn't want to be alone on date night," Brooklyn roared. She had gone into defense mode.

"That's not what I'm saying at all," Adair stated. "I agree that there's no way Cara can cancel the date. I have multiple reasons for this suggestion."

"I'd like to hear them," I offered.

"Thank you," Adair proceeded, "first and foremost, Cara already agreed to the date and this guy already knows where she lives and where she works. If he really is mad, do you think that when she cancels the date, he's just going to let it all go? No, no. He has invested time stalking her and money for the flowers --trying to woo her. He's not just going to leave her alone without a date."

"The second reason is that crazy man might not be crazy at all. He might just be socially inept. We've all heard of those guys who fall in love at first sight and begin acting insanely romantic. So basically, what I'm saying is that Dustin might not be obsessed today; he might just be trying too hard. However, if you break his heart . . ."

"Then he might become crazy," Cara finished the story.

"Exactly," Adair added.

"She's right," Autumn said and sipped her coffee thoughtfully. "You have to go on the date. You can cut it short if you want. You make up some reason at the end to never see him again, but you have to go tonight, even if it is just to prevent future run-ins with the fellow."

"You ladies do have a point," Brooklyn confessed.

"Okay, so it has been decided," Cara sighed loudly and placed her palms on the table, "I will go out with this hopeless romantic, yes?"

"Yes," we sang in a unanimous chorus.

"Just be careful," Brooklyn warned in her most maternal voice.

"I always am," Cara said. She looked up at us all with a winning smile, and I began to hope beyond all hopes that even if her judgments had been clouded in past relationships, that Cara truly would be on her guard tonight.

"Are you with Dan right now?" I said quietly into the phone. I had just left the Pond and I thought that I ought to call Hope and give her a heads-up. I would be home in about five minutes.

"Yeah," she whispered back.

"Are you decent?" I asked, with a little bit of an edge creeping into my voice. I still hadn't met Dan yet, so I was hoping that she wasn't already sleeping with him. I mean, she is my little sister, you know. I didn't always like to think of her like that, so vulnerable, but my innate protective side always seeped to the surface when I was dealing with Hope's gentlemen callers.

"Yeah," she said, and I could hear a man chuckle in the background.

"Then, why are you whispering?" I demanded.

"I'm whispering because you're whispering," Hope said, then laughed loudly to break the tension.

"I'll be home in a few minutes. Is it acceptable for me to meet Dan today?" I wasn't really sure why I was asking Hope this question. From the way she had talked about Dan since they started dating, I could tell that she liked him, but I also got the vibe that she wasn't ready to go public with their relationship just yet. I didn't know quite what that meant. I wondered if there was something wrong with him that she wasn't ready to share just yet, but I kept all of those thoughts to myself. I wanted Hope to be happy, and if she just wanted some alone time with her man for a while, I was willing to accommodate.

"I don't think today will work. He's actually on his way out." Hope said this quickly and I pictured her shooing him out the door at that very second.

"You know what--I actually need to stop at the store real fast, so I'll be a little bit longer getting home. Is that okay?"

Hope let out a brief sigh of relief, "Perfect, thanks!"

I couldn't really understand why Hope didn't want me to meet her new boyfriend, but for the time being, I was content with letting her keep him a secret. Besides, I had a first date to prepare for and I didn't want anything to spoil my good mood.

The funny thing about first dates is that they're deceiving, at least the majority of the time. Most people try to be on their best behavior during that first, most important date. The standard rules apply:

1. No cursing (Applicable for both men and women.)
2. No talking with your mouth open. (Men must fight hard to follow this rule.)
3. Don't say anything offensive. (For example: Claiming that people born in the north are all stuck up and full of themselves is a surefire way to lose the interest of a northern gal, such as myself.)
4. Give each other compliments (but don't go overboard.)

While my date went perfectly fine and all the above rules were regarded with care by both parties, that last rule really tripped up poor Dustin.

Initially, he'd told Cara that he would take her anywhere she wanted to go. As it turned out, when he said anywhere, he meant anywhere they wouldn't have to wait for a table. He took her to a little spot called Tripps. I like this establishment. Sometimes Steve Martin and I hang out there. It's quaint and they serve some good, greasy bar food. Cara, the true carnivore, ordered a juicy cheeseburger and sat back to try to enjoy his company. Before the waitress had even brought the drinks, the show began.

"I just want to tell you how beautiful you look tonight," Dustin began.

"Oh, thank you," Cara, said and tossed her hair, smiling easily as the waitress placed her water in front of her place. The waitress had heard the comment and was snickering above them.

"I really mean it," Dustin continued, "you are gorgeous."

"Thank you again," Cara sighed. She was now blushing. She was the kind of girl who was used to getting compliments, but this sort of idol worship was beyond even her comprehension.

"I am totally serious," Dustin said dreamily and offered his hand across the table. Cara refused to take it. She folded her hands neatly in her lap. He left his hand there and proceeded, "I mean, the other night when we were out, I decided that I just had to come talk to you because I was getting a strained neck from looking over my shoulder towards you and your beauty." Cara turned her head towards the wall so that he wouldn't notice her rolling her eyes.

"So," he said and took a sip of his Coke, "why did you decide to go out with me?"

"I'm sorry?" Cara felt the words sticking in her throat. She was terrified. What kind of question was that? Some might not be intimidated by this type of question, but Cara in all her dating career, had never met someone so bold as to come right out and say those words.

"I don't mean to catch you off-guard here," Dustin replied. "It's just that you're so amazing, I don't know why you would agree to date a guy like me." Cara couldn't decide what he was up to. She was definitely freaked out but didn't know exactly what was scaring her. She decided to level with the guy.

"Can I be honest with you?" She leaned forward. Dustin stretched his hand across the table again.

"I certainly hope you can," he said and looked deeply into her eyes. That longing, dreamy look should have been heart-warming for Cara, but since it came from Dustin, she found it revolting. He was taking himself and this date with her way too seriously. She quietly debated with herself the merit of just being frank with him and calling a cab.

Cara finally opted for honesty, but also felt obligated to give Dustin just a little more time on this date.

"Listen," she said and pushed back in her chair, "I was really drunk the other night . . ."

He cut her off. She could hear the temperature rising in his tone, "So, you only agreed to go out with me because you were drunk?"

"I didn't say that," Cara snapped, but kept her eyes fixed on the plaque that was posted above his head. "What I said was that I was really drunk Thursday night. I remember laughing a lot and having a really good time. I remember you being there. I just assumed that the fun we had the other night drunk might translate into having fun while we were sober."

He relaxed in his chair and said truthfully, "Oh good; I thought you were going to say that you wanted to end the date already."

"Why would I do that?" Cara scooted even further back in her chair.

"Because that's what women do," Dustin answered matter-of-factly. "They just leave."

Cara knew right then and there that Dustin wasn't crazy. She still found his wooing techniques to be highly alarming, but now she knew why he was so damaged. Something had happened to him before, and it had nothing to do with her. Chances were that some woman had broken his heart awhile back and now he was trying to compensate for that lost love. She almost felt sorry for the poor guy. But before she could soften up, he was back to the compliments.

"You really are a dream. I hope that we have this much fun for the rest . . ." Luckily, he was cut off. The waitress appeared with their cheeseburgers just in time. Cara's mind cringed at the words that would have come out of his mouth. He was a hopeless wreck.

As she began to tear her burger into halves and pick through her French fries, she noticed that he was drowning his entire plate in ketchup. Gross. She watched as he took a massive bite of the burger and then practically threw the sandwich back into its basket. She squeezed even further back into her seat. She felt like she was sitting in the Splash Zone at Sea World.

She quickly scanned her yellow tank top for residual ketchup. Luckily, she had been sitting far enough away that no tiny dots were evident. She made a mental note to check out the shirt as soon as she got home. The lighting was so dim in the restaurant, that it was really hard to tell either way.

As the meal continued, she began to find out some interesting things about Dustin. He was in the Air Force. He had grown up in the area and was currently on leave for a little while. He had done a small amount of traveling and, at one time had his life threatened while in Mexico. This last fact threw Cara for a loop because even though Dustin brought it up, he refused to elaborate on the situation. Why had he been in Mexico? Why did someone threaten his life? Dustin kept silent on those points.

In return, Cara tried to reveal as little as possible about her life but found that Dustin was more eager to talk about his life anyway, so it didn't really matter. As she munched on a few French fries, she noticed that he had not touched his burger since that first overwhelming bite.

"You don't like your hamburger?" she asked, trying to be polite.

"It's not very good," he said. She looked down at her own plate where her nearly devoured cheeseburger lay. She'd thought the meal was just fine.

"Hey, listen," Cara said, still trying to make the best of the evening. "We were planning to go see a movie tonight, right?"

"Yeah," Dustin replied.

"Well, what do you say we get out of here and head for the theatre?" Cara was putting on her best get-up-and-go voice.

"I already checked the movie listings; the show doesn't start for another hour or so. Do you want to go for a ride instead?" Cara did **not** want to go for a ride. If she were riding anywhere, she hoped that it would be right back to the safety of her apartment.

"Why don't we just go down the street," Cara said brightly. "There's a nice little sports bar; Hoops and Dreams. Have you ever been there?"

Dustin looked at her thoughtfully. It was as if he had a planned response to this question, but he swallowed whatever it was. He just simply shook his head instead.

"Well, let's go there then," she said. She waited for him to pay the tab and then headed for the door.

In the light of day, Dustin really didn't look too bad. He wasn't her normal standard of man, but he was sufficient. He had dark blond hair, blue-gray eyes, and a very small build. He was extremely skinny, not her body type, whatsoever, but she was trying not to fixate on that. She only had to make it through the rest of the evening. When he pushed up his sleeve to scratch an itch, she noticed a massive tattoo that covered the entirety of his arm. It was monstrous. Tattoos were okay in her book if they were minimal and meaningful. This thing was some big crazy, loopy design that seemed to be popping out of his arm.

As Cara tossed her purse over her shoulder, she thought for a moment gleefully that she was thankful that the rest of the date would be relatively silent. They would go to the bar for a bit and maybe watch some snippets of one of the ball games. Baseball was usually a safe topic for most dates. Then, they wouldn't really have to talk to each other during the movie, either. The great thing about watching a movie with a stranger is that talking isn't necessary, nor is it encouraged. For nearly two hours you can sit in a quiet theatre and enjoy a land of make-believe. That is, unless you go to the movies with Dustin.

He kept trying to ask Cara personal questions throughout the entire film. Even worse, he kept attempting to touch her. He would "accidentally" brush her leg or squeeze her hand at all of the suspenseful parts during the movie. She finally began to hold his hand to stop it from exploring any further.

Later that evening, she found that she was relieved to be back in his truck. At least the lights on the dashboard kept them from being in total darkness. Now she could see what move he was trying to pull. As they drew within nearly a block of her residence the conversation really began to venture into personal territory. Dustin wanted to tell Cara everything. He was only twenty-six years old and recently divorced. You guessed it: his wife had cheated on him and demanded a di-vorce immediately. Luckily, they had no children. And in case the thought had crossed your mind, Cara was the first person he had been out with since his ex-wife left him. Just as they were pulling into her apartment's parking lot, Cara began to grope for the door handle. He put the car in the park and put his arm around her.

"Where do you see this relationship going?" he asked her.

Cara tried to laugh it off, "I don't know. We just met."

"No seriously," he persisted, "what do you think about *us*?"

Cara swung her head around to face him. He was awfully close to her, so she backed away. "I don't think anything. We just met. That's all."

"Do you think I could come inside?" he ventured.

"You know what, I'm really tired. Maybe another time," Cara said quickly and pulled the door lever just as he leaned even further towards her side of the front seat.

She stood up and exited the vehicle. Just as she was about to close the door he yelled, "But I have to go to the bathroom!"

"There's a Shell station down the block. Have a safe drive," she replied and slammed the car door behind her. Cara raced up the stairs, flew into her apartment, set the alarm, and ran back to her room. She needed to get as far away from that date and Dustin as she possibly could.

"You're kidding?"

I was doubled over with laughter. The girls had come to my house for a Mario's Pizza party. It was Wednesday night and Brooklyn was forcing all of us to watch *American Jamboree*. I took a huge bite of cheesy bread to see if I could calm my laughter, but I couldn't get over the tragedy Cara's date turned out to be.

"Well, Ms. Perfect, I'm glad that you find my misery to be so entertaining," Cara snapped sarcastically.

"Oh, come on, Cara, isn't it a little bit funny?" I pleaded with her as I tried to suppress my laughter.

"Yes," Brooklyn said between laughing spells, "it is. The poor guy is in love with you."

"And he doesn't even know you," Autumn was giggling uncontrollably.

"Well, I feel sorry for the poor dolt," Adair said. She was busy picking the pepperoni off her pizza. "He sounds like he really needed someone to take care of him."

"Then you take care of him. He can drive you insane for a while," Cara declared and tossed a pillow at Jess that nearly hit her in the face. I was glad that Cara's work at Adair's agency was finished. She had helped set up a fine web advertising division for DieLou Records, but then had decided to move on. Now that she was no longer an employee of Adair's, the two could be a little more relaxed around each another.

"I'm just saying . . ." Jess began.

"You're just saying what?" Cara turned to face her. "You're just saying that I should be nice to the poor guy even though I'm afraid that he is stalking me? I get strange phone calls where someone hangs up now. No breathing, no number, and no voice: there is *no one* there. I have to run into my apartment because I'm afraid I see his white truck sitting out front. Now, what is it that you're 'just saying'?"

All the hilarity had vanished. It had been quite clear that Cara had been uncomfortable on the date, but we knew going into it that she wasn't going to love the situation. Even if Dustin had been incredible, all the pre-date attentions had made Cara uneasy. When she reported that the date was a disaster that had seemed natural, we tried to make light of the situation. But now that she was really expressing true concern, the entire group's perspective monumentally shifted.

"I didn't realize it was so serious," Adair said and cocked her head to the side in a contemplative sort of way.

"Sweetie, I don't think anybody did," Brooklyn said and patted Cara's hand. "Cara, is it really that bad?"

We all looked at Cara expectantly.

"Sometimes," she seemed to be considering what she was saying as she was saying it. "Sometimes, I feel bad for him. I want to call him up and tell him that all women aren't heartless, and all women won't cheat on him. Then other times, I want to run as far away from the memory of him as I can. When we were on that date, it was like he was *trying* to obsess over me. It was like he was trying to turn everything into a major connection, when really, I was just trying to be polite. I guess that's what scares me the most."

"I'm really sorry to hear that," I started.

"I'll bet you are," Cara laughed. She realized that her outburst had brought everyone down. She picked up a container of garlic butter and tossed it at Adair. "Sorry I snapped at you, dude. You didn't know." Adair began chewing carefully on her slice of pizza again.

"Now," Cara focused her attention on me. "Tell us about your first date with Poker Jonathon."

"There's nothing to tell, really," I said as I walked into the kitchen. I needed to refill my water.

When I returned to the room I announced, "Honest: I've got nothing to report. The date was fine. It was just like a few friends, hanging out. We were very relaxed. I have to admit," I said as I plopped down onto the floor, "I was relieved that Savanna and Stephen were there too. I don't really think Jonathon enjoys the theatre."

"Big surprise," Brooklyn interjected. I giggled at her comment.

"It was nice having another couple there that appreciated musical theatre because it not only gave me someone to discuss the aspects of the show with, but it gave him some binoculars."

"Huh?" Autumn asked.

"Oh, Savanna brought binoculars because she knew our seats weren't so hot. He borrowed the glasses for almost the entire performance. At one point, I thought he might be sleeping behind them."

"Sounds like a snoozefest to me." Adair pointed to Autumn. "Now, tell us about your hunky football coach."

"He was fine," she said and focused her attention on the crust of her pizza.

"Fine?" Adair asked. "What does 'fine' mean?"

"'Fine' means that we had a good time," Autumn provided.

"Could you elaborate?" Brooklyn probed.

"Sure," Autumn sighed deeply, "we chatted nonstop. I liked the football game. He seems to really enjoy his job. You know-- all the normal first date stuff."

"But?" Cara threw in.

"I don't know. But nothing, I guess," Autumn responded. We all looked at Adair to decipher the code. It was as if Autumn was trying to use a riddle to throw us off her scent.

"Adair!" Jess snapped to as Brooklyn barked in her direction, "Does Autumn like Mr. Football or not?"

"Curtis," Jess began, "is a really nice guy."

"And?" I prompted.

"And the thing is . . . there's nothing." Autumn finished.

"Oh, come on, Autumn. Quit beating around the bush. What's the problem?" I asked.

"Okay, okay, geez, you're so inquisitive. I mean that we have plans to meet again tomorrow. I volunteered to cook him dinner."

"What about you cooking dinner for a boy implies 'nothing'?" Cara tapped her chin in a questioning manner.

"I would say there's something," Brooklyn said with a wink.

"Nope," Autumn coughed and threw her crust onto her plate. "The thing is this; we had a good time. I enjoyed his company, but at the end of the night, I wanted him to leave. The date was over, and I didn't want to chat anymore."

"You mean, like, you really didn't want to talk to him anymore. Was it that bad?" I asked, suddenly wondering if Autumn's night had been as fretful as Cara's.

"What she's saying," Adair began to explain, "is that there wasn't any chemistry. Curtis is a very good-looking guy and it's very easy to be attracted to him, but Autumn doesn't feel any physical desire for him."

"So why are you bothering to cook the man dinner?" It was Cara's turn to be confused.

"Because..." Autumn said, "I didn't feel anything on the first date, but maybe I will this time."

"Ooohh," we all nodded in unison.

We live in complicated times here, ladies.

Autumn's second date with Curtis turned out to be just as mediocre as the first.

"I mean," she said into the phone, "he is a really nice guy."

"Sweetie," I said, "I just don't get it. If you think he is good-looking, smart, and nice, then what's the problem? Is there something that you're just not sharing?"

"The problem's that I feel nothing for the guy. Everything with Curtis is so relaxed and so comfortable."

"And how is that a bad thing?" I questioned.

"Because when you're hanging out with someone for the first time you should at least feel a little nervous. You should at least experience some butterflies. The kiss good-night ought to be a little unnerving."

"So, he kissed you good night?"

"No, and I didn't want him to," she answered.

"Wow, A, it certainly sounds like you're growing up. You've stopped . . ."

She cut me off, "Oh, I'm getting a beep." She paused, "It's him. What do I do?"

"Nothing," I answered. "If you aren't interested in the guy, why make him believe that you are?"

"You're right, I won't answer." She seemed not entirely sure about the choice she was making. We talked for only a few more minutes when Autumn said she needed to go feed her dog because it wouldn't stop barking. I hadn't hung up the phone for a grand total of two minutes when Autumn's number appeared on my Caller ID again.

She was laughing uncontrollably, "Okay, Missy, I apologize for calling again, but I don't know whether I should be alarmed or laughing hysterically."

"Sounds like you picked the second one already. What's so darn funny?" I wanted to know.

"Well, I felt bad about not answering Curtis' phone call, so I decided to call him back and explain that I just wasn't interested."

"I knew you would crack," I sighed and grinned into the receiver.

"Anyway," she continued, "he didn't pick up the phone. Well, actually I don't know if he picked up or not."

"What do you mean?" I was intrigued.

"Well," she began, "after his phone rang approximately twice this voice came on. It sounded a bit like one of those old-fashioned fake professional wrestlers."

"And what did this voice have to say?"

"He said, 'I like school and I like football and I'm going to keep doing both!' When I heard that I clicked the phone off immediately. I don't know if it was a recording, a real person, or if he just had his phone near a television."

I cackled at the top of my lungs, "That is the funniest effing thing I've ever heard. Awesome." I began to chuckle softly as the moment faded.

When we calmed, she asked, "Why would anybody want to do that or say that?"

"I don't know Autumn, but aren't you glad he's the crazy one and not you?"

"Most definitely," Autumn said and seemed to breathe a sigh of relief. "It's amazing what a girl has to go through nowadays."

If I had any sense in my head whatsoever, I would have taken Autumn's bizarre phone call as an omen. Neither I nor anyone else I knew was meant to go out that evening. I should've just stayed at home and laughed it up with Autumn. If I could have seen what was coming, I would have.

"Let's go out," Hope said and looked at me with big eyes.

"What?" I squawked.

"I said," she repeated as she rolled from the couch onto the floor, "let's go out. I never get to go."

"Ahh," I moaned. "I don't really have the energy, and it's Thursday."

"Oh yes, you do!" She grabbed my hand and yanked me onto the ground beside her.

I stared at the clock on the wall. "Alright, let's go." She began to jump up and down excitedly. "But we can't stay long." Even as I said the phrase I knew that I didn't believe it. I just had the feeling that tonight was going to be a long night.

We strolled into Chucklin' Charlie's and found a group of friends perched near the door. Come to find out, there was going to be a poker game there that evening. Savanna and Eve were both in attendance.

"Hey, ya'll," Savanna called. She was gingerly sipping her glass of wine and seemed to have just spotted us from over the rim. Only Savanna would go to a bar called Chucklin' Charlie's and order a glass of Chardonnay. Somehow, she made it work, though.

"Hey, roommates!" Eve said loudly. When Eve has been drinking, she tends to get quite brash. It's not exactly an obnoxious loud; it is more of an entertaining sound. She was in fine form this evening. Everyone was. Not only was a poker tournament scheduled at the pub for that evening, but there was also the same football game being televised on every screen in the place. I had forgotten that the Panthers were playing an out of season exhibition game tonight. From what

I'd heard the Panthers had been in the Super Bowl earlier in the year. People in Charlotte were obsessed. They loved their Panthers. I suddenly felt very uneasy about being out. While I do love a good crowd of drunken sports fanatics, I can't stand a crowd of super-drunk sports fans. There is a fine line that divides the two, but it exists.

At that moment, the most hammered individuals in all of Charlotte came strolling through the door: Jonathon and his roommate Tony were practically falling all over each other trying to get into Charlie's. They were dressed in Panthers memorabilia, complete with jerseys, caps, rally towels, and large buttons. I watched as they waltzed towards the bar and ordered a round for everyone wearing Panthers garb.

Jonathon walked towards our table. He clumsily sat down across from me. Upon closer inspection, it was certain he was drunk. He was beyond drunk. He was toasted. His eyes were bloodshot and hardly open. His head was swaying slightly from side-to-side. He looked as if he might pass out at any moment.

"Hey," he slurred. "Savaner? Is that you?" Savanna laughed her light laugh.

"Yes darlin', it's me," she said and laughed again.

Eve interjected, "Jonathon, how long have you been drinking?" She arched her eyebrow in his direction. We all knew that she had been drinking for a while, but her drunken antics couldn't hold a candle to Jonathon's.

"I've been drinking since . . . hey . . ." He had finally spied me across the table. "Missy, how are ya?" Everyone laughed.

"Looks like he spotted you," Eve chuckled and elbowed me.

"Hey," he repeated in my direction.

"Hey," I laughed.

"How ya doing?" He said, "You want a drink?"

"No, no, Sweetie, I think you've had enough for the both of us," I replied amiably.

"You are," he hiccupped, "right about that. Bartender," he yelled, "bring over a round for my friends." A cheer went up from our group. Jonathon stood up to cheer and stumbled away. Something else must have caught his attention.

"How was your date last weekend?" Caroline asked. Caroline was a poker regular, and she had apparently been informed of mine and Jonathon's blossoming relationship.

"It wasn't a date, was it?" Hope had been busy checking out a guy at the next table, so she was only half-listening.

"It most certainly was a date!" Savanna cooed. "I'm shocked at you! I was there. I know it was a date."

I patted Caroline's arm, "It wasn't a date. Savanna took Stephen and I took Jonathon. It was a group outing at the theatre."

"Honey, call it whatever you want, but do you think *that*," we all stared in the direction she was pointing, "would go to the theatre for just a group outing?" I shook my head. Jonathon was busy hugging everyone in the bar. He was still offering to buy the entire bar a round of shots, but Tony seemed to be continually reminding him that buying *another* round was a bad idea.

I shrugged, "It was no big deal."

"Sure," Eve mimicked, "it was no big deal. That's why the entire world stopped when he finally caught sight of you across the table."

"But he didn't even notice her initially," Hope jumped into the conversation, trying to help.

"Yes," Caroline said, "But . . . he noticed her." She winked at me, grabbed her drink, and headed for her poker table. I blushed and ducked my head. I really didn't want people to think that Jonathon and I were dating. He was a good guy, but I still hadn't decided what I wanted from our relationship. Why ruin a friendship if you didn't need to even go there?

"Tables are ready," the tournament director said. He was striding around informing everyone that the games would be starting in a few minutes. We all parted, and I plopped down at a table near the door.

I wasn't doing too badly during the game, but sometimes I get bored. It is like I've said before: I enjoy playing the game of poker because I like seeing other people's reactions and I love talking to poker characters. The game itself is fun, sort of, but after about an hour and half at the poker table, I'd suffered long enough. My poker time was up. I went all in on a King-three off-suit and hoped that Savanna would win the hand. We had been lucky enough to be placed at the same table. As fortune would have it, Savanna did win the hand, so she got to keep all my chips.

I pushed in my chair then and began to saunter towards the bar. I was planning to buy a beer and have a drink with a few friends I'd spotted. Mike and Sharon were sitting at the Megatouch machine, and I sidled up next to my pals. They were playing a naughty photo hunt game. Not exactly my cup of tea, but I could live with it. Just as we started our conversation, I spotted Jonathon. He was weaving through the crowd and headed in my direction.

"Hey," he called, and in a surprisingly smooth motion, looped his arm around my shoulder. "What're *you* doin'?" He wavered back and forth and fell into my arms. I was now practically hugging him. Mike and Sharon turned around long enough to laugh in my direction. Jonathon started to nuzzle his face into my neck. I became uncomfortable very quickly.

"Oh Jonathon, stop that," I whispered.

"Stop what?" he asked and looked up at me with half-closed eyes. He pulled me closer to him. Caroline came up behind me.

"So, he doesn't like you, huh?" she chuckled. He began to snuggle into me even closer. "Oh, he likes you." She continued to laugh as she walked away. I didn't know what to do. I felt like I was backed into a corner. Just then, he let go. He pushed his way up to the bar. I took the chance to escape. I saw Tony standing across the room sipping a mixed drink. I decided to see if he was doing any better than Jonathon.

Tony attempted to grab my behind. He whistled and shouted, "Hey," as I glided by him. His eyes were bloodshot as well.

"What's the good word?" I said and leaned towards him.

"You taking care of Jonathon?" he asked and nodded in his buddy's direction.

"Not exactly," I said and sat down at the table.

"You should," he said and took another sip of his drink.

"Why do you say that?" I wanted to know.

"Because he needs a friend like you right now."

"But you're his friend. Why can't you take care of him?" I questioned.

"Because..." Tony paused and leaned in close. "He needs a friend like *you* right now."

He's got to be kidding.

Only a man would be thinking about getting laid when he's that plastered. Women are open to the idea of having sex while they're drinking, but forget about it once they become really intoxicated, because they know what happens. Every woman knows that when she gets really drunk, she's bound to do one of three things during sex: The first is just lie there; the second is pass out; and the third is vomit all over her partner. No woman in her right mind wants any of those events to occur. Men, on the other hand, can't seem to fathom anything going wrong when they're drunk.

I began to walk towards Hope's table to see how she was doing, when Jonathon lurched across the bar and grabbed my hand.

"I've got to go to the bathroom," he breathed.

"Okay," I said and tried to release his hand. He only held my hand tighter. "Do you want me to walk you there?" He leaned up against me again. "I'll take that as a yes," I said and began to push our way through to the restroom. Jonathon tried to elbow his way into the men's bathroom.

"Where do you think you're going?" some small, stout man barked in our direction.

"Go ahead," I apologized, "sorry about that." The man walked past us and gave me a weird look.

Jonathon took the scrunched quarters as an opportunity to get closer to me. He maneuvered me up against the mirrored wall and began making out with my neck and the side of my face.

"Stop, Jonathon! What are you doing?" I shrieked as his hands began to rove. He was having the time of his life as I was trying to push him away. Just as his hands were sliding up my shirt, Mike walked around the corner. He looked almost as shocked as I did.

"Help me!" I said. Mike walked up behind Jonathon and grabbed his shoulder. He gently pulled Jonathon away.

"Leave her alone, man," Mike said. Just as Jonathon seemed to be relaxing, the door to the women's restroom swung open. Somehow, Jonathon quickly grabbed my hand and threw me into the bathroom with him. The scene that had happened outside the bathroom repeated itself. He began to grope every inch of my body. I felt like I was paralyzed. I kept telling him to quit it, but I knew he couldn't even understand. He was beyond gone.

"Jonathon," I squirmed out of his reach. "It's time for you to go home." He pushed himself back as if I had slapped him.

"You go home," he ordered and unlocked the door to the restroom. I ran out of the room ahead of him. I wanted to run away, but Tony was waiting right around the corner.

"Where's Jonathon?" he asked. I turned around to see Jona-thon stumbling towards us. He threw his arms around me.

"Take him home," Tony ordered and walked in the other direction.

"What?" I said. "Why don't you take him home?"

"Because you owe him."

"Owe him?" I reiterated.

"You heard me. You owe him," Tony roared.

"I don't owe anyone anything," I yelled back. "You owe him. He is your best friend and chances are that you got him this drunk." Tony had already walked away. What was I going to do with this incredibly obnoxious drunk that wouldn't let go of my hand? Just then, Hope came walking in my direction.

"What is this lump of crap?" She picked up Jonathon's hand and let it drop back down to his side.

"Tell me about it," I scoffed.

"Well, what do you plan to do with him?"

"I don't know. I guess we should take him home," I shrugged underneath his weight.

"Do you know where he lives?" Hope asked.

"I can only vaguely recall, but it requires passcodes and special keys to get inside."

"It would," Hope said sarcastically. "Alright, let's load him in the car and take him to our place."

"Where's Eve?" I said. I was hoping she could help us carry Jonathon to the car.

"She left about thirty minutes ago," Hope replied and linked her arm around Jonathon's. "She can help us get him up the stairs when we get home."

I had forgotten that we had stairs. We were in trouble.

Getting Jonathon into the car and the car ride home felt like a terrible use of positive energy. I expended so much strength just trying to make him understand that we were getting into a car, that it hardly seemed worth the trouble. I thought, after Hope suggested it first, that leaving him by the curb might actually be a viable option.

After that, it took approximately five minutes to convince Jonathon that we *weren't* going to leave him by the side of the road. Hope jumped into the driver's seat, while Caroline and I tried to bundle Jonathon in together. (Luckily, she saw us struggling and came to assist). He was trying to fight us, so it made the job even more difficult. Then as suddenly as lightning strikes, he nearly collapsed into the car. It was like the alcohol had finally impaired all his bodily functions. We took the opportunity to push his dead weight around. I crawled into the car behind him. Someone needed to hold his head up the entire ride home so that he wouldn't get a kink in his neck. I was the lucky girl to make sure his head didn't roll around.

When we got to the apartment, things got worse. First, Jonathon refused to get out of the car.

"Jonathon," I said softly, "time to wake up and go inside."

"Maaaaa," he groaned, "where are we?"

"Home," I said.

"Blah," he smacked his lips together and turned over in the seat. Hope had gone inside during this time and had brought Eve to our aid.

"What is this?" Eve chuckled.

"This," I pointed to the blob curled up in the passenger seat, "this is Drunk Jonathon. Not to be confused with Poker Jonathon. Drunk Jonathon is a different sort of beast altogether."

"Well, I guess we better get him out of the car, right?" Eve said as she stepped closer to me.

"Okay, Jonathon," I focused my attention back on him, "we are going to take you out of the car and into the apartment."

"No!" he ordered. "I'm staying here." He tried to get comfortable in the seat and in the process made a mess of Hope's car. He turned over and kicked an air freshener down.

"He is ruining my car! He knocked over my air freshener." Hope was upset. Her car was a mess most of the time, but when it was clean she didn't want someone else mucking it up.

"Come on, Jonathon!" Eve and I continued to try to coax him out of the car. We figured if we had his help, this operation would go a lot more smoothly. However, he still refused to leave the car. He kept kicking and flailing about, trying to make himself comfortable in the tiny Honda.

"That's it," Hope was ticked. "I've had enough being nice. Grab a corner." She yanked on a corner of his jersey. "Get out of my car, Jonathon," she said and tugged on him. Only his shoulder moved slightly. We tried to follow suit, but his legs still wouldn't budge.

"Jonathon," I moaned, "you're going to have to help us."

"So, this is what it feels like to lift a dead body," Eve groaned as we pulled Jonathon out of the car and threw his legs out after him. Hope slammed the door shut so that he couldn't regain consciousness and crawl back in. We tried to stand him up, but failed, so we just let his body sink to the pavement. We forgot to protect his head on the way down, so his head landed with a clunk.

"Whoops," I giggled, and the other girls laughed, too. We were already exhausted, and we hadn't even made it through the hard part.

"So, how are we going to do this?" Eve asked. We were taking a breather and trying to plan our next course of action. I'd noticed that Eve was now alert. I'd thought that she'd been hammered herself a few hours ago, but having to take care of Jonathon was certainly sobering her up.

"I say we push him," I said. "It seems like it's easier to push something than it is to pull it. Let's give it a try."

"How are we going to push him on pavement?" Hope looked at me like I was totally losing it.

"Oh," I looked at the ground, "well, what's your idea?"

"I say we lift him," she and Eve said simultaneously.

"We'll both take his legs," Hope said and pointed to herself and Eve. "You take his head," she ordered and pointed to me as we all bent over to retrieve our piece of Jonathon's body. He just laid there. He was motionless. It really was like picking up a dead body.

"Now lift," Hope instructed. They hoisted his legs into the air as I was only able to lift his head about five inches off the ground.

"Lower him," Hope commanded.

Eve ran to my end. "Switch me," she said. "I'll take the head, you take the middle, and Hope can take the legs." I tried to navigate exactly which part of the "middle" would be best to hold as Eve began to raise Jonathon's head.

"We can't just leave him here," I argued.

"Why in the world not?" Hope asked. "He has done nothing to help us."

"But I feel like we should . . ."

"We don't have to do anything," Eve interrupted me. Then she looked at him sprawled on the ground. "Ugh-- he's so help-less. The homeless will eat him alive."

Hope grinned too and conceded, "Let's get him inside."

This time as we began to lift, Jonathon struggled to put his legs on the ground. Just as we came to the stairs, he stopped moving his legs. We draped his arms around our shoulders and tried to nearly carry him up the stairs.

"Okay, okay, okay," Jonathon groaned, and tried to kick his legs out. I think it was his idea of helping the process. He looked like a baby giraffe that was learning to walk for the first time. He was bending his knees and then kicking his legs out in front. It didn't help at all.

As we pulled him up over the last stair and into the apart-ment, I had never been so grateful to see the couch right beside the door.

"On three, we throw him down," Eve said through deep breaths.

"One, two, three," Hope counted. As we began to toss Jonathon onto the couch, he grabbed my arm and hurled me under him. I couldn't breathe. Not only was he lying on top of me, but he had thrown his arm up over his head and it was cutting off my air supply. The girls struggled to roll him off me. I finally burst free and sat on the floor, attempting to catch my breath. After I gulped down some delicious air, we all began to laugh uncontrollably. During our laughter, Jonathon regained consciousness.

"Where am I?" he growled.

"You're at my apartment," I said in a very annoyed way.

"Your apartment? Where the hell is that?"

I didn't answer. I knew this game could go on forever because he would never understand where he was. Hope and Eve took this conversation as their cue to go back to their daily lives. Hope headed towards the restroom, probably to wash her hands, and Eve bolted straight for her bedroom.

"Missy, I've got Dan on the phone right now. He says that he'll come over here if we need him."

I thought about that idea for a millisecond and then told her that it wasn't necessary.

She spoke very loudly and clearly into the phone then. "We don't need you right now, but if things get any worse, I'm calling you back." I imagined that this fierce show was for Jonathon's benefit, but he had totally ignored the whole thing. He was now splayed across our living room sofa.

I propped his head up on a pillow, put a glass of water within reach, and placed a trash can near his head. As I changed into sweatpants, I decided that it was necessary for me to lie within his sight; if he woke up in the middle of the night without knowing his surroundings, chances were that he would wake us all up trying to find out. As I laid my tired bones down on the couch opposite him, I slowly drifted off to sleep.

Approximately three hours later I awoke to the sound of:

"What the . . ?"

It was Jonathon.

"Where am I?" he asked.

"You're at my house," I replied groggily.

"Who are you?" He asked.

"I'm Missy," I responded, allowing the sarcasm to creep into my voice.

"Why am I here?" He asked.

"Because you were too drunk to walk," I said.

"If this is your place, why are you sleeping out here?" He did present a good point.

"I'm sleeping out here so that if you woke up you would know where you were," I said, then yawned and rolled onto my side.

"Why is there a trash can by my head?"

"In case you woke up and had to puke," I answered angrily.

He tossed the trash can out of his way and sat up. You could actually see his head spinning, so he quickly put his head back down.

"Who is sleeping in your bed?" He asked a second later.

"No one," I answered. We then laid in silence for approximately thirty seconds. The next thing I knew, Jonathon was off the couch and running down the hallway in the direction of my room. He left the door open, and from where I was sitting, I watched him strip off his top layer of clothing. All that was left was an undershirt and his tighty whiteys. He quickly crawled into my bed and threw the covers up around his head. Gross, now my covers were going to smell like disgusting drunk guy. I picked up my blanket and pillow and went marching back into my room.

"What do you think you're doing?" I asked as I shut my bedroom door.

"Ahhh," he growled.

"Move," I said and pushed him over. If he was going to sleep in my bed, then I was going to sleep in my bed. I was sure to pull my own blanket around my body, and I was glad that I did, because as soon as I lay down he began to try and paw all over me again.

"Jonathon, quit it," I ordered.

He giggled. That's right. He giggled, just like a girl. Then he rolled over and promptly passed out. I laid there for about an hour pondering what had happened. I couldn't even explain it. Every time I tried to rationalize the situation; I kept getting upset. It was as if he and his friend, Tony, expected me to put up with these shenanigans just because we had gone on one date together.

I just couldn't understand this excuse. Sleep finally caught hold of me, and I relaxed completely.

I woke up about an hour later to Jonathon trying to climb over me to get out of bed.

"Stop," I said automatically and pushed him down. I moved off the bed and let him exit. He raced to the bathroom. He left the door open, so once again, I got the wonderful chance to hear him pee. I dragged my limbs out of bed and began to walk towards the kitchen.

"Do you want something to drink?" I asked, as I thought I heard him walking in my direction.

"No thanks," Eve said, coming into the kitchen. I jumped as I heard her voice instead of Jonathon's.

"Hey, buddy," she said and began busying herself making coffee.

"What are you doing up this morning?" I asked. I started to rummage through the cupboards for some food that I could give Jonathon that would be good for his stomach.

"I have to go to the gym," Eve said, and she turned to face me. "Do you want me to take Jonathon home?"

"Oh, yes, please!" I breathed a sigh of relief. "That would be a tremendous help. I can't deal with much more today." Even as the words were coming out of my mouth, another situation was in the making. Jonathon appeared around the wall, riding out into the living room on Eve's bike. Eve and I began to laugh deliriously.

"Hello," Jonathon said and stopped the bike. He put his legs onto the ground and stood up proudly, with his hands on his hips. Eve and I laughed even harder. He was still only wearing his underwear. Apparently, he had wandered into Eve's room, found her bike, and rode it into the kitchen.

He suddenly looked very bashful. "I didn't realize you were out here," he said in Eve's direction.

"Where did you think you stole the bike from?" Eve called after him. He had already retreated towards the bedroom. Moments later, he reappeared. This time he was fully clothed and not riding a bicycle. He greedily helped himself to a cup of coffee and began scavenging through our refrigerator. I didn't even ask what he was looking for. I was exhausted. I could not handle any more antics.

At that moment, Eve emerged from her room, ready to leave. She collected her things and started to push Jonathon towards the door. He left without saying good-bye or so much as a thank you. My tired feelings overwhelmed my perturbed nerves. I wasn't even in the mood to think about it. I tried to crawl back into bed and fall asleep but wound up watching an episode of "Roommates" instead. Just as I was about to hop in the shower and get ready for work, my phone rang. It was Eve. What else could have happened?

"What an interesting night," she laughed into the phone.

"Interesting--to say the least," I laughed, too.

"How did this all happen?" Eve said.

"I don't really know," I said, then breathed deeply.

"Oh, sure you do," Eve replied, "you didn't just volunteer to bring Jonathon to our house. Did you?"

"No," I said slowly, "I didn't volunteer." The events of last night had all suddenly come rushing back to me. "I by no means volunteered. I was *forced* to take Jonathon home." My voice had begun to become angry.

"What do you mean you were forced to take him home?" Eve was bewildered.

"Well, I told Tony that he needed to take Jonathon home and he refused. He told me that I owed Jonathon and that it was my responsibility to take care of him."

"What the hell was he talking about? You don't owe Jonathon anything," Eve replied, also sounding a little angry.

"Exactly," I shrieked. I took time to pause and evaluate the situation.

"You don't think Tony meant that I owed Jonathon something because he had gone on one lousy date with me, do you?"

"Well, I'm sure that's what he meant, but I don't know why," Eve responded. "You most certainly owe Jonathon *nada*. You two only went on one date. That means absolutely nothing. You owe him not.a.thing, especially now." Eve paused. "Do you know that when I dropped him off, he didn't even say thank you or apologize for his behavior?"

"I know," I nodded my head, "he didn't thank me, either."

"He sucks," Eve said into the phone.

"Tell me about it," I agreed.

"Do you think you'll ever go out with him again?" I knew Eve was joking, so I just snickered.

"I hope I never get that desperate. I mean," I began, "I understand that he was drunk, so most of those actions were induced by the alcohol, but I don't want to have to deal with that on a regular basis. I only went on one semi-date with him, and now apparently, I'm his babysitter."

"I think that's a very good decision. Jonathon is *not* boy-friend material."

"I guess not," I said.

"And listen, Missy," Eve started, "you really don't owe Jona-thon anything. You never did. You guys are friends and he took advantage of that. Tony tried to make you feel bad and it worked. All that meant was that he didn't have to take care of his wasted friend then. It's not your fault."

"You're right," I said, and I knew that she was. As Eve and I said our good-byes, I began to once again ponder how much a girl owed a guy after one date.

I sent Steve Martin, my fount of knowledge and new best friend, a quick text message:

> Hey pal! How much do you owe someone after one date?

His reply hit me back within thirty seconds:

> Enough for cab fair
> LOL

And I did laugh out loud. I texted back instantly:

> Meet me for brunch in thirty?
> The Pond?

His response:

> The Pond? Lame. Barney's Bagels. It's on the way to work.

Even though I had suggested the Pond, I was glad that he declined. It felt wrong to go there for brunch without the girls. But I was happy to have someone to share a meal with this morning. I thought about knocking on Hope's door and invit-ing her to join us, but reconsidered when I heard her already talking on her own phone. I assumed that she was filling Dan in on the entire story from last night. He probably had been worried about her after the late night phone call.

About fifteen minutes later, I walked out the door of my apartment. I was dressed for work, barely. My hair was a bit disheveled, and my outfit didn't entirely coordinate. I was praying that Ross didn't send me on some wild goose chase today through the streets of Charlotte. If I did my math correctly, Steve Martin and I would have just a few minutes to grab our bagels and go before he needed to be in the makeup chair, and then he could prepare for his segment with Melody today.

As I ventured out into the bright morning light, I got to contemplating first dates.

My conclusion is this: After one date, a girl owes a guy absolutely nothing. She doesn't have to call him; she doesn't have to allow another date; she doesn't have to take care of his drunken, slobbering alter ego; and she doesn't even have to acknowledge his presence. A girl *may* choose to do any of the above, but in my experience, I have learned the following: If a guy is already demanding something of you after one date, then he's not worthy of your time, or mine.

Chapter Seven

Do People Actually Date Strippers?

"Oh, you guys, I can't believe you started without me!" I yelled as I came back through my apartment door.

Adair's wedding was just a matter of weeks away and it was hot as all get out, so my voice traveled out the open windows and down into the street. Amid my living room my friends Brooklyn, Autumn, Eve, Savanna, and Hope, were all gathered around the bride-to-be, Jessica Adair. Along with my close circle of friends, the rest of Adair's wedding party had congregated. Sydney, the slightly obnoxious girl who had been in our sorority in college, was seated to Adair's left. Janet, Adair's little sister, flanked her right side. And Jess was seated in the center of the group, glowing, as usual.

I had just returned from the airport, borrowing Hope's car to pick Bree up. She was originally from North Carolina, but upon graduation, she had moved to Oregon. Even though Bree was a few years older than the rest of us, we had all been great friends while at school. I was more than happy to drive to the airport to pick her up, and she was more than happy to rearrange her schedule so that she could fly in to attend Adair's bachelorette party.

"Start what?" Bree asked. "What are they doing?"

Before I had a chance to answer, Renee came bounding through the door. Renee was dripping with sweat, and I started to wonder if she had run all the way here from her new apartment. Renee was also a member of the Philalethean Society, but she had just become a recent alumna. Renee graduated from UNC-Charlotte this past May. She quickly moved off campus and into one of the apartment buildings that was about two blocks away. I was happy to have Renee living close by because she was such a sweet girl. I was even more excited to see that she had arrived just at this moment. That meant that with the exception of Cara, the gang was all here, but she was scheduled to meet up with us later. Now we could get the party underway.

But still, I was bummed that the girls had started playing my favorite game without me.

Renee rushed towards me and gave me a big tight squeeze. I had seen her only once since graduation, and I have to admit that it was wonderful to see her again. She was such a big ball of sunshine. Renee was short and a little bit round. She had lost probably ten pounds since graduation, but she still had a circular shape to her body. Renee had a very bright smile-- I swear that she bleaches her teeth, but she maintains that she's naturally blessed. And she has stunning bronze-colored locks. She usually wears it long and bouncy. Tonight was no exception; her lustrous brown hair was flowing down her back. I patted it gently as I finished giving her a hug.

She then moved on to Bree. The two girls exchanged pleasantries and I realized that with the two of them occupied, I was free to go back to my scolding. I focused my attention on Brooklyn.

"Brooks, how could you start *Hot Pursuit* without me? You know that it's my favorite."

She gave me a sly grin. "We wanted to play without you."

"Huh?" I was bewildered.

"You're so competitive that you always get so worked up over the game. We just thought that we'd give someone else a chance to win," Autumn explained.

"That sounds like treason, ladies. I can't help it if I'm the best at the game," I laughed, but still felt an angry pang dancing around in my chest.

Bree came up behind me then. "I don't understand why you're so mad. What game are they playing?" Bree looked at me quizzically. She had this weird sort of stare that she would use occasionally to halt the speech of all those around her. She was fixing that gaze on me right now.

Adair chimed in, as she was oblivious to Bree's warping scrutiny, "We're playing *Hot Pursuit: British Edition.*"

I groaned, "You're playing the British Edition without me. You know that it's my real favorite!"

All of the girls laughed, and Renee started clapping her hands. "Oh, oh, I love the British Edition. Is it too late to join the game?" She circled around the group of girls and finally found an open seat on the floor between Brooklyn and Autumn. She grabbed a pillow from the couch, threw it on the ground, and plopped heavily onto the cushion.

The girls all laughed again.

Bree was still fixing her eyes on my facial expressions. "What is this game?" She asked for a third time.

"All right, all right," I said. "I'll tell you." I grabbed her hand and led her over to where the girls had the game cards spread out in front of them.

"Are you certain that you never played *Hot Pursuit* with us in college?" This was Autumn. She was wrinkling her nose in Bree's direction. Autumn and Bree had shared a suite in college for a year.

"I'm positive," Bree said as she gave Autumn a quick hug.

"She really couldn't have played with us," Brooklyn answered while looking from Bree to Autumn. "Remember, A?

You, Missy, and I invented this our junior year. Bree was long gone by then." Brooklyn reached out and patted Bree's hand. I don't remember them being very close in school, but since Bree had graduated, the bond between her and Brooklyn had gotten stronger. Now they probably spoke to each other online more than any of us did.

"You *invented* this game?" Bree asked as she scrunched up her brow.

"Of course," I answered. I handed her a pile of cards and started explaining the game.

"The game is called *Hot Pursuit*. There are many different ways to play this game, but we either use the American Edition or the British Edition, most often. I, personally, am a fan of the British way . . ."

"Because you're an Anglophile," Adair said and stifled a yawn.

"Yes, well, I do love my Brits," I finished with a small smile. "Anyway," I continued, "everyone starts the game with ten chips. The chips can be real money or fake; that doesn't matter."

"Okay," Bree said, and she reached into her purse, milling around the bottom of it. She pulled out a palm full of change and started to count out ten coins. I allowed her to finish this task. While she was at work with that, Renee also began sorting through her small clutch, looking for loose change. Adair handed her a few pennies, and I was off with the rest of the explanation.

"Next, the timer is set for five minutes. Each player has access to an unlimited number of note cards and writing utensils. In those five minutes, each player needs to write down as many things that they can think of that have to do with the topic: 'England.'"

"Okay," Bree said and grabbed two or three note cards. She quickly scribbled "Big Ben" on one and "London" on another.

"Is this what you mean?" She held up the cards for my approval.

"Exactly," I said cheerfully. "Everyone takes these first few moments to prepare their cards. Now don't forget," my head was currently on a swivel, and I could look around at all of the other girls while I said this, "you can put anything British on your cards. That includes celebrities, athletes, cities; anything that you can think of that would come from Great Britain." Everyone nodded enthusiastically. Since most of the girls had already started playing the game, they had been through this step, so the ladies were sitting quietly. I did notice that Eve was adding a few note cards to the deck. She is nearly as competitive as I am, so I imagine that she was still coming up with new ideas every few seconds.

"When you're finished, you place all of your cards into the deck." Savanna grabbed the small deck of cards and passed it in my direction. I added my pile, and then handed the cards to Renee. She put her cards in, too. Bree looked hesitant but still made her contribution.

"Now that we have a playing deck, a dealer gives everyone five cards each. Who was the dealer this round?" I looked around my group of friends and passed the deck back to Savanna. She had her hand raised. Of course, the professional poker player would be the first official dealer. Savanna delicately dealt out five cards apiece to Renee, Bree, and me. I took my cards quickly up into my hands and turned my attention back to Bree.

I continued giving directions, "In your hand, you now have your playing cards. In just a minute, the dealer, Savanna," I said and motioned to Savanna, "will turn over a card on the 'topic' deck. The topic deck is different from the regular deck because it lets us know which kinds of cards we are to play." I couldn't remember if I had ever properly introduced Bree to

Savanna, but I thought that they would get to know each other pretty quickly tonight anyway.

Bree gave me that quizzical look again and I knew that I had lost her.

"Ladies, can we just show her what I mean?" They all nodded in consensus as I turned back to Bree. "We will play a practice hand and you can see how it goes. Okay?"

She nodded as Savanna flipped over a card on the topic deck. It read "actors/actresses."

"Yes," Autumn said through a small smile. Brooklyn gave her a strange look and switched a few cards around in her hands.

"Left to the dealer goes first," I reminded everyone as the girls all took another good look at their hands.

Eve threw her hands up in the air, "I've got nothing. Pass," she said while looking more than a little annoyed. I snickered a little but decided that this would be an important thing to point out.

"If you don't have any cards that match the topic of 'actors/actresses,' you can always pass onto the next person."

Bree nodded and looked again quickly at her own stack of cards.

Hope was next after Eve, and she put "Sienna Miller" onto the pile.

"Good play, good play," I cheered. "I love Sienna Miller."

"That's only because you look like her," Hope said in a teasing manner. But it was true; I had been told at least a dozen times that I resembled Ms. Miller.

Sydney, Adair, and Janet all passed. It was now Renee's turn. She was bouncing happily in her seat.

She threw down "Andrew Garfield" and looked around at the group satisfied. We all nodded in approval. On my turn, I was forced to pass because I didn't have anyone better than Andrew Garfield, and then we skipped Bree for the sake of playing a practice round.

Brooklyn was now up, and she took a second to eyeball Renee. She gave her a sinister look and reached into her pile of cards. Ever so delicately, she placed "Robert Pattinson" on top of "Andrew Garfield."

"I declare 'war,'" Brooklyn said in a mischievous manner.

"Yes! This is my favorite part," Hope said, looking at our crowd of girls. Hope wasn't very good at playing *Hot Pursuit*, but I had to agree with her, the war part of the game was the best part. Unfortunately for Renee, Brooklyn was the best at war. She knew everything about pop culture, and she could wipe others out almost instantly.

I turned to Bree and tried to quickly explain before the war actually began. "Declaring 'war' on someone else is how you win points in this game. You can take someone else's money at this point, depending on how much they are willing to bet. Most people usually wager four of their own tokens during each round of war." Brooklyn and Renee were no exception. They each placed four coins on top of their deck to indicate that they had made their bids.

"The point of the game is obviously to be the person who ends up with the most money, so declaring war and winning the battle is very important." Bree tipped her head slightly to show that she was paying attention.

"Now, what just happened here," I pointed to the deck of cards, "was that Brooklyn decided to challenge Renee's degree of hotness. In this case, Andrew Garfield and Robert Pattinson are both 'hot,' yes?" Everyone around the table nodded.

"But only one can be victorious, right?"

"Right," Brooklyn agreed with a sneer and Renee laughed heartily.

"So now," I pointed to Brooklyn and Renee, "they go to war."

"Okay," Bree scratched her eyebrow piercing, "but how do they do that?"

"The first thing they do is begin by citing either the good claims or the bad claims. For example . . ." I gestured to Renee, and she picked up the reins.

"Andrew Garfield is hotter than Robert Pattinson because Andrew was in the movie *The Social Network.*"

"Ooohh," some of the girls moaned, while others nodded their heads approvingly.

Before Brooklyn could jump in to defend her actor, Renee was back on the case.

"And . . ." she said, "Andrew Garfield is *the* Amazing Spider-Man."

"Ain't it the truth?" Adair nodded her head enthusiastically. We all looked to Brooklyn for her rebuttal.

"Spider-Man, please," she stretched out the words. "That's kids' stuff. I cite Robert Pattinson as both Cedric Diggory and Edward Cullen. You *can't* beat that."

"She's right," Janet, Adair's sister, nodded in Renee's direction. "You can't beat that."

Sydney agreed, "That's hot."

But Renee was not ready to accept defeat. "Sure, I can," she shrugged and narrowed her eyes in Brooklyn's direction. "While I hate to burst your bubble, ladies Robert Pattinson just went through a very serious breakup, and his woman was totally unfaithful." A couple of boos and one hiss escaped the mouths of my friends. Renee had just struck a low blow.

Brooklyn seemed to be mulling over her options. In the time it took for her to do this, Renee sealed her victory. "Even though Pattinson wasn't to blame, and they eventually got back together, he still looked pretty lousy in the tabloids. But Andrew 'Spider-Man' Garfield is dating Emma Stone, and everyone knows that she's perfect. That just adds to his hotness."

"Agreed," Autumn said and gave Brooklyn a bashful look. Brooklyn shot Autumn back an intense stare, but then she scrambled to find someone who would agree with her. Her eyes searched the crowd until they fell on Savanna.

"Judge?" she questioned, "Does that argument hold up in *Hot Pursuit*?"

We all waited patiently while Savanna deliberated. She gave one firm nod, and Renee cheered enthusiastically.

Savanna finally spoke, "In this round, Renee appears to be the victor of this war, ya'll. In this case, Andrew Garfield matches and defeats Robert Pattinson. Hope," she looked in her direction, "because you played a person in this round, you owe Renee one chip. And Brooklyn, 'cause you challenged Renee, you owe her four chips."

Brooklyn grudgingly reached into her pile, ticked off the four chips, and passed them in Renee's direction. "I can't believe you brought up the breakup. The man *suffered*." She said this in a saddened tone but gave Renee a small smile.

"Wait, wait, just a second," Autumn said. Before Brooklyn could pass her monies over to Renee, Autumn's hand clasped down on the change.

"I would like to call 'trump' and claim this prize." As she finished this statement, she threw a "Prince William" card onto the top of the deck.

All the girls gasped and then some started laughing.

I quickly explained. "You see what Autumn just did right there? She used her trump card, 'Prince William,' to claim Renee's prize. Now, technically, Renee doesn't lose anything except the prize that she rightfully won."

"But why is Prince William a trump card?" Bree asked.

"Do any of these other people have their own castle?" I replied.

"You're kidding, right?" Bree was shaking her head back and forth. She threw her cards down on the table. "This is the most ridiculous game ever."

"What?" I asked, a little bit shocked, but also finding this hilarious.

"Let me get this straight," Bree said loudly. She had now stood up and she was looking around the room at all the girls. "You rank people and places from the U.K. based on their hotness?"

"Yeah," Eve said with a snort.

"And that doesn't seem a little superficial to you?" Bree asked again as she scanned the crowd.

Brooklyn answered her, "Sure, I mean, it's not like rocket science or anything, but it is a game and it's all good fun. It's not like we're hurting anybody. It's just a test of knowledge. A little bit like *Jeopardy!*"

"It's nothing like *Jeopardy!*" Bree laughed.

We all laughed with her. If she didn't like the game, we'd never get her to come around. There was no point in arguing the merits of *Hot Pursuit* with someone who didn't want to go there.

"Okay, okay," I said, "you don't have to play if you don't want to."

"I don't want to," Bree said and shook out her flat ironed hair, chuckling again. "You girls must have been awfully bored at school to be forced to create this game in my absence. But I'm here now, so let's do something fun!"

"Well, what do you want to do?" I asked with a big smile.

"I made something special for everyone in honor of Ms. Adair's bachelorette party," she said, and all eyes focused on Adair. Adair's face turned slightly pink, and she tossed her hair, indicating that she had no idea what the surprise might be. Bree began to rummage around in her bag, and she pulled out a familiar tin that was filled with chocolate.

"Rum balls, anyone?" She held the container high in the air, and then walked it across the room so that Adair could pick one of the chocolate-alcohol confections first. Adair reached inside delicately and pulled out a piece, being careful not to get her fingers caught up in the rest of the chocolate.

"What's a rum ball?" Janet asked as Bree brought the candy right in front of her face.

"Oh, you'll see," Bree laughed and turned to wink at Autumn. The year that Autumn and Bree lived together, they made rum balls on a regular basis. Then they would have a small tasting party. About three balls in, we would all be so plastered that we would start drunk dialing people across campus. The way Bree made rum balls was legendary. I reminded myself to warn the people who had never tasted the sweet chocolate of just how potent these little treats could be. We didn't want anyone passing out before we got to the real party.

"I can't believe that Eve and Savanna didn't want to come to this!" Brooklyn yelled. She grabbed my hand and pulled me back beside her. I was leading the way into the club named "Powerhouse Players." We had never actually been here before, but I was eager to get inside and survey the territory. A few of the girls were a little skittish.

"Oh, you know them," I shouted over the loud music. "They always prefer playing poker over anything else." That was true, Eve and Savanna had ditched the bachelorette party to go up-town and play poker. But that was not the full truth of the matter. The real story was that they didn't agree with strip clubs, so they decided that they would rather play cards than come on this leg of our journey.

"I can't believe that anyone would want to willingly pass this up!" Adair shrieked as she bolted to the front of the group. Her sister, Janet, grabbed her hand as she plunged forward and the two nearly tripped over Brooklyn and I.

I laughed in her direction, "Yes, this is exactly what I was hoping it would be." I took a moment to drink in the spectacle that was surrounding us.

The club that we had just entered, Powerhouse Players, was different than any other place I had ever been. We emerged through a large set of double doors, then after paying the hunky doorman we were presented with three options. We could either take Aisle A, which led to the female strip club; we could choose Aisle B, which would take us to the common area that contained a dance floor; or we could choose Aisle C. This option would take us into the heart of the male strip joint. There was no hesitation. We raced through the velvet ropes and into the area marked Aisle C.

After the earlier quick game of *Hot Pursuit* and the rum ball taste testing extravaganza, we prepared ourselves for this outing. While everyone was changing into their black party dress--we all elected to wear black so that stylistically we would easily be able to spot each other in the crowded club-- Savanna and Eve were arguing with me about the night's activities. They really wanted to come and celebrate with Adair, but they refused to go to a strip club.

"It's gross," Savanna said, laying on her accent even thicker than normal.

"It's not gross," I said and rolled my eyes.

"How do you know?" Eve was challenging me.

"I don't know; I just know," I answered back.

"But you neva even been to one, Missy. You don't know how disgustin' it's gonna be," Savanna said, wringing her hands.

"I mean, really," Eve said as she grabbed my shoulders, "strip clubs are uncivilized. All of the men will be ugly and they'll be shaking around wildly and . . ." she trailed off and seemed to be trying to hold back the vomit.

"Girls, relax," I sighed and eased Eve's hands off my shoulders. "First of all, neither of you have ever been to a strip club, either so how can you be so sure that it will be repulsive?" I didn't give them time to answer before I charged ahead.

"Second, I've heard really great things about this place. It is supposed to be a lot of fun. Third," I held up my hand to stop any interjections, "Adair *wants* to do this. She wants to go see the Powerhouse Players. If the club sucks, then we leave."

Eve and Savanna looked at each other quickly, but Eve shook her head. She had already made up her mind.

"I'm not going, Missy. I like Adair, but I just don't want to do this."

"We could go play poker instead . . ." Savanna started to add this statement but cut herself off.

Eve picked up where she left off. "That's a great idea!" Her eyes brightened. "Listen, Missy, we'll go and play poker at Calamity Jim's. If the Powerhouse Players Club stinks, give us a call. We'll meet you anywhere else you want to go."

"You guys, this really isn't about me. This is about Adair . . ." I started to give this argument, but Eve cut me off.

"Oh, come on, you know that you've been dying to get inside that place. This just gives you a valid excuse." Eve looked at me with a challenge in her eye. She was right. I really did want to know what all the hoopla was about. I couldn't deny it any longer.

I agreed that I would call them if we decided to leave the club, but I hoped that it would be spectacular.

And I wasn't disappointed.

Because Adair was wearing her "Bride-to-be" sash and tiara, our party was led to a group of tables that surrounded the main stage. Presumably, the show would be starting in a few minutes, and it looked as though our crew would be seated front and center.

Self-consciously, I scanned the crowd of women who were also perched around the stage. They looked excited, too. There were a couple of other bachelorettes planted among the crowd and there was even one girl who was wearing a "Birthday Girl" sash. As I was surveying the crowd, my eyes fell on Adair. She was grinning from ear to ear.

"Why are you smiling like that?" I asked as I leaned towards her.

"Didn't you notice? We're in a strip club and we're the prettiest girls here!" She yelled over the crowd.

"So?" I raised my eyebrows.

"So?" She answered back and laughed at my response. "So, pretty girls get the most attention from the strippers."

"Yeah, but the strippers are paid to give everyone special attention," I tried to reason.

"Sure," she said again, her eyes sparkling. "But one could always take a special liking to you and slip you his number."

"Do strippers do that?" I asked, feeling like a child.

"Do strippers do what?" Autumn had caught the tail end of our conversation.

"Do people actually date strippers?" I wondered aloud. Adair laughed brightly and pointed to the stage. The show was about to start.

The lights went down, and the music started playing. A flock of men dressed in various overgrown Halloween costumes entered the scene. When the lights flooded the stage again, the music was rocking and so were the bodies of the men on stage. I felt my heart jump into my throat. I immediately developed a crush.

It sounds pathetic, but the guy who was dressed like a police officer had my heart beating faster and faster. I couldn't tear my eyes off him. It seemed as though most of the women in the crowd were also paying close attention to this officer of the law.

He was probably six feet tall and built in a nice way. He had lots of muscles, but they were the muscles of an athlete, not a meathead. He had really dark hair that was spiked neatly under his cap. His eyes were intense, and I couldn't identify the color because the lights kept washing them out and making them look completely black. As he began to peel off his clothing, I noticed the definition of his arms and the curvature of his ab muscles. The waitress arrived not a moment too soon with our drinks. If I did not distract myself immediately, I would have been in very grave danger of pitching myself onto the stage to get closer to this stripper.

As the first number wound down, the emcee began introducing the men. Of course, they were all using stage names, so they each had a name that sounded like it came out of the *Stripper's Handbook.* Ace and Maverick were introduced first, and then Pedro came next. When it was the cop's turn, I listened closely. Gabriel was his name; like the angel, I thought.

When the introductions were over, the music began blaring again and the strippers really started discarding clothing. They were getting down to the bare essentials here. As Gabriel in one fluid motion flung aside his trousers, I saw the woman nearest him laugh loudly. He turned to wink at her. In that second, I saw what she was laughing about. Tattooed on his behind was the phrase, "Naked and Famous." I chuckled, too, and continued sipping my drink. I pointed out the tattoo on his posterior to my posse and they laughed with glee. We were already thoroughly enjoying ourselves and the night had only just begun.

A few hours and multiple drinks later, we were starting to wind down. Despite the awe-inspiring show, we had been partying most of the day. Some people, like Bree, had been on a plane that morning, and she just wasn't sure how much longer her eyelids would stay open. We were just thinking that it was about time to leave when Gabriel came back onto the stage. I couldn't go quite yet. When I turned to explain this matter to my friends, I noticed that I didn't need to. They had all backed gracefully into their own chairs. They were ready to catch this act, too.

The pulse-pounding beats started to play over the loud sound system. During the course of the night, Gabriel had changed his costume many times, but now he was back to being a police officer.

He did a quick dance routine that required lots of hip popping and locking. Then, he started to circulate through the women sitting around the stage. He would perform little acrobatic feats in front of some and then he would rub up against others. All the while, the women were eagerly screeching and pushing dollar bills into his G-string.

In preparation, I began rummaging through my purse. If I had any money, I would have given it to Adair earlier in the evening. While it was fun to have the strippers pay special attention to me, this was Jess' party, after all, and I had chipped in to make sure that the guys brought her up onto the stage for an extravagant display. Penniless, I sat back in my chair feeling defeated. I had waited all night for Gabriel to come over and grind on me, and now that I couldn't even afford to slip him a dollar bill, I would just have to sit back and watch while he played with the other girls. I felt a bit huffy, and I probably sound like a baby, but I don't really care. I wanted Gabriel.

As he came around the corner, he recognized Adair from her trip onto the stage earlier in the evening. He did a small routine directly on her lap and then gave her a quick peck on the cheek. I appreciated that he didn't totally humiliate her as some of the other guys had tried to do throughout the night. Still working his way through our group, I watched as he grinded on Autumn, took a dollar bill out of Hope's cleavage, and used his teeth to remove another bill from the collar of Brooklyn's dress. I was so envious I could hardly breathe.

Just as I thought that he was about to turn away, he came gliding up to where I was sitting. Even though I showed him that my hands were empty, he started dancing anyway.

"Hey," he breathed as he leaned into me. He was playfully licking my ear while his body was gyrating against my lap.

"Hey," I felt myself heave out the phrase, as if the words were going to be caught some place inside. He ran his mouth down to the side of my face, giving me small kisses as he went. I relaxed completely at that moment and waited for more to happen. Quickly, and with what I can only imagine was a well-practiced move, he transitioned from my lap back to the stage and went on about his business.

Once he was out of earshot, I began to breathe heavily.

Autumn put her hand on mine. "Are you okay?" She was laughing while saying this. I must have looked like I was having a heart attack.

"I'm fine," I replied, and my hand immediately flew over my heart.

Autumn laughed at my apparent discomfort, and she nudged Renee, too. Both girls moved in closer to check on me, but also to revel at my very obvious embarrassment.

"Hey," Hope said and had a hold of my hand suddenly. "Snap out of it. We're going." I turned to look in the direction she was standing. Everyone, except for Autumn, Renee, and me, was already crowded around the exit. Apparently, the bachelorette and the rest of the girls were ready to call it a night. But I just wasn't ready to go; I didn't want to leave the club yet.

"Hey," Autumn said quickly as she came up behind me and grabbed my other hand. "If you go now, I promise that I'll bring you back later."

I turned and took one more look at the stage. Gabriel was just exiting.

"I'm going to hold you to that promise, you know?" I said in Autumn's general direction.

"I know, I know," she said and shook her head, laughing deeply. "And even though you might not believe this, I'm actually looking forward to it." She nodded her head in the direction of another stripper, Roman. He was standing on a platform toward the back of the room. He was dressed only in camouflage pants, and he was grinding away as if his life depended on it. Maybe I wasn't the only one leaving the strip club with a crush that night.

Chapter Eight

Why Can't I Just Get On Board with This?

"Hey girl. Where you is? J/K. Seriously where are you?"

That was the message I had waiting on my phone on Sunday morning. I'd had such an amazing time at the Powerhouse Players Club that I'd silenced my phone altogether. So, this little text from Nathan was just sitting there, hanging out, waiting for me to respond.

Fueled by the memories of the night before, I deleted it quickly and decided that perhaps I *was* a confident woman and perhaps I *could* just ignore a message or two.

When I was telling Hope about my bold move later that day, she quickly reminded me that I still did have to talk to Nathan. He was scheduled to be my date for Adair's upcoming nuptials and if I blew him off now, I would be dateless.

I didn't want that, and after a few moments of contemplation, I decided to return his call.

All summer long, ever since I let it slip that I was still in love with him, I had purposely been avoiding Nathan. We would still talk, text, and email occasionally, but our conversations weren't like they had been before. Instead of going to him with my troubles, I usually called the girls, or I would text Steve Martin. I realized, as I found Nate on my speed dial, that we might actually be growing apart.

But as soon as I heard his voice, all those thoughts vanished. I could ogle strippers, and I could call up my best pals in town when I needed them, but it was Nathan who made me feel at home. We spent almost three hours on the phone that day. As the afternoon wound down, I felt as though our talk had nourished my soul.

When I turned in for bed that night, my prayers were especially grateful, as I was finally starting to feel like my life was filling up again.

On Monday morning, I was still feeling so grand that I was pumped to go in to work.

"So, how's life?" Kevin, my cameraman, was wrapping the camera cord neatly under his armpit when he asked this question.

"Life's good," I answered and gave him a shrug.

"Don't shrug while I'm doing your makeup," Ethan sighed deeply and gave me a pinch on the shoulder before he went back to applying my eyeliner.

"Sorry," I said quickly.

I was prepping to head out on the town for my latest news story. There was going to be a new store opening uptown today. Even though it wasn't a giant piece of news, Ross Neil, my boss, thought that it might make an interesting feature story for the nightly broadcast. The newscast had been verging on boring lately. This summer had been hot, so the weather didn't really have anything brilliant to bring to the picture. The NASCAR season was proceeding as planned; there were no big shakeups, no major injuries, and no underdogs making a run for the cup. So, sports were a little blah, too.

In short, my life as a news reporter was perfectly sufficient, but hardly exciting. It was nice to live near the city and I was grateful to be working in such a fabulous town, but sometimes I wondered what it would be like to live in a place where something newsworthy and incredible was always happening.

I thought momentarily about what my life would be like if I moved to New York City, but I quickly abandoned that dream. I probably wasn't New York City material.

"So, how's your life?" I posed this question to Kevin a little delayed, but he didn't seem to mind. He and I had worked together for so long now that he was starting to understand how my mind operated. He knew that I had been off in my own little world for a few seconds, but now I was rejoining the conversation.

"My life's all right," Kevin said slowly and closed the latch on the camera case.

"What's wrong?" I inquired. I could see his heavy brow furrow and I thought instantly that he was hiding something. He lingered over the camera container, and I was wondering if he was contemplating sharing his secret with me.

Just as it looked like Kevin might shed some light on the situation, Ethan came around so that he was standing directly in front of me. He started to mouth something, but I couldn't pick up on his silent words.

"Deidra and I broke up a few days ago," Kevin said finally and shrugged his shoulders.

"Really?" I asked. I was a bit shocked. Kevin and Deidra had been dating for a long time. If I remembered correctly, he had, as recently as last week, been engagement ring shopping. I wondered what the problem was, but Ethan seemed to be attempting to telegraph me something, so I decided to stay out of it.

"Really," Kevin replied and allowed his shoulders to move up and down again in a careless way.

"I'm really sorry to hear that," I told him, and I meant it. Ethan nodded approvingly and then made a weird motion with his head. It was as if he was trying to tell me to find a way to get rid of Kevin. I wasn't really following his signals well, though.

Ethan finally put down his pencil and stepped away from me. "There's something wrong today," he said in an annoyed way. He pouted his thin bird-like lips and stepped back even further. The way he was looking at me made me feel really uncomfortable, but I would rather that he would fix me up now than let me go on camera looking like a fool later. I sat still, willing myself not to budge during his inspection.

"Kevin," Ethan said and turned to him, "I need you to go into Melody's dressing room and get her deep rose-colored lipstick. Can you do that for me?"

Kevin produced a baffled expression. Ethan had never asked Kevin to help with my makeup and hair before. Even further, Ethan wouldn't usually even think of sending someone into the lion's den unaccompanied. Melody Castina was the lead anchor at WSTA Charlotte. She was a masterpiece on camera, but in real life, she was a bit more abrasive. She and Ethan had been dating for a few years, so normally, if Ethan wanted to borrow something from Mel, he just took it himself.

Even though Ethan's request seemed off, even to me, Kevin nodded his head absentmindedly and turned away, wordlessly. He quickly bounced back around and made a scrunched-up face. "You said deep rose lipstick, right?" Ethan nodded his head and devoted his attention back to me. Evidently, Kevin was dismissed.

As soon as Kevin disappeared around the corner, Ethan pounced on me.

"How could you do that, Missy?" he accused.

"Do what?" I was totally bewildered.

"How could you allow Kevin to talk about Deidra?" He spat this at me. I had no idea why he was so angry.

"What are you talking about?" I felt almost a little afraid of Ethan. He's not exactly an intimidating person, but I guess that I've never really seen him angry before. This whole new demeanor of his was a weird sort of revelation.

"Kevin isn't supposed to be talking about Deidra. It'll reduce him to tears." Even as the words were coming out of Ethan's mouth, I couldn't believe them. I had known Kevin for a long time, and he just wasn't the type to cry, especially in public.

When I didn't say anything, Ethan continued. "Where have you been all morning?" He grabbed my shoulders and gave me a small shake. In time with his shake, I rocked my head back and forth.

"I've been here," I nearly yelled at him, as I pulled back from his reach and stood up out of the cosmetologist's chair.

"If you had been here--really been here-- then you never would've let that conversation happen. Poor Kevin is probably lost right now in Melody's dressing room, crying his eyeballs out." Ethan took a step towards me.

"If you were afraid that he'd get lost in there, then why'd you send him?" I took a step towards Ethan. If he was going to challenge me, I wasn't going to take it lying down.

Ethan suddenly started laughing, backing away a few steps simultaneously. "You really are clueless, aren't you?" He kept laughing. "You know, I always try to defend you, but sometimes you really do get lost in your own head." He sat down in the makeup chair then, which really surprised me. I felt as though my position had been usurped.

Still feeling a bit threatened, and not exactly comfortable with his latest comment, I took a step towards Ethan. "Could you please just tell me what's going on already?" I tried to bat my eyelashes at him but that only made him laugh harder.

"That won't work on me, Lawrence. You forgot that I was working on your makeup. I only finished with one eye. You're totally lopsided right now." He sighed heavily, then he pitched himself out of the chair and pushed me back into it.

I took a deep breath, in and out. I have to admit that I was starting to be annoyed by Ethan today. I noticed that he was acting a little batty lately, but I figured it had something to do with Mel. I usually try to stay out of my coworkers business, but now he was really beginning to frustrate me.

He put his hands on my shoulders and used one finger to slide my chin towards his face. "Poor Missy is starting to get annoyed, huh?" I gave him an icy glare as a response.

"It's cool," Ethan said with nonchalance. "You can be mad at me all you want, but I'm not the one who is neglecting their friends in their time of need."

"Stop it now!" I slammed my fist on the makeup tray. "Tell me what's going on?"

"Sheesh!" Ethan blew hot air up across his own face. "Here's the story, Ole Miss." He leaned in close, as if we were co-conspirators. Ethan had a flair for the dramatic and he wanted to set the stage perfectly before he dropped a huge bomb on me.

"Last week," he began, "Kevin came to me and said that he was so excited because he had finally picked out a ring for Deidra. He was going to give it to her on Friday night. If she agreed to marry him, he planned to surprise her even further by taking her away for a weekend in Asheville. You know how beautiful the mountains can be this time of year." I nodded my head as both an affirmation and a signal that he should continue with this tale.

He continued, "The proposal went off without a hitch. He got down on one knee, Deidra said yes, and they packed their bags. Everything seemed perfect . . ."

"Sure," I said sarcastically, at which Ethan gave me a critical look. He kept going with the story anyway.

"On the road to the lodge, Kevin and Deidra smooched all over each other. She was overjoyed. She was on the phone calling her parents. She even called her sister in San Diego to share the good news. By the time they reached their cabin, Deidra had called most of her family and Kevin had also called him mom."

"Uh-huh," I said for the sake of keeping the story moving. Ethan took a deep breath and looked around us. I knew, just as he did, that Kevin would be back in a matter of minutes, and that meant that Ethan didn't have much time to get on with it.

Ethan nodded, cleared his throat, and took off with the story. "So, Kevin grabs all their bags and goes to get them checked in. He leaves Deidra in the car because she says that she wants to make one or two more phone calls before she goes inside and loses reception. They were in the mountains after all, and sometimes calls would fade in and out. It wasn't always a big deal, and this explanation seems logical enough to Kevin, so he goes on inside. An hour later, it has become dark, and he has still not heard from or seen Deidra. He tries to call her phone, but no one answers. He starts to think about the absolute worst possible things that could have happened. What if someone stopped her and hurt her on the way into the hotel? What if someone attacked her while she was sitting in the car?"

I shook my head.

And he kept going, "With these terrible images floating through his mind, he runs to the front desk and begins asking questions. No one there has seen Deidra, either. While this is a small resort and it is probable that someone had to have seen her, he also is feeling dread creeping into his stomach because they're up in the mountains."

I groaned. "Just get on with it. Where's Deidra?" I whispered.

"Deidra," Ethan paused for effect, "was sitting in the car . . . crying with all her might."

"What?" I asked and felt my voice crack.

"Yeah," Ethan leaned in closer. "Deidra told Kevin that she loved him but that she wasn't ready to marry him. She said that she realized it when she was on the phone with her grandmother. Her grandma offered her the use of the family wedding veil and Deidra said that even though she wanted to accept the family heirloom, she just couldn't do it. She just didn't want to marry Kevin."

"Ouch, that seems harsh. What happened next?" I asked.

"Well, Kevin coaxed Deidra out of the car. He was sure that if he could just calm her down that he could talk some sense into her. He was certain that she'd just become too overexcited and that she needed a little time to breathe. Maybe calling her relatives so quickly had been a mistake."

"Maybe," I agreed.

"But it wasn't a mistake, Missy. Deidra really *didn't* want to marry Kevin. Once he got her out of the car and into the lodge, a whole deeper, darker story played out. Deidra said that she'd been in love with Kevin for so long that she forgot what it was like to breathe of her own accord. She had depended on him for so many years that she forgot how to be independent. She said that she had been waiting and waiting for a proposal, but that when it finally came, it didn't feel the way she expected it to feel."

"Well, what had she thought that it would feel like?" I asked.

"I don't know," Ethan picked up a blush brush and twirled it around. "I imagine that she thought it would be a welcoming breath of fresh air. She could finally say that she was getting married. She could finally call Kevin her fiancé."

"But?" I coaxed.

"But..." he went on, "it didn't feel that way to Deidra. Instead of feeling carefree and happy, she felt stifled and chained. For so long, she wanted him to propose, and then when he did, it just wasn't enough."

"'It just wasn't enough,'" I repeated.

"Her words, not mine," Ethan said with a halfhearted shrug.

"So?" I asked.

"So," Ethan replied, "Kevin packed up their things and drove back to the city. He dropped Deidra off at her apartment and he went on to his own house. He spent all day Saturday reevaluating the situation, and on Sunday he ventured over to her apartment and took his ring back."

"Huh?" I felt like the wind had been knocked out of me.

"Missy, you know Kevin pretty well. He's a nice guy and he works hard, but he doesn't really beat around the bush and he doesn't want to be pushed around, either. He just decided that if Deidra didn't want to marry him, then she didn't want to marry him. End of story."

"Is that really the end?" I felt a little peep of sadness sinking into my stomach.

"Not exactly the end, no," Ethan said and began doing my makeup again. "Even though Kevin put on a brave face in front of Deidra, he broke down the minute he came into work. Even though he wasn't supposed to be here, he came in on Sunday. He spent ninety percent of that time crying. The guys in the video room actually had to kick him out because he was crying too much during the editing process. He was driving them crazy. I found him this morning hiding out in the back lot. He was just sitting on the sound stage, picking little fuzzy tufts off his shirt."

"Oh, he sounds so sad," I said, truly feeling disheartened for Kevin.

"He *is* sad," Ethan said matter-of-factly, "and you didn't even notice." He turned me around in the chair so that I could look directly at myself in the mirror. "And you're supposed to be his friend."

"Autumn, do you think that I'm a bad friend?"

I had to know, and if anyone would be honest but gentle with me, it would be Autumn. She didn't hesitate for one second.

"You're a great friend, Missy. Why do you ask?" She looked at me with big eyes. I could tell that she was slightly worried about me.

Autumn, Brooklyn, and I had decided to meet at the Pond on Monday afternoon. We had invited Adair, but she was busy at work. She was staying late to collaborate with a new artist. Brooklyn had invited Cara, but Cara had declined. She had a party that she needed to attend for work. So, it was just the three of us. I couldn't help but to feel the absence of Jack and Benson. I missed them so much.

"Everything's fine, Autumn. I just feel really bad about Kevin," I said quietly. I had already explained his whole story to the girls, and they were sympathetic.

Brooklyn uncorked her pot of lip gloss, applied a thin sheen, and smacked her pout, "I don't really think that you should worry about it, Missy. Ethan was being very unfair to you. It's not your job to keep up on everyone else's social lives. You had a very busy weekend and no one at work got involved in your personal affairs. Did they?" She looked at me with her perfectly tweezed eyebrows arched high.

I shook my head no. "But I feel bad." I whined a little. "I feel like I should have been there for Kevin."

"How exactly should you have been there?" I knew that Brooklyn was getting irritated by this conversation. The tone in her voice had taken on an almost angry tenor.

I shrugged slightly.

"Listen, Missy, because I'm only going to go over this one more time with you." She grabbed my hand so that I would pay attention. "You don't have to please everybody all the time. It's not your job to be everyone's rock. Yes, Kevin had a lousy weekend, and yes, he cried over it afterward. But you know what? Kevin is allowed to grieve without you sticking your nose into his business. If I were Ethan, I would be a little bit ashamed that I even made you feel bad about it," she finished with a huff and dropped my hand with finality.

Autumn turned in my direction. "I agree with Brooklyn." She looked me dead in the eye. "I'm sorry for Kevin's troubles, but they're not yours. You've got plenty of your own business to deal with right now. Plus, if Kevin had specifically wanted your help, don't you think that he'd have come to you?"

I had to admit that the girls had a point. The only reason that Ethan knew what was going on was because he had found Kevin, alone and crying. Maybe Kevin just wanted to be alone and work things out on his own. It was Ethan who was butting in and making the situation worse than it needed to be. I wanted to send Ethan a quick text message to let him know all these conclusions, but I decided to take the high road. Instead, I chewed on a French fry thoughtfully.

"Hey," Brooklyn said and smacked my hand, "Get your own fries." I hadn't realized that I was eating her food. I was lost in thought.

"Sorry," I said while putting the half-eaten fry down.

"Cheer up, please," Autumn commanded and threw four French fries onto my plate. Apparently, she had been eating French fries, too, and I hadn't noticed.

Brooklyn pushed her plate away and started to look around at the clock. I knew that she was getting antsy. She really needed to get home to Duke. He was helping her prepare for her next interview tomorrow. She had a couple of interviews this afternoon.

"Hey, I have good news," Brooklyn said out of nowhere, and I was a little surprised that it wasn't accompanied by her picking up her purse to leave.

"You do?" I asked.

"Yeah," she replied. "I heard from Benson yesterday."

"Good!" I exclaimed. Suddenly a small bit of warmth had filled my heart. It had been about a week since we had talked to each other, and I was missing her dreadfully. She hadn't been able to attend Adair's wedding shower, nor was she able to fly in for the bachelorette party. And it was too bad, too. She would have really liked both events.

"How is she?" Autumn asked as she popped a singular fry into her mouth.

"She's well," Brooklyn stated as she took a sip of tea and swished it around. "She sends her love to all of us."

"Well," I was almost bursting, "Give us the details. How *is* she? What's going on?"

Brooklyn laughed lightly, "She's fine, like I said. She's staying busy, and she even saw Jack the other day."

"Really?" I asked, feeling a bit of relief flood my system. Even though I had been outwardly worrying about Kevin, I was inwardly thinking about Jack. Since Jack had moved to L.A., I had not heard from her even once. I emailed Benson regularly, we talked on the phone weekly, and we even tried Skyping a few times, but I hadn't heard word from Jack. Even Benson's updates were bleak and not really informational.

"How is *she*?" Autumn asked, putting emphasis on the last word.

"She's fine," Brooklyn replied and tossed her hair. "She's Jack."

"That's not good enough," I moaned. "Tell us more."

"Okay, okay," Brooklyn groaned, checked the clock again, and relaxed back into her seat. "Benson said that Jack came by the apartment on Tuesday night. She said that Jack looked pretty normal, except that she had lost a bit of weight."

"Really?" Autumn's eyebrows shot up. It was hard to imagine Jack working out. When she decided that she wanted to be recognized in the music industry, Autumn and I had both volunteered to exercise with Jack, but she had vehemently refused all our offers.

"Yeah," Brooklyn nodded, "Benson said that she looked good. She said that she looked healthy. Anyway, Jack came by the apartment for a few minutes and let Benson know that she would be moving out in the next few weeks or so, but not to worry because she would still pay her half of the rent."

"Why?" I asked.

"I don't know," Brooklyn answered.

"But where's she going?" Autumn asked.

"And how will she have money to pay more than one rent check?" I wanted to know.

"I don't know, and neither does Benson. Jess was just grateful that Jack resurfaced. She wasn't willing to push her luck by asking too many questions."

"That's understandable," I said and nodded my head. Suddenly, my heart didn't feel so heavy. Jack was okay. Benson was satisfactory. I felt a little better just having that knowledge swimming around in my head.

"Well, ladies, I must be off. It's interview prep time, you know." Brooklyn slid up and out of her seat before she had finished her sentence. She leaned down and gave me a hug. "Don't sweat it, Ma. You don't have to be everybody's confidant. You just be you. Ya dig?" I knew that she was messing with me, so I gave her a gentle push away, but I was quick to laugh so that she knew I was being playful.

Brooklyn also hugged Autumn quickly from behind and made her exit. Then, Autumn and I were left at the Pond alone.

I looked at her thoughtfully and said, "It's Monday night, you know."

"I do know this," she replied in the same calm tone. She picked up a French fry and nibbled on the end.

"What do you want to do?" I asked, trying to keep the excitement from spilling into my voice.

"We can't," she said in a chiding tone. But she added a wink in my direction.

"But I want to," I whined.

"No really, Missy. We can't go to Powerhouse Players tonight because it's not open. The male revue only runs on Saturday night."

"How did you know that?" I asked.

"I looked it up online," she answered sheepishly. I started to laugh but she cut me off. She held up her hand. "I made you a promise and I intend to keep it."

"Girl Scout's honor?" I questioned.

"Absolutely," she said and held her hand over her heart.

"So, if the strip club isn't open tonight, what are we going to do?" I asked her again, scanning my own brain for viable options.

"Well, aren't Eve and Savanna going to go play poker?" She looked at me and started to gather up her own things.

"Indubitably; that's what they always do."

"Well," she said breezily, "why don't we go out with them?"

"Autumn," I said her name cautiously, "you don't like playing poker. Why would you want to do that?"

"You're right. I don't like playing poker, but I know me, and I know that I want to go out. I don't want to overdo it, so poker seems like the obvious choice." I thought over her logic for a minute and then finally agreed that it made sense.

I gathered my bag and we headed for the door.

"I'll meet you at your apartment in a few minutes. I have to run a quick errand first. We'll pick up Eve, okay?" Even though this was a question, she said it more like a statement.

"Deal," I replied.

"Why can't I just get on board with this?" I was looking at Eve in the mirror and groaning as loudly as I possibly could.

"I have no idea," she was dancing sloppily around the room and yelling back in my direction. "It makes so much more sense." She spun clumsily towards my bed, bounced off, and then came sauntering over towards me and the mirror.

We were preparing to go out for the evening. Since Autumn had not had the chance to go home and change her clothes after work, she was now sorting through my closet, looking for an article of clothing that would be appropriate for pub poker.

Eve and I were having a very similar discussion: what sort of outfit was appropriate for going out on the town?

"Listen to me," Eve said loudly. She had already knocked back a few beers, so I knew that her genius idea had been fueled by hops and barley.

"I'm going to call my new project 'Get Ugly, America.' It's gonna be great. Look at you, just look at you." Eve motioned to my form as it was reflected in the mirror. I was looking.

"Look at you all dressed in a floating little sundress. Your hair is done," she shouted and grabbed my hair, pulling a little. "Your makeup is done," she pointed to my eyeshadow. "You're dolled up for a night on the town," she accused.

"Okay?" Autumn asked as she peeked out of the closet. She had found a tank and skirt that would go together nicely, and she was changing into them now.

"But here's the problem, Missy. You took a half-hour getting ready, and that was just the time it took you to get ready for *pub poker*. How long does it take you to get ready when you want to go out to a real club?"

I shook my head, "I don't know."

"That's right because you don't keep track of the time. You stay at it until you look perfect, right?"

"Right!" Autumn chimed in. I'm not exactly sure that she was helping.

"Okay," Eve laughed gleefully. She was picking up steam here. "So, here's the problem. You spend hours fixin' yourself up so that you can go out and impress a bunch of guys at a bar, right?" Eve was gesticulating wildly, and frankly, I thought that she might fall over.

"Right!" Autumn said again. I gave her a sharp look and she went back to pulling on her own outfit choice.

"Here's the problem, ladies," Eve said, then paused for dramatic effect. She steadied herself, in a manner that I would have guessed to be impossible at this point. She was really quite drunk. "You spend all this time getting ready and then you just intimidate the guys. Come on, let's do the math. If you go out twice a week, how many times a week would you say that you actually get approached by a guy?" I didn't know. I had never really thought about it before.

"Are you counting guys that are sloppy drunks?" Autumn asked for clarification.

"Nope," Eve answered quickly. "I'm asking you this question: Even though you spend hours getting yourself ready to go out on the town, in the end, how many guys do you really meet who you actually want to spend time with later?"

I stayed silent. I was thinking about the point that she was making. When was the last time that I had gotten all gussied up for a night on the town and I actually met someone who I found interesting? Even further, when was the last time I gave my number to a guy that I met out at the bar? I couldn't recall.

Eve clapped her hand down on my shoulder and pulled Autumn in front of the mirror, too. She spoke directly into our ears. "You're not meeting guys when we go out because you're intimidating the living daylights out of them. They take one look at you and think, 'Nah, she's too hot. She won't want a guy like me.'" I started to argue with Eve, but she slapped her hand against my shoulder again.

"Stop frightening guys. Stop making it hard for them to approach you. Come on, *Get Ugly, America!*" She said that last piece like it was a cheer.

I turned and laughed at her, straight in her face. "Oh, come on, Eve. You really mean to tell me that you're going to go out tonight dressed like that?"

We all looked down at Eve's attire. It took just a minute to soak her all in. It almost looked like she was trying to imper-sonate a homeless person. It was a very sad sight, indeed. Her short red hair was pulled into a pitiful ponytail. She had on an aged pair of jeans. There were paint stains near the bottom.

Her tennis shoes were old and badly in need of a wash, or perhaps they just needed to be tossed into the trash. She had on a pale blue T-shirt that was left over from her days of cleaning the dishware in the B.D. Petey's kitchen. She looked like she was going to do laundry, not out for a night on the town.

"Absolutely," she said without blinking an eye. "I'm going to strut my hotness down to Calamity Jim's tonight wearing this exact outfit. I'm going to play some cards, smoke a few cigarettes, and flirt with a half-dozen guys."

Now, Autumn laughed at Eve. She was being ridiculous.

"Oh, you two think you're so funny. You think that you know better than I do. Well, would you care to place a little money on this experiment?" Eve's eyes were wild now with excitement.

I nodded at Autumn and she dipped her head at Eve. "Okay," I agreed. "We're game. What's the wager, exactly?"

Eve thought it over for a minute and then said, "I'll bet you each fifty dollars that I'll have more guys interested in me by the end of the night than the both of you do, combined."

"Hold on, hold on," Autumn said swiftly and held up her hand. "Those terms are a little vague. If we're going to bet money, I want specifics. For example, what do you mean by 'interested?'"

"Okay, alright," Eve was bouncing back and forth on her heels. I took a wistful glance at her tennis shoes. It would be nice to wear tennis shoes out to the bar instead of heels. But I just couldn't make myself dress like a bum out in public. I did have a reputation to uphold.

Eve finally got her thoughts straight and presented her proposal. "I'm willing to guarantee that using my new idea 'Get Ugly, America,' I will be more successful at attracting men than either of you will be. To that end, I'm willing to bet you fifty dollars each that more men will approach me tonight AND more men will ask for my phone number than both of you combined."

"Wow! Those are some pretty big stakes," I said and looked at Eve again in the mirror. "Are you sure that 'Get Ugly, America' can work that kind of magic?"

"I'm absolutely positive," Eve said with a curt nod. "Guys want a girl that they're not afraid to talk to. You two," she pointed at us, "are too unapproachable. You might not even get a single bite tonight."

"Man," Autumn laughed. "I hope that you're wrong."

"Me too," I chuckled and swung my purse over my shoulder. I took one look back in the mirror before exiting out the front door. "Man, I hope she's wrong . . ." I repeated this phrase as I turned to lock the door behind me.

As luck (or maybe not so much luck, but fate) would have it, Eve was right. Get Ugly, America was a success. Not only did Eve have three guys ask for her phone number, but another actually promised to take her out the next night. Even worse, while Eve racked up the attention of four proper suitors, Autumn and I attracted none.

Final Score= "Get Pretty" Zero: "Get Ugly" Four.

Chapter Nine

Am I the Marrying Kind?

"There's just not enough evidence. No jury in their right mind can convict her of the crime. It's just not a possibility," Steve Martin explained, expounding on the latest scandal erupting all over Charlotte. I was waiting in the wings, watching him work.

It was Tuesday afternoon and I had just left my desk. I'd come in that morning at four. I probably shouldn't have gone out with Autumn and Eve last night, but I'd forgotten that I needed to be at the station so early the next day. When I woke to my alarm blaring in my ears, I wasn't a happy camper, but I put on a brave face. I had an appointment to film the lead-in shots today that would be used for the morning broadcast and if I didn't report the news, no one would be able to watch it a few hours later. (Maybe that wasn't entirely true, but I liked to think of it that way. I knew perfectly well that one of the other field reporters, like Sandy, were capable of waking with the dawn to catch some of the news stories, but I never really wanted to give up any assignment. I considered it a personal point of pride that I never shirked my duties and that even if I was under the weather, I could still make it to an important shoot anytime of the day or night.)

The report had gone off quite nicely. I hadn't been able to snag an interview with the accused (a forty-year-old female on trial for the murder of her husband), but I had been present when she turned towards the courthouse with tears streaming down her face. Since the sun hadn't cleared the horizon yet, she was able to hide some of her anguish simply because it was dark outside, but she couldn't conceal everything.

Her posture gave away her grief. Her shoulders were rounded. Normally this happened because the handcuffs would pull a person into that sort of position, but for some reason, this woman wasn't being restrained this morning. I wondered if this had anything to do with her innocence, or rather, if they knew she was guilty, and they were giving her a moment of freedom. Either way, I stood quietly off to the left-hand side of the steps and watched as she made the long climb upward.

I wasn't exactly proud of myself for catching her at her most vulnerable, but this was a facet of my job. I had to show the public how criminals (or the innocent—we'll find out in a few days) react when they finally come face-to-face with the overwhelming courthouse steps.

Since I'd put in my time this morning like a good little soldier, I now had the opportunity to hang around on set and watch Steve Martin. I never get this pleasure. Even though we work at the same place we are both always so busy with our own gigs that we hardly ever see each other. Today was a special treat and I wanted to really soak up Steve's on-camera personality.

He was really stunning Mel today. Not only was he practically radiating confidence and subtle sexuality, but he was also defending the accused. I don't think that Mel had been prepped for this interview with him very well because she seemed to be floundering. Now, don't misread that. Mel's a professional. She knows how to handle herself-- even if it's im-promptu--but there was something off about her interactions today. Her speaking halted in places and at other times she would just stare at Steve with her mouth slightly agape. When

I saw her shuffle a few papers on the desk about halfway through the interview, I noticed from my vantage point that there was nothing written on the pages. She really was winging this portion of her program. This was so unlike her personality that I had to pause for a moment.

I was deep in thought, so much so that I didn't realize when Ethan was right at my elbow.

"Dazzling, huh?" Ethan whispered quietly.

Even though no one else could have possibly heard his soft voice, I jumped nearly a mile in the air, so most certainly they saw my reaction. I spun to see Ethan smirking triumphantly. He had a giant grin that would stretch the expanse of his very small face. He didn't smile this way often (I think that it embarrassed him), but when he did, I couldn't help but respond with my own gigantic smile. (FYI: I look really silly when I do this. Unlike Ethan, who has a very slim face, mine is a little more fleshed out. When I smile from ear to ear, my cheeks billow up like hot air balloons and my face looks like it's about to liftoff. I reserve this smile for very special people, and I like Ethan enough to consider him in that category.)

"Yeah," I finally replied softly.

"You know, Mel's really going to miss him when he's gone," he said quickly and took a step closer so that our conversation would truly be guarded.

"She's not the only one," I sighed heavily and turned my attention back to Steve and Mel.

Ethan laughed dryly. "You women. You get so attached so easily." His superior attitude caught me off-guard. Ethan didn't usually lump Mel in with women like me. While Mel and I had many things in common, we weren't exactly the same people. Sometimes, even when Ethan thought that he was reading my emotions well, he could be totally off the mark because I'd never tell him the full story. Women like Mel were easier to understand. Mel always told Ethan exactly what she wanted when she wanted it. It was easy to follow Mel's orders because they were always precise, and she never accepted any last minute substitutions or alterations.

I turned around to look at Ethan momentarily. "Is something bothering you?" I asked so that only he could hear me.

"Nah," he shook his head slowly. "I'm just thinking."

"Hmm . . ." I pursed my lips and nodded thoughtfully. I didn't really want to pry into Ethan's personal affairs. Even though he had harpooned me recently about not being involved in Kevin's life, I still couldn't bring myself to force my way into anyone's personal business. It didn't feel right. Ethan and I knew each other well, and I figured that if there was something to share, he would eventually get around to it.

"You going out after work?" Ethan asked and checked his cell phone casually.

"I wasn't planning on it," I said and shrugged. That wasn't entirely true, I realized as soon as I said it. I wasn't prepping to go out to a club or anything, but Steve and I did have dinner plans. I was waiting for him to get off work so that he could take me out for some much-deserved eats. (On top of getting up early today, I hadn't made time for breakfast or lunch. I was famished.) But I didn't think that Ethan needed to know all of this.

"You know, not every man can pull off a white suit," Ethan said in a small voice. I could hear the laughter (and maybe a bit of awe) tucked behind that statement.

"Yeah, Steve is pretty . . ." I stopped and thought about how to finish that sentence.

"Yeah, Steve's pretty," Ethan finished it for me. He shifted uncomfortably from one foot to the other and I smiled a little at his statement. It hadn't been exactly what I meant, but it kind of covered the basic idea. We both turned our heads back to the news platforms. Mel was sitting on one side of the table and Steve was at her elbow. Mel always had a way of sparkling when she was on film and today was no exception. She was wearing a turquoise jacket that gapped only slightly at the neck to reveal a black ruffled camisole. Her look was understated but the colors magically lit up her face and hair. Even though Mel was striking, Steve managed to steal the spotlight from her.

Today he was wearing a gleaming white suit that seemed to be tailored to his custom measurements. (I would guess that most of his suits were custom-made because his measurements would have been hard to purchase under normal conditions. He was extremely tall and had very broad shoulders. He was built well, but he had awfully skinny legs. I liked to bug him about them when we went to the beach. Consequently, he was a tiny bit shy about this one feature and he almost never wore shorts as a result.)

The shirt beneath his jacket was a playful lilac color. If only a handful of men can pull off a white suit, even fewer can pair it with light violet and come away looking amazing. And that he did. Steve looked breathtaking. Even though he was one of my best friends, my heart did a tiny happy dance just looking at his well put-together ensemble.

As I was busy ogling my buddy, I noticed that Ethan wasn't exactly watching his girlfriend. He was standing right beside me, and he appeared to be enjoying the broadcast, but his body language was deceiving. His features were fixed pleasantly enough, and his stance was relaxed, but his eyes were worried. They would dart back and forth between Mel and Steve so quickly that I started to wonder what he was really looking for.

"Do you want to go out to dinner with Steve and me?" I asked Ethan this on impulse. I assumed that Steve wouldn't mind. Besides, even though he was feigning happiness, he didn't look the part--not entirely.

"I thought you said that you weren't going out?" Ethan lifted a fine eyebrow in my direction.

"We're not going out," I replied calmly, "but I'm letting Steve take me out to dinner."

"Do you and Steve go out often?" Ethan asked in a tone that I had never heard him use before. It sounded almost protective.

"Yeah," I said as nonchalantly as possible.

"Are you dating?" Ethan asked with a new spark finding its way into his voice.

"No," I shook my head politely and smiled in a secretive way. Many people at the office had assumed that Steve Martin and I were dating simply because we spent time with each other whenever we could. I actually wished that I could see my friend more often, but even this miniscule relationship blip at the T.V. station was bound to show up on someone's radar and raise a few suspicions.

"So, I wouldn't be interrupting if I came along then?" Ethan ventured.

"I wouldn't have invited you if it were an imposition. You know that," I said easily and gave Ethan a small pat on the arm. He looked a bit relieved. I wasn't quite sure what was eating him today. If I didn't know any better, I would say that he was jealous of all the attention Mel was lavishing on Steve. Watching them on camera felt like watching magic in the making. They had great chemistry and both personalities flew off the screen. Mel's afternoon program ratings had jumped almost ten points when Steve joined her broadcast. Finding Steve next door had been a real coup for Mel.

I took a brief minute to watch the pair at work. Mel's manner had calmed considerably since the beginning of the program and now she was easily bantering back and forth with Steve. I wondered if after he graduated from school, the station would try to create a co-anchor position for him so that he could sit in with Mel every day. The thought was bittersweet for me, and a small pang of envy rose quickly through my body. I wanted that anchor position. I loved Steve, but I wasn't going to just happily move aside so that he could take the spot I had coveted for so long.

I was so deep in thought that I nearly missed the end of the newscast. Ethan slid away from me a step and began to glide towards Mel. As soon as the cameras clicked off and the lights began to dim on the set, Mel jumped up from her desk. She shook Steve's hand and realigned her papers. A pleasant smile floated across her visage when she noticed Ethan breezing up in front of her.

"E," she breathed lightly, "what did you think?"

"Fantastic, as always," he said and gave her a genuine grin.

"And . . ." she started to say something else but noticed that I was standing behind Ethan. My presence cut her off briefly, but Mel, the eternal professional, rebounded very quickly.

"Missy," she said with a little too much enthusiasm. "What are you doing on this side of the studio today?" She peered up at me through her heavy eyelashes and I wondered what accusation she was really trying to make. I had made the attempt to get along with Mel because I was a devoted friend to Ethan, but his girlfriend was not my favorite person in the world. Clearly, I wasn't her cup of tea, either.

"I just came to pick up my man," I said and ran around the side of the desk to link arms with Steve. He laughed playfully and tossed a lock of my hair over my shoulder.

I wish that I could've taken a picture of Mel's face at that moment because it was priceless. While Ethan looked slightly amused, Mel was dumbfounded. I know that I had just told Ethan that Steve and I weren't dating, but I couldn't help playing with the hearts and minds of my colleagues just a wee bit.

Her voice cracked slightly as she tried to recover. "And what are you two up to this afternoon?" She looked at Steve when she asked this question.

He laced his arm around my shoulders. "I'm taking my best girl to dinner. She got up early and needs to catch a quick supper," he said and fixed a sparkling smile on his lips.

"That sounds nice," Mel replied in a phony voice.

We all looked at each other awkwardly for a brief second as it was clear we were fresh out of things to say.

"Well," Mel finally broke the ice, "I have to go do some editing on a piece. I'll call you later." She winked at Ethan, and he nodded sadly. I think that he was imagining her actually joining us for dinner. Dating Mel couldn't be easy on him. Not only was she domineering, but she also didn't really like to socialize with the rest of the staff and crew. Ethan would almost always choose Mel over the rest of us, but I could see where sometimes he just wanted the two worlds to collide.

"You're still welcome to join us, you know," I said to Ethan brightly.

"Still?" Mel said in a high-pitched voice. Her facial expressions matched her tone. Her eyes floated over to her boyfriend's face, and I must admit that he looked guilty, even to me.

"Oh, it's nothing," Ethan began slowly, but suddenly the words began tumbling out of his mouth. "While we were watching the two of you work, Missy invited me to join them for dinner. They're not dating and so it wouldn't be a big deal."

I laughed a little and Steve tried to hide a smile. That was about the oddest thing that anyone had ever said.

Mel watched Steve and I both nudge each other slightly. I saw a flicker of understanding cross her face quickly and she turned away from us so that she was looking Ethan in the eyes.

"Don't be too late. Okay, baby?" She leaned in and gave him a peck on the lips. I was shocked. Literally, I was astounded. Mel and Ethan had been dating for years, and I had never once seen them kiss. Ethan blushed profusely and nodded in Mel's direction.

"Ya'll be careful now," Mel said in a warm way that was totally unreflective of her usual self. First of all, I still couldn't believe that she had kissed Ethan in front of us. Second, my mind was having trouble processing the fact that she had just called him 'baby.' I was willing to bet that had never happened before. Finally, and perhaps most importantly, did Mel just call us 'ya'll'?

Steve pinched me on the shoulder and brought my out of my stupor.

"Let's go, kid," he said and smiled at me in a bright way.

"That was the weirdest thing I've ever seen," I said, still feeling like I was trapped in a dreamlike state. As I said it though, I registered that Ethan was standing right beside me now. "Sorry, E," I apologized quickly and patted his arm.

"It's cool. That was odd. Mel never acts that goofy." He was still watching her retreat into the distance. "It must be you," he said and nodded in Steve's direction.

"Ya think?" Steve said and I could tell that there was a little part of him that was trying to be sarcastic. I imagine that he knows the effect he has on women. (Not to mention the fact that I've told him this repeatedly.)

"Is it too early for a drink?" Ethan looked in my direction for approval. I laughed lightly and Steve clapped him on the back.

"Come on, I have the feeling that we all have quite a bit to talk about today." With that statement from Steve, we finally felt as though we had been officially dismissed from work for the day and then we were on our way to Tripps.

I was practically starving and utterly dumbfounded all the way to the restaurant. Ethan was acting strange. Mel's behavior was totally mind-blowing. For the first time, I began to wonder if there was something actually going on with the two of them. They had always been sort of an odd couple, but that was just a figure of speech. Today, in a surprising twist, they had become truly bizarre.

We decided to go to Tripps this afternoon because it felt too early to go to a bar. Plus, I wasn't exactly jazzed about the prospects of eating bar food. When I'm not cooking at home or eating at the Pond with the girls, my restaurant selections are generally limited. I like certain types of food, but loathe others, so I try to stick with what I know. Since I was so hungry today (and feeling pretty agreeable), I let Ethan pick the destination and we were at Tripps about ten minutes later.

Once I had a cool glass of ice water perched within my reach and I had placed my order (a petite steak and a side order of sautéed mushrooms), I thought it might be appropriate to interrogate Ethan. He was clinking ice cubes around in his glass, the gin and tonic threatening to spill over the side. The poor guy looked so distracted that I took a second to think about my questions. Should I really harass him right now? Ethan had very recently given me grief for not participating in the lives of my co-workers, so maybe I would need to get involved here. Still uncertain how to approach the topic, I watched him take a large gulp of his drink, and it seemed to brighten his complexion considerably.

Steve Martin was busy studying the pair of us. I knew that he was trying to calculate exactly what I was going to say to Ethan, and I had a feeling that he was just about to stop me from doing something rude, invading Ethan's private thoughts. As always, Steve saved the day again.

"So, I'm excited. I heard from my landlord this morning and he said he's going to go easy on me with the whole breaking the lease thing."

"That's a relief," I said and faked a smile in his direction. I was grateful that he had stopped me from confronting Ethan, but I really wanted to know what was going on with him and his girlfriend.

Before I could explore this thought any further or Steve and I could continue our small talk, Ethan drained his glass and looked at us both with wild eyes.

"Do you think you'll ever get married?" His thin lips pursed together immediately after the words were released. It was like they were trying to clamp down on any further comments.

"Huh?" I squeaked quietly.

Ethan rolled an ice cube around in his glass, watching it as it chased small drops of liquid. He looked up at the both of us and smiled shyly. He repeated himself, this time in a much more reassured manner. "Do you think you'll ever get married?"

Instead of focusing on the answer to his question, I focused on the motive. Why was he asking such a thing? It didn't make any sense at all.

"Do *you* think *you'll* ever get married?" I countered. Steve Martin shot me an 'easy there, girl' look and I abruptly sat back in my seat.

Ethan shifted uncomfortably and then answered quietly, "Well, I always thought I would."

He lifted his empty tumbler slightly in the air and nodded in the direction of our server.

"And now?" Steve asked.

"Well," Ethan said slowly, "well, now I'm not so sure."

"I know I asked you this before, but is something wrong with you?" I gently laid my hand on Ethan's arm as I asked him this.

He nodded.

"Is it Mel?" I asked quietly.

He nodded again.

"Do you want to tell me about it?" I felt like I was pulling teeth here. While some would characterize Ethan as a reserved individual, he had always been forthcoming with me. We just had that type of relationship. Maybe it was because we had been working together for years, but we never had a communication problem before right now.

He patted my hand and nodded in Steve's direction. "You already know what's wrong, don't you?"

Even though it was a shocking accusation, Steve didn't look even a little bit surprised. He just stared back at Ethan in a cool way.

"You do, right?" Ethan looked at Steve with big eyes. He was waiting for some kind of reaction and Steve wasn't giving him the satisfaction.

While they were playing cat and mouse, I was getting annoyed. I was tired and hungry. I had looked forward to my dinner with Steve all day long (he was leaving to go back to school very soon, after all), and now I was perplexed by the mind games that these men seemed to be playing with each other. Feeling totally excluded, I stood up brusquely.

"I'm going to the ladies' room. When I come back, you two better have it together." With that, I turned on my heel and stomped towards the back of the restaurant.

In all actuality, I was intrigued by the strange dance that seemed to be unfolding between Ethan, Mel, and Steve. Was it possible that something was going on and that I had been oblivious to it all?

As I sauntered back out of the bathroom, I was greeted by a welcome sight. Steve and Ethan were both engaged in an enormous laugh. Both were trying to contain their mirth in a most gentlemanly way, but they just looked silly to me. I was immediately relieved.

"Now that all of that garbage is out of the way, can someone please tell me what's going on?" I knew that my tone was a little bit biting, and I hadn't meant to be that way. I was seriously glad that these two had lightened up the atmosphere. Just as I was settling back into my chair and looking between the two of them for an explanation, our dinner's arrived.

A few bites of steak later, I was feeling even better and not so annoyed, but I still had a few qualms about the whole situation. Was something going on between Steve and Mel? If so, why wouldn't he have told me?

"All right," I said, pointing my knife at both men in turn, "someone give me the details."

Ethan purposely shoveled a spoonful of food into his mouth at that moment and shrugged at Steve good-naturedly.

Steve gave his signature "I'm amazing" laugh and looked at me with happy eyes. "We've all just had a major misunderstanding," Steve said and placed a piece of salmon in his mouth. He chewed thoroughly and then continued, "Ethan thought I was trying to steal Mel."

"You?" I laughed in a pointed way.

"I set him straight," Steve said with a shy smile.

"Honestly," Ethan piped up, "at first, I really thought the two of you were dating. Then, when you denied it earlier, that completely threw me for a loop. I figured that Steve had to be after Mel because they just clicked so well together . . ." he let his voice trail off. Even though I was certain that Steve had explained everything to Ethan and that he had undoubtedly assuaged many of his fears, I could still tell that he felt dubious.

"You do work well, together. I'll grant you that much," I said and stabbed a few mushrooms with my fork.

"I'll take that as a compliment, Miss Lawrence," Steve sighed and rolled his eyes in my direction.

I thrust the food into my mouth and took a moment to digest the information and the exquisitely buttered vegetable. (Yes, yes, I know that technically mushrooms are not vegetables, but they look like them—sort of.)

I put my fork down and shifted in my seat. Even though the boys appeared to be playing nice now, none of it made sense. This whole afternoon felt like one big riddle to me, and I found that I was displeased. I didn't feel like any true problem had been solved. I looked quickly from one man to the next and realized that I had to ask a couple more questions. Maybe I was just really tired, and my brain wasn't processing at a very high rate.

"Okay, so let me get this straight. Ethan thought that Steve and I were dating. Then he thought that Steve was trying to steal Mel. Now you know that neither of those is the case and suddenly everything is cool again. Right?"

"That pretty much sums it up," Ethan said between slurps of his tomato soup. I looked from Steve to Ethan, and I noticed the small smile playing on Steve's lips. He knew that we didn't have the entire story, either.

"No, no, that doesn't sum it all up. You're still hiding something." I looked at Steve for approval and he nodded his head.

Ethan gave me a sad puppy dog look.

"Do you think I'm the marrying type?"

I was a little surprised by this question. I needed some clarification. "What do you mean?"

"I don't really know what I mean." Ethan dropped his head and took another slurp of soup. I watched as he crushed a few crackers into the bowl and stirred them around.

"I think I get it," Steve said, wiping his mouth with a napkin. "Are you worried about your future with Mel?" Steve looked pointedly at Ethan. It seemed like a simple question, but it appeared to make Ethan extremely uncomfortable. Instead of answering, he just nodded.

We all sat in an absorbed silence for a minute. I had never really thought about Ethan and Mel being married before. I mean, they were a couple for sure, but I never pictured the two of them tying the knot. That's not to say that I imagined them breaking up, either. I realized that I didn't have a clear perspective on this whole relationship. I waited patiently for Ethan to shed some light.

A full minute later he took a final bite of soup and placed his spoon gently on a napkin beside the bowl. He looked at the two of us very carefully. I could see him weighing his options in his mind. Did he tell us what was going on or did he brush the subject off? I was really hoping that he would find us worthy and decide to share his story with us. It might have been the news reporter in me, but I felt like I had come too far in this story to be turned away now before the climax.

"Okay, okay," Ethan sighed slightly. "First of all, if you want me to talk about my issues, you're both going to have to stop giving me the 'news' eyes. You're doing it right now and it's creeping me out." I turned my head slightly and saw that Steve and I were giving Ethan the same expression. It was a hint of interest mixed with sympathy. I shook my head to try to wipe the look away. This seemed to appease Ethan.

"Here's the thing: I was pretty upset when I heard that Deidra and Kevin had called it quits. It really bothered me. You remember?" He said and nodded in my direction. I grunted back at him. I most certainly did remember his reaction to their breakup. He made me feel awful and I wasn't even involved in the debacle.

"I had a hard time processing. They had dated for such a long time that marriage just seemed like the next logical step. When Deidra balked at the idea and Kevin decided to dis-regard the whole notion, I seriously began to evaluate my own situation."

My eyes widened as he said this. I felt like I should have seen this coming. I should have known that the reason he had given me such a hard time about the breakup was that he wanted to make sure I wouldn't leave him hanging in the moment that he'd need me. I began to wonder if this was going to be that moment.

"Anyway, I thought all weekend about marriage. I'm pretty sure that I want to marry Mel, but I don't really think she wants to marry me. Just look at the way she acts around him." He gestured towards Steve. "She's captivated," he sighed heavily. "She's *never* looked at me that way."

"Ethan, Ethan, don't say that. Everyone looks at Steve that way. Come on, even though I know he's gay, even though he told me it in the first hour that we met, I still drool all over him," I said.

Steve nodded in affirmation. "It's true. Missy's practically obsessed with me." I hit Steve playfully on the arm and this seemed to thaw Ethan's mood momentarily.

"You see, that's the one thing that's missing," he sighed and pointed at the two of us. "That's the only way I know that you really aren't trying to steal Mel. You never flirt with her like that." I started to say something but instead I tried to look at the situation through Ethan's eyes. He was right. Mel did seem to be infatuated with Steve, but she never did anything about it, and she certainly never flirted with him.

"Point taken," Steve said casually.

"Ethan," I ventured. I had been milling a question around in my head and since I couldn't banish it to a dark corner, I figured I might as well ask it already. "Ethan," I repeated, "were you going to ask Mel to marry you? Are you getting cold feet?"

"Lord no," Ethan gave a sharp laugh. His fine features contorted up into a bright smile. "I would never dream of asking Mel to marry me."

"I don't get it," I said, thoroughly confused.

"I always pictured that Mel, and I would get married, but I also never planned to propose. I just figured that she would suggest it one day and I would agree. The next day we'd go pick out a ring and then I'd let her take over everything else."

Steve laughed and I stared at Ethan in dismay. "Did you really never intend to ask her to marry you?"

"I still don't," he replied. "But see," he leaned towards us, "that's the problem. Like I said, I always sort of pictured her popping the question. But now . . . I'm not sure that she wants to marry me at all." He looked a little sad by the thought and I instantly felt sorry for him. My mind flashed forward to a future where Ethan and Mel had to work together but had stopped dating. That would be miserable for everyone. Mel would go back to bossing *everyone* around (not just her boy-friend) and Ethan would probably just be sad all the time. Even worse, Ethan would probably quit working at WSTA if he and Mel were to hit the skids. I had never even contemplated the idea.

"Ethan, I really wouldn't worry about it, if I were you," Steve said. It was a manly thing to say, and I appreciated that he was trying to liven up the dinner party by suggesting that Ethan toss aside his worries. "I'm certain that Mel loves you."

"Certain?" Ethan asked.

"Certain," Steve confirmed and nodded briskly.

"But does she want to marry me? Am I the type of guy that a girl like her should marry?"

My maternal instincts went into overdrive. I wanted to reach across the table and pet Ethan's head. I wanted to whisper sweet reassurances in his ear. He was my friend, and he was suffering. I wanted to help calm him down, and at the same time, wash away his fears. But I couldn't do any of these things. I had never really seen eye-to-eye with Mel, so I didn't feel like I was qualified to make assumptions about her feelings.

"Oh, come on, E, getting married is not so glamorous. Look at Adair," I said and took a quick sip of water. "She loves Wesley, but she's not really into the whole marriage thing. She's only doing it because he asked, and she knows it will please him."

I felt a little guilty telling this lie. Adair was actually enjoying all of the wedding attention. I tried to cover up the situation.

"Speaking of Adair, you both know her, and no one ever would have guessed that she was the marrying type."

"That's true," Steve said.

"I guess so," Ethan sighed again.

"No, seriously, think about it. Jessica Adair was the girl least likely to get married in this whole city. Then one day she meets a great guy and just decides that she thinks she'll go for it. It sounds crazy, but even though she never seemed interested in the idea, it actually suits her quite well." Now, that was not a lie. I was surprised how gracefully Adair had taken to all of the wedding formalities and functions. At the beginning of their relationship, she had tried to push off her feelings for Wesley, to hide how she felt, but as soon as he put the ring on her finger, she melted into a pile of love. I had truly believed that Adair would never get married, and now, here it was a matter of days from her *big day*.

"Where are you going with this?" Ethan asked, suddenly pulling me back to the conversation.

"I'm just saying that you don't have to be the marrying type to get married. I mean, look at me—am I the marrying type?"

"Yeah," Ethan grunted.

"Of course," Steve added.

"Huh?" I felt my eyebrows shoot up. They had answered that question awfully fast.

"You're kidding, right, Missy?" Ethan asked and took a small sip of his drink. "You were born to get married."

"What's that supposed to mean?" I felt myself start to blush as I said this.

"He's right," Steve looked at me thoughtfully. He reached over and began playing with a strand of my hair. "You're just the kind of girl that guys want to marry. Someday real soon someone's gonna come swooping in here and make a little wifey out of you."

I swatted his hand away from my hair. "You guys, this is real nice of you to say and all, but it doesn't compute. If I was the marrying kind, wouldn't I have a boyfriend? Wouldn't I be out on a date with him right now?"

Both guys looked at each other and then back at me.

"Oh, Missy," Steve patted my shoulder reassuringly. "You're so overdramatic sometimes."

Ethan nodded in agreement. "I mean, imagine, you not getting married. If you don't get married what kind of hope is there for the rest of us?" Steve seemed to think that final statement was hilarious, and he let out a barking laugh.

"What does that mean?" I asked, feeling defensive.

"Miss," Ethan leveled me with his eyes, "stop this nonsense. You know that you'll get married someday. It's inevitable."

I just sat and looked at him. "Inevitable?" I questioned.

"Sure, girls like you get married," Steve said simply.

"And guys like you don't?" I countered on him quickly.

"No," he said, with a look of regret floating in his eyes, "no, guys like me don't get married. Yet," he threw that last part in there and gave a small smile.

"No, I guess you're right. You would have to find the right guy and live in the right state to get married, wouldn't you?"

"Yep, that's about right. So, I guess it's not even debatable whether or not I'm the marrying type. I probably would, if the perfect opportunity presented itself, but it's going to be a little harder for me than for either of you." A flash of guilt swept over me as Steve delivered this speech. Steve was a little bit like Adair. I never actually pictured him getting married. But now, come to think of it, he (like Adair) would probably be a very respectable spouse. He would most likely be very well suited to the challenge.

"So that brings us back to the original question: Am I the marrying type?" Ethan said and began drumming his fingers nervously. I really wanted to give him a good answer. I didn't want it to necessarily be something that he wanted or needed to hear. I wanted to deliver the right answer. I would have to think about this.

I leaned back in my chair and took a small sip of my water. If I thought really hard, could I picture Ethan getting married?

I could. The image came to me very quickly and I felt my insides light up as the warmth of the idea spread in my mind's eye. I could see Ethan standing underneath a beautiful archway. The wooden creation had been decorated in lovely cream-colored roses. The sun was shining brilliantly, only to be outdone by the power of his smile.

Ethan himself was looking quite dashing. (I have never lumped Ethan into the "dashing" category before. He's usually not my type, but on the wedding day that I was picturing in my mind, he was striking.) He had recently received a haircut and he had acquiesced to trim his facial hair. His eyes were sparkling with the tears that he would inevitably release as he watched his blushing bride glide down the aisle.

In my imagination, I listened to Pachabel's Canon in D Minor play in the background and saw that he and his beloved had chosen to get married in a natural environment. The trees that were growing up around the area denoted a forest of some sort. This was an immediate problem. I felt a pang of anxiety creep into my stomach. I knew instantly that Ethan would get married someday, but Mel wouldn't be the bride.

Even though my mind was begging me to let go of this little fantasy, I felt like I had to see it through to the end. I wanted to give Ethan an answer to his question. He was sincere, he was determined, but most importantly--he was suffering because he had come to a crossroads in his relationship and now, he needed a little guidance from his friends. I felt that I owed this to him.

I continued to stare off into the distance and I saw a bride quickly flash before my eyes. Thank heavens; it wasn't anyone that I recognized. Slowly, I allowed myself to return to reality. I was surprised to see both Ethan and Steve staring at me intently. I thought that I had only been focusing hard on Ethan's future for a matter of seconds, but from the way they were looking at me, you would think that I had passed out.

"Missy, you okay?" Steve held out his hand to me and I tapped the top side of it lightly.

"Yeah, why?" I asked.

"Nothing's wrong with us, but you were staring at the door as if it was moving on its own," Ethan said in a breathless tone.

"What? What did I do?" I couldn't figure out what was going on. Maybe I *had* passed out and dreamed about Ethan getting married. I thought it was only a few seconds, but I suppose that it could have been more.

"You closed your eyes and started humming something. At first," Ethan laughed uncomfortably, "I thought that you were trying to mimic one of those television psychics."

"Really? Did I look like that?" I asked, glancing in Steve's direction.

He shook his head, "You're a weird girl. I'll give you that much."

"Well," I said shaking out my blond hair slightly, "I wasn't trying to be strange or rude or anything else, I was just trying to give Ethan an honest answer. But first, I had to think about it—really think about it."

"Okay," Steve said slowly. "And?"

"Ethan," I started and placed my hand so that it covered his, "you're definitely going to get married someday."

"That's good news," he said and visibly breathed a sigh of relief.

"But..." I began and then caught myself. I didn't want to tell him everything that I imagined. What if he and Mel broke up because I made some stupid comment? Mel would certainly hate me, and Ethan would undoubtedly be miserable. If Ethan was going to break up with Mel, I didn't want it to be because I had said something out of line.

"But..." Ethan repeated and his eyes seemed to beg me to continue.

"But I don't know. What do I know anyway?" I finished in the most lighthearted way that I could.

"I don't . . ." Just as Ethan was about to grill me for my innermost thoughts, his phone buzzed. He clutched at his pocket and made a tortured face.

"It's Mel, I just know it," he said through gritted teeth.

"Answer it; I'm sure she's worried about you. We've been out much later than we should have been." As I said this, I allowed my eyes to survey the rest of the restaurant. None of the patrons currently in the establishment had been here when we arrived. I searched the crowd to spot our waiter. Just as I was doing this, a young woman sauntered over to the table.

"Miss, did you need something?" she asked politely. "Would you like a refill?"

I looked at her with questioning eyes and she anticipated my question: Where was our waiter?

"I'm Connie. Ty had to take off for the day, so I took over his remaining table." She rattled off this information very quickly and gave me a triumphant smile. We had been here so long that our server had thrown in the towel and gone home.

I patted Steve on the arm, "We really should think about going soon, right?"

He looked from me and then up at Connie. "I don't know. Maybe," he smiled smoothly. Connie blushed.

"Actually," Steve said and leaned in her direction, "I'll take another beer and my girl here will have a margarita." I shot Steve a warning glance. I hadn't been drinking all evening on purpose. I didn't really want to start now.

He totally ignored my silent protest and looked at Ethan with a large question looming in his eyes. "Ethan, you want another round, or do you want to go home?"

Ethan shoved his cell quickly back into his pocket. I was sure that was a sign that he was staying, but I was wrong. He gave us both a big apologetic grin.

"I'm sorry guys. I really am. I didn't mean to bring you both down tonight. I don't really know what's going to happen with me and Mel, but I appreciate you both being here and trying to help me through it."

"No problem, man," Steve said and offered his hand to Ethan across the table. "I'm just glad we got our issues resolved." Ethan took Steve's hand and shook it quickly.

"I'm glad about that, too. I would hate for you to leave with me hating your guts." Ethan smirked a little at Steve.

"I'd hate that, too," Steve said.

"And you," Ethan turned to face me as he was standing up, "I know what you're thinking. You think I'm not going to marry Mel-- and maybe I'm not--but I'm glad you didn't say it. Thanks for holding back."

He leaned in and kissed me quickly on the cheek. I sat motionless until he was out the door. Apparently, I had given him the right answer after all.

"Now that he's gone, what the hell was that?" Steve asked and flicked me on the shoulder. Sometimes he teased me like we were related. I liked this about our relationship. It always made me feel comfortable.

"Oh hell, I don't know. This has been the weirdest day ever."

"I blame Ethan," he said with a conspiratorial grin.

"I do, too," I said and laughed aloud. It felt good to emit a real laugh. This entire day had felt ridiculous. Ethan had been so serious all day long that I felt like he had totally drained all the energy that I had on reserve. It was at that moment that I realized Ethan was in big trouble.

Here was the problem: Ethan *was* the marrying kind. Just like I had pictured, Ethan would eventually find a nice girl and he would have an outdoorsy ceremony. But that girl wouldn't be Mel. It would be someone who didn't boss him around quite so much. It would be someone who put his needs before her career. I don't really think Mel would ever be capable of doing that.

I thought about Steve next. He was so beautiful that anyone would be lucky to have him as their lifelong partner. I wished, not for the first time, that I could just live with Steve forever.

As for me, I was the real mystery of the group. The men had, without blinking an eye, dubbed me the marrying type. I was bound to get married to someone, and according to Steve, I would probably be taking the vows pretty soon. That seemed a little unreal to me.

Don't get me wrong, I don't have anything against marriage. I really don't, but I wasn't one of those little girls who practiced the ceremony growing up. I couldn't picture the flowers or my dress. I never even contemplated the cake. I was just never that sort of person.

It was bizarre: I could picture Ethan's wedding, but I couldn't even fathom my own. What did that say about my prospects for marriage?

Even if I found the right dress and I finally decided that I wanted to settle down, there was still one ultimate question that loomed largely in my mind: Who would want to marry me?

Chapter Ten

Do You Have to Change Who You Are?

I can't quite explain to you why I'm baking cookies right now, but I am. I have so many things going on this week that spending time in the kitchen seems like a waste of resources, but I can't help myself.

It's Wednesday, and instead of going to Cardio Fusion with Autumn tonight, I elected to stay home and bake cookies. This sounds counterproductive, I know, but my motivation is shot right now. This week has been totally draining already and it's only Wednesday. I figured that I was going to need some cookies to help get me over this hump.

I'm mixing up a batch of chocolate chip cookies--my mother's recipe-- and Hope is sitting at the kitchen table telling me about her day. She's a little peeved that I decided to bake cookies right now, because she's on the Atkins Diet.

I hate it when she decides to go on diets. Hope is a beautiful girl, and even though she probably should lose a little weight, she never goes about it the right way. Instead of decreasing her food intake and starting an exercise program, she always tries some wacky diet. I do realize that Atkins isn't considered out of this world, as far as dieting goes, but it also isn't a desirable lifestyle. I mean, really, who wants to live their entire life without drinking milk? I love milk, so I could never even consider this for a second.

As I pop the first batch of cookies into the oven, I think about Autumn having to find a new partner in Cardio Fusion class. I do feel a little badly about all of this for two reasons: The first reason is that I'm letting Autumn down. I'm the one who insists that we go to the gym, so I should keep up with it. The second reason is that I have to fit into my "Pool Blue" bridesmaid gown in just over a week's time, so I really should be making smarter choices. But after my dinner with Ethan and Steve yesterday, I just feel spent. I guess feeling exhausted is better than feeling angry. Earlier today, I was in such a rough around the edges kind of mood that I snapped at Steve, and I upset Autumn.

I called her quickly from work to tell her that I wouldn't be accompanying her to the gym tonight. She didn't give me any grief about the situation, but she asked if something was wrong. I said that I was okay, but I think she knew that I was hiding something. Because she's Autumn and she knows better than to pick at something, she let it go and totally changed the subject.

She started to tell me about a date that she had last night with Paul. I could hardly keep up with the Paul relationship. I knew that I had been dating a smattering of men lately, and that none of them had been serious, but I thought that my love life was much easier to understand than Autumn's. At least when I went out with a guy a couple of times, I could easily explain to my friends what was going on in the relationship or why I (or he) had chosen to end the whole thing. But Autumn and Paul were different. They couldn't decide which way to go.

Autumn was telling me that Paul had taken her to Imperfection the night before. This was sort of a ritual for them. He had taken her there on their first date and she had enjoyed it so much that they made it a point to go there monthly. I don't think that it was meant to celebrate any sort of anniversary or anything, but Autumn always treated the occasion like it was something special when the opportunity did roll around.

Anyway, they were out for dinner when the topic of Adair's wedding was broached. Interestingly enough, it wasn't Autumn who brought it up. Paul said that he knew Autumn was going to the event next weekend and he offered to take her if she wanted him to go.

I said that I thought that was a nice thing to do. Going to a wedding alone can be a little depressing, so I figured that Autumn would be excited to have her (sort of) boyfriend onboard. But when I said this, Autumn got really huffy. It wasn't like she was mad or anything, but she just seemed disappointed in me.

It was like she wanted me to say something else, but she didn't want to tell me what to say. Frankly, I didn't know what to do. The truth was that I didn't think that Autumn should be dating Paul anymore. I felt like he had made it clear a while ago that his interest was waning, and honestly, I felt like Autumn had gone on enough dates with other people that this whole issue with Paul should have been resolved. I couldn't say any of these things to her because I didn't feel that they were appropriate; just look at my wedding date. If I was going to start picking apart her man, then she would start in on Nathan and that really wasn't what I wanted. I just wanted us both to have a great time with our respected dates at Adair's wedding. I thought that would be simple enough.

It wasn't quite so easy though. By the time Autumn and I had ended our conversation, I think that she was mad at me. Part of me wants to believe that she wanted me to tell her to drop Paul. I want to say that she needed some reassurance of sorts, but I'm just not the person to do that. Maybe I could have told her what I was thinking, and that would have made things better, but I highly doubt it. Autumn had to figure out her feelings for Paul on her own. If I put my nose in her business, both of us would surely regret it.

When I told her that, she sighed loudly. I pictured her blowing her hair up and out of her face at the time. I promised to call her later. I reminded her that we had discussed going to the Powerhouse Players Club again this weekend and the thought seemed to cheer her momentarily, so I was glad to say that we ended on a happy note, but I really hated disappointing Autumn. She was right on top of my list of favorite people, and I didn't want that to change. I wasn't sure what was going on with Autumn and Paul. I also wasn't entirely certain how it all affected me (or if it should even be any of my business), but I couldn't focus on that right now. I had cookies to bake.

I turned my mind back to the process of making small, rounded balls out of the dough. Baking, to me, was cathartic. I felt like everyone, including myself, was on edge this week, and I just wanted to do something that would ease the pressure. If Eve had been home, I might have suggested running down to the Triple Play and grabbing a drink, but she had left early this morning for San Antonio. She and Savanna had a huge tournament this weekend and they were going a little early so that they could spend some time hanging out together before all the madness began. It was hard to believe, even when they complained about it repeatedly, but working together didn't necessarily mean that they got to spend time with one another. Eve and Savanna could be in the same place all week long, but only see each other a handful of times. They said that this was pretty common on the tour because most of the contestants tried to keep a low profile, but it just felt off-base to me. They had to have downtime. Why couldn't they hang together then? I didn't know the answer to that question, and it always slipped my mind anytime I had this conversation with either one of them.

The little oven timer pulled me from my thoughts, and I grabbed the red oven mitt that was stationed close by. Hope carefully moved her stuff off the table. She had been sorting through some photographs and made a way so that I could put the cookies down.

"Could you not put those directly in front of me, please?" Hope whimpered a little as I began to put the cookies down. My poor girl. She had even pooched out her lower lip in a sad little pout. I knew that she was just joking, but I got the point either way. She needed to avoid temptation.

"So, how's the diet going?" I asked casually.

"It's all right, I guess," she said and began shuffling her photos in her hands.

"Do you want to go sit in the living room while the rest of the cookies bake?" I barely had the words out of my mouth before she was off and moving. I hadn't realized that the urge to have one had been so strong for her. I admired her will-power. I turned back towards the oven quickly and set the timer. I ran my hands under the kitchen sink, rinsing away any remaining cookie dough, and then found my way to the living room. I plopped down next to Hope on the couch and tried to peer over her shoulder at the photographs.

"That's a good one, "I said thoughtfully. There really was no pattern or reason to the collection of photos. I thought that maybe Hope was just looking at them for something to do. I could spend hours looking through her pieces, so I didn't find this practice to be unreasonable at all. She continued leafing through the pictures for a few minutes, and I would politely comment every so often.

"Oh, Dan!" I said excitedly. Hope had been dating Dan for the majority of the summer and they seemed to be hitting it off. I wondered what Dan had to say about Hope's attempts to lose weight. I stared at the picture of him that she was hold-ing, and I thought that maybe they were doing this whole diet thing together. Dan was a cute kid. He was a bit large around the middle and he had heavy legs. In the photograph, his thin blond hair was flying all over the place. I couldn't tell the exact location from the picture, but I could tell that they had been trapped in one of the wind tunnels created by the buildings uptown. Dan had a huge smile plastered across his face and I smiled back at the picture.

"I think Dan's mad at me," Hope said suddenly. Her tone was neutral, which was surprising. She definitely caught me off-guard.

"Why's he mad?" I asked.

"I yelled at him last night," Hope said and shrugged her shoulders.

"What did he do?" I questioned. I turned slightly in the seat so that I was no longer looking at the photos, but I was now zeroing in on Hope's face. I wanted to gauge her reactions. As far as I knew, this was their first argument.

"Technically," she said with a small snicker, "he didn't do anything. It was all me."

"Okay," I said, trying to lead her to give away more.

"I'm such a jerk sometimes. I just don't know what's wrong with me." She looked at me with her big gray eyes and I couldn't tell if she was being funny or sincere. I gave her a small smile in return, hoping that she would continue with the story.

"All right," she said loudly, and dropped the photos onto the coffee table, "I made a huge mistake last night." She looked a little sheepish as she made this admission. Just at that moment, the buzzer sounded on the oven, and I looked at her for approval.

"Go! Go! I don't want them to burn," she said in a scolding tone, and I hopped up off the couch.

"I want to hear about this!" I called over my shoulder, as I raced to the kitchen. I pulled the golden-brown cookies from the oven and set them on the countertop. I flicked the knob on the oven to the "Off" setting and I quickly washed my hands again at the kitchen sink. I took one longing look at the cookies and shook my head. Even though I had spent the time preparing them, I didn't think that I would actually eat them. I really did have to fit in a bridesmaid dress next weekend. (Okay, maybe I would sneak one later, but then I promised myself that I would take the rest of them into the office so that everyone else could enjoy them.)

This time when I went back into the living room, I settled into the brown couch that was opposite the one Hope was sitting on. I didn't want her to feel like I was invading her space. Plus, I really wanted to see her face as she was telling her story.

As soon as I sat down, I motioned for her to begin, and she obliged.

"Last night, Dan took me out to Mickey's Steakhouse. We love going there, so this wasn't a big deal."

"Okay," I said and shrugged my shoulders.

"Okay," Hope repeated. "You know that we both started this diet together, and Dan suggested Mickey's because we could still follow all of our rules by eating there."

"Okay," I said shortly, but mentally I logged the note that they were in fact taking on this diet challenge together. I gave Dan props in my head for working with my little sister on this endeavor. She would need a buddy to help keep her grounded.

"Anyway, as soon as we were in the restaurant, something happened to me. I don't know if I'm emotional because I'm supposed to start my period soon or what, but I just flipped out."

"Why?" I asked quickly.

"I don't know. I just looked around the restaurant and threw a fit. There were bowls of peanuts on each of the tables and I knew, I just knew that I couldn't have any and that really ticked me off."

I grinned, but didn't say anything, so she continued with her tale.

"Then, when we were finally seated, the waitress started out the evening by bringing these big old round rolls to the table. I nearly started crying. I wanted that roll so much."

"Aww, Hopey," I said in a comforting tone.

"Ugh," Hope made a sigh of disgust, "so, I ordered my meal--steak with steamed broccoli and a side salad--and I sat back and just stared at those rolls and peanuts. It's like they were taunting me. It's like they were saying, 'Come on, Hopey, I know you want a bite.' I just couldn't stop thinking about eating the roll."

"So, what did you do?" I asked cautiously.

"Well, I picked up one of the rolls and started buttering it." As soon as she said it, my hand flew to my mouth. I knew that eating a white bread roll was against the basic principles of the Atkins Diet. It probably contained more carbs in it then she was allowed to have in two days combined.

"Don't worry, crazy pants. I didn't eat it or anything, but I really wanted to."

"All right," I gave a sigh of relief and laughed lightly.

"But I did see Dan's eyes get wide just like yours did right now, and I flipped out on him."

"You did? What'd you do?"

"I threw the roll down on the table and started yelling at him, 'You think I'm fat! You think I'm fat, don't you? That's why you don't want me to eat the roll!'" She hid her head underneath a throw pillow.

"Hope! You didn't!" I yelled at her.

She ducked out from underneath the pillow and sneaked a look around at me.

"Oh yes, I did!" She exclaimed. "I started yelling at him and asking him if he thought I was fat."

"What did he do?" I asked.

"He didn't do anything at first. He just kind of stared at me, dumbfounded."

"Poor guy," I said with a hint of a laugh coloring my tone.

"Poor guy's right because I got worse. After I threw the roll down, I started to reach for the peanuts. As I had my hand in the bowl, I saw him giving me a puzzled look. Then he said something in a small voice like, 'Are we allowed to eat peanuts?' That's when the stuff really hit the fan." She looked at me with red now creeping up her face. I didn't know how to react. I just waited for her to continue with the story.

"As soon as he said that I started yelling at him again. In response, he began eating the peanuts himself."

"What?" I asked loudly.

"That's right," she laughed bitterly. "He started popping the peanuts in his mouth, shells and all. He said, 'Baby, baby, it's okay. See? You can eat peanuts if you want to. See? You can eat anything you want!'" Now, she was doing an impersonation of him popping peanuts into his mouth. I just pictured poor Dan trying to appease Hope and started laughing.

"Why did you freak out like that?" I had to ask the question, but I was sorry as soon as I said it. She immediately stopped laughing and looked at me curiously.

"I have no idea," she said thoughtfully. "I think that I just really wanted to eat the roll."

"Aww," I sighed and tried to hide the smile that was still lurking underneath. "Hope, if you wanted to eat the roll, you should've done it. You could have worked off the extra carbs later."

"Maybe," she said and shrugged nonchalantly, "but I wanted to make him happy."

"It doesn't really sound like you made him happy with your whole outburst."

"No," she conceded, "I probably didn't make him happy with that, but I wanted to please him overall. You know?"

I shook my head, "Not exactly."

"Well, he's the one who wants to do this whole diet thing. Even though I know that I need to lose weight, I'm not exactly committed to it. Carbs are like my favorite thing in the whole wide world, so I really hate the idea of giving them up."

"Do you really want to change who you are and what you like for this guy?" I asked the question quickly before I had time to consider what I was saying.

Hope looked at me with big eyes. "Do I want to change who I am?" She echoed my statement.

"I don't know. Do you?" Now, it was my turn to stare at her.

"I don't know. I never thought of it that way. Maybe that's why I overreacted like that," she said and sat back in the sofa. She really seemed to be contemplating this possibility.

"Maybe," I agreed, and I sat back in my chair, too.

For a few minutes, we just sat together in a comfortable silence. We were both thinking, I imagine, about how much we were willing to change to be the perfect version of ourselves for a guy. I was having a tough time with this concept because I didn't have a committed boyfriend. I didn't have anyone that I would need to change to please. Just then, my Calypso ringtone began sounding. I had left my phone in the kitchen. I looked over my shoulder and then back at Hope.

"It's all right," she smiled in my direction, "you go on and answer it. I really need to call Dan and apologize again." She looked a little more confident as she unfolded her legs and stood up from the couch swiftly. Apparently, Hope was willing to give up a few things for Dan.

I grabbed my phone just in time. It was on the final ring before voicemail would pick up.

"Do you want to go to Sounds with me tonight?" It was Adair, and from the background noise that was coming through the wire, I pictured that she was already at the club.

"Why?" I asked quickly. I liked going to Sounds if the live musician who was scheduled to play was talented. If it was just open-mic night, I would try to stay away from the place altogether.

"There's a new artist playing that I need to check out. The show's only going to be here tonight and then once next week, but I'll be so busy with the wedding next week that I have to come tonight. Are you in?"

I thought about it for a second and then quickly agreed. Even though I had been out every night this week, I still wanted to see Adair. She and I hadn't gotten to spend enough time together since the wedding madness had begun. I figured that this might be my last chance to hang out with her, just the two of us, before she walked down the aisle. I jumped at the chance.

"I can be there in fifteen," I said quickly into the phone. I didn't even wait for her to reply before I hung up.

"I hope you're drinking champagne tonight, because I already ordered," Adair said as I wandered up beside her table. I wasn't really wandering; one of the bouncers actually left the front door to show me to Ms. Jessica Adair's special reserved spot. She was a permanent V.I.P. at Sounds because she helped launch so many careers for the artists who played there. Anytime Jess was in the house that meant that someone was likely to leave feeling very grateful and extremely fortunate.

"Champagne's cool, I guess," I said airily as I slid into the leather seat next to Adair. "What are we celebrating?"

"What else?" She laughed haughtily. "What are we always celebrating nowadays?" She winked at me in a playful way, and I chuckled under my breath.

"Your wedding? Again?" I teased in a mild way.

"We're always going to be celebrating my wedding," Adair said with a grand smile, "but, we're also toasting the artist who's about to take the stage."

"That's nice of you. Did you invite him to join us after his set?" I asked.

"*Him*? What makes you assume that it's a *him*?" She arched her eyebrow in her signature way, and I sat back a little in my seat.

"I guess I just thought . . ." Now that I was thinking about it, I couldn't remember the last time that Adair had signed someone who wasn't male. That's not to say that she didn't have females working at her record label. She had quite a fine selection of female artists--really talented women--but she was just more likely to recruit a man than a woman. I didn't have any problem with it and I certainly never questioned it (except in Jack's case), so my assumption had actually seemed pretty fair to me.

Just then Adair's cell rang, and she held up a finger in my direction. I loved watching Adair work, so I didn't mind when she was forced to take a phone call. I wasn't like other people who got all offended if she had a call or text that would interrupt our conversation. Jessica Adair was a very important woman and I considered myself lucky to be her friend. If I had to share her with a few other people from time to time, that didn't bother me in the slightest.

I took a brief reprieve to survey my surroundings. Gosh, Jess and I (and Jack and Benson once upon a time) had been coming to Sounds for years. I loved the live music scene and Charlotte had plenty of places that provided this sort of entertainment, but Sounds was our favorite spot. I took in the atmosphere and tried to figure out why we had ever decided to designate this as our spot.

The club wasn't much to brag about. It was rather small, which I preferred for live music. I liked the intimate feeling that I got when I sat close to the artist. The stage was set accordingly in the center of the room, and there wasn't a ton of room for backup singers or a band. That usually didn't make much difference anyway, because most of the performers were solo acts. There was a bar off to the left side of the stage and the entrance was on the other side.

Jessica and I were seated in the back of the room, on a platform that was clearly marked "V.I.P." I don't remember the sign being there the first few times we came here but leave it to Jess to make her mark in some way. This club wanted its patrons to know that the owner of DieLou Record was a regular and they had clearly put up a small sign in honor of her sponsorship.

As for the decoration of the place itself, it was much like any other small club. There were a few booths scattered throughout and most of the people in the place sat at small round tables or stood around the perimeter of the room. The tables were covered in a sticky black plastic cloth and the chairs had purple pleather cushions. Our booth was covered in the same material. Small candles were placed in the center of every table and the lights were always dimmed.

When a performer came onstage, a small set of stage lights would shine on the platform. They didn't do a great job illuminating much but the singer's feet. This really wasn't a huge thing to complain about, though, because we didn't exactly come to see what the performer looked like; we came to hear the music.

As I was thinking about this club that we had considered a place of refuge now for so many years, I noticed that Jess was attempting to flag me down. She needed to take her call outside. She looked a bit annoyed, and I said a silent prayer that it wasn't Carmen, her secretary, on the phone. I had a soft spot for young Carmen, and I didn't want Adair to give her a hard time. I motioned for her to go on with her work and that I would be just fine. I even took a small sip of my champagne to prove that her absence would not bring me down. I was immediately sorry that I took a gulp of the drink. It was a tad bitter, and I had a hard time swallowing it.

As I managed to force that small swig down, I turned in my chair ever so slightly to watch Adair head for the exit. She didn't look upset—it took a lot to make her lose her cool in public—but she didn't look pleased, either. I noticed as she was walking away that she had lost probably five pounds over the last two weeks and that her normally fitted candy apple red pencil skirt was flowing a little more loosely around her knee area. I only wondered about this briefly and then I remembered that Adair was a bride. That meant that she had probably been secretly dieting to look exquisite on her big day. I don't know if I'll ever get used to Adair being married.

Minutes later, Adair was returning to the table. She shook her head slightly and ruffled her own blond hair. She casually unbuttoned the highest button on her white blouse. Even though I had watched her leave, I hadn't really realized that she was still wearing her formal work attire. She simply looked so nice all the time that she could go from day to night in the blink of an eye. Adair noticed that I was watching her, and she gave me a sly smile.

"What am I going to do with that man?" she asked quietly. In a normal club, I probably wouldn't have heard this statement, but since this was Sounds and we were sitting in the V.I.P. section, I caught every word.

"Your husband giving you issues?" I asked teasingly.

"It's not his fault, really, it's not. He just gets so worked up over everything." She shook her light hair again and pointed towards the stage. This was a clear change of subject. "This artist is nice. I like his voice. Do you know his name?"

I didn't. I pointed to the little light blue leaflet that had been left on our table. I picked it up and scanned the document. "Says here his name is Peter Charming." I gave Adair a funny look. "That can't be his real name, can it?"

She laughed lightly. "I'm sure it's a stage name, but it's cute and catchy. Plus, he's pretty good." She drummed her fingertips lightly on the top of our table, seemingly enjoying the entertainment.

"Is he the reason we're here tonight? If so, I probably better start paying more attention," I said quickly and shifted in my seat so that I was now facing the stage head-on.

"No, no," she sighed in a resigned way, and pointed down the program a few spaces. "We're here to see the final act: Cora Collins."

"Cora?" I asked.

She nodded.

"I like that name: Cora Collins. It sounds . . . It sounds . . . Well, I don't know how it sounds, but I like it. What kind of music does she play?" I looked up from what I had been reading and slid the leaflet back onto the table.

"She plays a lot of softer rock. She's not exactly bohemian, but she has kind of a folksy feel to her style. I like it a lot," Adair said.

"That sounds different," I said quietly and gave Adair an anxious look. In all the time I had known Jess, she had never signed a folk-rock artist; that sort of music really wasn't Adair's taste. It's not like she represented a bunch of rappers or metal bands or anything, but she didn't usually pick up on the folk singers, either. I was intrigued.

"Are you going to miss this?" I asked and gestured to Sounds. Ever since she had returned from her call with Wesley, she was just letting off this serious vibe. It was like she was paying special attention to the performers. It was as though she was prepping herself because this would be the last time she got to come to Sounds and scout for young talent. I began to wonder if she was even interested in Cora Collins. Maybe this was just an excuse to go out and do something that she loved one last time.

"*Miss this*? What do you mean?" Adair looked at me with a mystified expression.

"I mean, once you get married, aren't you going to miss going out with me and looking for hot new recruits?" I felt like I was spelling it out for her, and maybe I was.

"What makes you think that I would give this up?" Adair gave me a hard look. It was almost a challenging sort of glance, but there was also something behind her eyes that betrayed her true feelings. She knew exactly what I was talking about.

"I just guessed that once you got married that you would have to, or maybe you would want to spend more time at home hanging out with Wesley. I sort of just assumed that you'd delegate this duty to someone else. I was pretty glad that you called me in for your last big hurrah." I was sorry that I gave this speech the second that it left my mouth because now Adair looked sad. She glanced at me and then she looked back at the stage quickly.

"Missy, I'll never stop going to clubs and I'll never stop scouting for new talent."

Even though she said it, I could hear the pain behind her voice. She didn't want to give this part of her life up, but she knew it was inevitable. Something had to give. She couldn't work all day long and still managed to go out with her friends every single night. She might manage to go out for recruiting purposes every once in a while, but she would probably also need to hand this job over to someone who could do it on a more permanent basis.

"Okay, Adair, either way, I'm glad you called me. This is one of my absolute favorite things to do. And I'm glad that I get to share it with you," I said softly and then reached out to squeeze her hand. To my surprise, she gave me a firm squeeze back.

"Damn," she said softly. "I hadn't thought about it that way."

"I know," I replied and released her hand gently. "Hey," I thought that maybe I should try to lighten the mood, "are you really going to change your last name to Jefferson?"

She laughed unexpectedly. "Jessica Jefferson? I don't think so. I'm Jessica Adair. I built my company as Jessica Adair and I'm going to stay that way."

"Jessica Jefferson!" I echoed and then thought about it. "Is Wesley okay with you keeping your own name?"

"Missy." She gave me a matronly look. "We all make our little sacrifices."

Just as I was about to say something about this, she pointed to the stage. Cora Collins was carrying a guitar and pulling a stool up to the microphone. She slowly began strumming the opening chords for a cover of the song "Let It Be" by the Beatles. I thought it was appropriate, so I kept my mouth shut, and just enjoyed the show.

I made a promise to myself that after I returned from my workout with Autumn that I would stay in my apartment on Thursday night. No matter what sort of mayhem or wonderful time I could have on the streets of Charlotte, I absolutely had to relax and get some sleep. I'd had a draining week. This weekend looked to be even more eventful, and then the capstone would, of course, be next weekend with the wedding.

After I bid Autumn *adieu* and made my way back to my apartment, I made a conscious effort to do some cleaning. I always try to do my household chores when I'm dirty and sweating because I figure that I'm already a mess, so adding a little more dirt and grime to the fold doesn't make a whole lot of difference.

My short list of chores was knocked out pretty quickly and I happily hopped into the shower. As I was wrapping myself in a dry towel afterwards, I was delighted to hear my little sister calling me to dinner. She had made a very simple chicken breast, but since it had been marinating all day, I imagined that it would taste wonderful. I wasn't disappointed--it was a nice little meal. Shortly after dinner, Hope excused herself so that she could take a few minutes to call Dan. She had elected to stay in tonight as well, but I think it wasn't because she wanted to be alone. I think it had more to do with needing a little space to reevaluate her relationship with this man. I washed the dishes quickly and headed back to my bedroom.

I don't often find myself with a few spare hours before bedtime. I am usually on the go or surrounded by friends. In my minimal solitary moments, I generally read a book or a magazine, so I'm always occupied. This felt like a rare occasion. I decided to weigh my options very carefully. What did I want to do tonight?

Before I could make any grand decisions, my cell began buzzing. For a millisecond, I considered not answering it. This was "me" time after all, and I felt like if I picked up the phone, this blissful peace might be destroyed. However, since I'm not the type to ignore a phone call, I grabbed the cell off my desk and picked up.

"Misdemeanor," Jack said, and I just knew that she was smiling.

"Jack-o-lantern!" I squealed with delight. It was Jack! It was really Jack. She was finally calling me. I got so excited so fast that I had to force myself to sit down.

"Where are you? What are you doing? Why haven't you called me?" I bombarded Jack with questions immediately and I was relieved when I heard her chuckle on the other end of the line.

"Okay, Mom, calm down," she said simply.

"Jack," I moaned a little, "seriously—where have you been? It's been months."

"I've been . . ." Jack began and then took a second to breathe. "I've been reinventing myself."

"Huh?"

"Is your computer on? Are you sitting at your desk?" Jack asked these questions, and they felt a little out of the blue.

"Yeah," I said slowly.

"Excellent," she replied. "Do me a favor and pull up a browser. Whatslife will do."

I listened to her instructions, still feeling bewildered. I hadn't talked to Jack in months, and now here she was, calling just to ask me to look something up online for her. It felt awkward. I shifted the phone in my hand and quickly began typing.

"Oh, hold on a sec," Jack said, "Don't type in Jack Swammie; try Jackie Rose instead."

"Who's that?" I asked sardonically.

"Me . . . Duh," I could hear the sarcasm dripping off Jack's words.

"Jackie Rose?" I questioned. "What's that all about?"

"Jackie Rose is my new stage name. Do you like it?"

"Do *you* like it?" I asked quickly. I had known Jack for quite a few years now and I knew two things for certain: 1. the only person who called her Jackie was her Aunt Claire and she despised it. 2. No one--and I mean no one--was ever allowed to call Jack by her middle name. It was way too feminine for her tastes, and she had explained that to us at great length many years ago.

"I like it, Miss. I promise."

"Okay, well then . . ." I paused to contemplate my answer. "If you like it, I like it." Maybe this was what she was talking about when she claimed that she was reinventing herself. She had already changed her name to something I would never have dreamed possible. (To be fair: her name is Jacqueline Rose Swammie, so it's not like she really altered her name. But this still felt bizarre, and I wasn't entirely sure that I was psyched about it.)

"Good," Jack said, "now type it into the search engine and tell me what you see." I took a moment to follow her directions and was greeted by a bevy of options. I chose the one that said "musician" after it. I figured that it was the safest bet.

Boy oh boy.

I couldn't have prepared myself if I'd tried for what I saw. If I had happened on this site upon my own, I swear that I wouldn't have even recognized it as *my* Jack. She was so different.

"Is this you?" I asked cautiously. I didn't want to offend her, but seriously, the girl on the screen didn't look a lot like the Jack that I knew and loved.

"Yes, Miss, that's me. Take a minute to let it sink in."

"Okay," I agreed readily. I actually thought that I would need a minute to adjust to this new Jack, so I was glad that she gave me permission.

The website itself was very well put together. The colors were neutral and didn't grate against the nerves. There were quite a few pictures of Jack, a blog, a couple of YouTube videos (presumably performances), and then a few links so that her fans could follow her on Twitter and Like her on Facebook. The page looked good; it looked professional. I was fairly pleased with what I saw on the surface.

Just below the surface was the problem. The girl in the pictures didn't look like Jack. First, she had lost probably twenty-five pounds. Back in the day, her hair had been a strawberry blond color and it had either been pulled back into a pony-tail or it was scrunched up by using an inordinate amount of styling gel.

In these pictures, Jack's hair was a white blond, a kissed-by-the sun color. It ran all the way down her back in deep waves and hung loosely so that small pieces would occasionally cas-cade in her face. Her face had taken on a little different tone as well. Jack had always been extremely tan, but this person in the picture was not the same bronzed hue. She wasn't pale, but she definitely didn't have the same coloring that I had come to associate with Jack's complexion.

In most of the photos, Jack was holding her guitar. I found this to be a bit out of character because even though Jack played the guitar, she usually elected to use her keyboard and sing along. The interesting thing is that the guitar had not changed, even though the girl holding it had.

The photographs themselves appeared to have been taken in a field of wheat. The sunshine was dipping on the horizon, and it made Jack's hair glow like a halo around her head. For the first time since I started looking at the photo slide show it struck me: Jack was pretty. Now, Jack had always been pretty, but this Jack, this softer, tamer Jack was actually *pretty*. She looked like maybe she could be a country star now; she just had that charm exuding all around her.

"So," Jack drew the word out nice and long, "what do ya think?"

I hesitated. I didn't want to tell Jack that I thought she looked pretty because I didn't want to hurt her feelings; I didn't want her to think that I meant she was ugly before. That wasn't at all what I was trying to say. Instead, I stumbled and said something else equally stupid. "What happened to you?" I finally croaked. I immediately slapped myself upside the head. What an idiot.

"I changed, "Jack said calmly.

"I see that," I answered quietly.

"Missy, do you like it?" She was echoing her previous question, I knew that. But she phrased it differently now. This time around she was directly asking for my approval.

"Jack, I like it. I really do. It's just different, that's all."

Jack blew out a huge sigh of relief. "Did you watch the music video yet?"

"You have a music video?" I asked before I could stop myself. I slapped myself again. Of course she had a music video; she wouldn't have brought it up otherwise.

"Yeah," she said briskly. "Take a minute and watch it. Okay?" I could feel her enthusiasm sifting its way through the phone. "Look, I'm going to give you a minute to watch. I'm hanging up now, but I'll Same Time you in a minute. Just make sure that you have your Facebook account open. Okay?"

"Jack wait!" I yelled quickly. I hadn't heard from Jack in months. I didn't want her to hang up on me now.

"Missy, I'll wait five minutes and then I'll hit you up on Facebook. We can message back and forth from there. Okay?" she asked again. I nodded because I didn't feel like I had any other choice.

"Okay," I grumbled.

"Good. Talk to you soon!" Jack said in a most chipper way.

"Bye," I responded. I turned my phone off and turned my attention to the computer. I quickly opened a separate tab and logged into my Facebook account. I was ready for Jack to get a hold of me. I wasted a minute or so worrying and then remembered why she had hung up in the first place. I was supposed to watch her music video.

The video was unlike anything that I'd ever seen before. It was for the love song "Movin' On." Jack had received her record deal because of this number, so it was logical that her first single (and subsequent music video) would be this tune. I enjoyed the song more than I ever had before. She sang it beautifully.

The music video itself was simply shot. It was a mixture of Jack, sitting in various spots strumming her guitar and singing her song. She looked like the girl in the pictures Jack, not the girl I recognized. When the camera wasn't following Jack around it was showing her running through a field. The sun was in the same position as it had been in her cover shots, so I assumed this video and the photos must have been taken on the same day. The video was sweet and when I finished watching, I felt satisfied. It was a good song, but I knew that a long time ago.

As the credits rolled afterwards, I took a minute to reflect on this experience. Hopefully, Jack would be messaging me in a few seconds, and I would have to tell her something. I could easily tell her that I loved the song because that was the absolute truth. I thought it was wonderful. I can honestly say that it was even better than it used to be, because it was.

To be perfectly frank, the new Jack was kind of amazing. I was a little bit in awe of her. Jack had successfully morphed into someone I could see selling millions of records and performing in front of large audiences. But if that was the case, why did the pit of my stomach keep turning over and over? What didn't I like about the new Jack?

I checked the time on the side of my computer. It had been about eight minutes since Jack, and I had hung up. She was late—per usual. I decided to give her three more minutes before I tried to dial the number that originally popped up on my phone. I actually needed these extra minutes to help me work my way through my own issues.

I closed the music video portal and hopped back to Jackie Rose's webpage. Okay, aside from the name (which for the record, I loathed), what did I dislike about this image change? I was just about to roll through the slide show again, when I saw a page entitled "wish list." I laughed a little because this had always been a big deal for Jack. Her wish list had always been as follows:

Get a record deal.

Meet Ozzy Osbourne.

Find a place where I can have a regular performance gig.

Jack's life had always been that simple. She had always been about the music, and her musical tastes had always leaned a little towards the hard side. (As a matter of fact, "Movin' On" had been the only ballad in her previous repertoire. We never thought that it would become the song that made things happen for her because it was so outside of her usual genre.) On this new wish list, I was surprised to see the following:

1. Sell a million copies of my single "Movin' On".
2. Perform with Stevie Nicks.
3. Find a place where I can have a regular performance gig.

I read number three and felt a wave of happiness wash over me. Up until that point, I thought that I was going to vomit. So much had changed about Jack. As soon as I read number two, it all came together. Jack had gone soft. The girl I knew liked to wear bright orange jack-o-lantern pants and pound heavily on her keyboard. The new Jack apparently liked to walk through abandoned fields and strum on her guitar. The old Jack wanted to party with Ozzy. The new Jack wanted to sing a ballad with Stevie. I couldn't believe it.

Just as I was about to freak out completely, my instant messenger pinged. Jack had followed through. There she was.

Jack: So—what do you think?

Me: Your song is better than ever.

Jack: Really?

Me: I'm totally impressed. You nailed it.

Jack: Do you like my new look?

Me: It's nice.

Me: You look pretty.

Jack: Thanks, friend.

Jack: What about the name?

Me: It's awful.

Me: Sorry, I can't help it.

Jack: LOL. It *is* awful. My manager recommended it. She said that it suited my new image better and I kinda agree.

Me: I can see that. I guess.

<Long pause>

Me: Your hair looks nice in the pictures.

Jack: You like it?

Me: I do. I promise.

Jack: I know I'm not tan anymore, but my skin feels better—less dry.

Me: Okay—sounds reasonable.

Jack: Do you really like it?

Me: Yes.

<Long pause>

Me: Can I ask you a question?

Jack: Yeah.

Me: Why?

Jack: Why what?

Me: Why Stevie Nicks?

Jack: Why not?

Me: Seriously—you've always been so hard rock. What happened?

Jack: It was time for me to change. Time to grow up, I guess.

Me: You don't have to give up what you love to grow up, do you?

Jack: Sometimes.

Me: But Jack, Do you really want to change who you are?

Jack: Yeah.

Me: Really?

Jack: Really, really.

Me: But Jack, you were awesome the way you were.

Jack: I'm still awesome.

Me: I know, I know. I didn't mean it like that.

Jack: I know that you didn't. I know this is a lot to take in.

Me: I'm sorry.

Jack: I'm sorry, too. I should've told you about all of these changes earlier, but I wanted to unveil it all at once and have it be a big surprise.

Me: Well, I certainly am surprised.

Jack: Good—that's what I was going for.

Me: Okay

Jack: Can you share my page with the rest of the girls?

Me: You're not going to call them? They would love to hear from you.

Jack: I'm pretty busy.

Me: Okay.

<Long pause>

Me: Yeah, I'll share it with them.

Jack: Thanks, Miss.

Me: Will I ever have to call you Jackie Rose?

Jack: Only if you want my legions of adoring fans to know who you're talking about.

Me: Okay, I could do that.

Me: Jack, are you sure you really have to make all of these changes?

Jack: I appreciate the concern, but I got this, girl. I'm cool with the changes. This is who I want to be. Promise.

Me: If you're sure . . .

Jack: I'm sure.

Me: Miss you.

Jack: Miss you, too.

Chapter Eleven

Why Must All of the Men in My Life Leave Me?

"I'm not sure that I can take much more this week," I said heavily. I was sitting beside Steve Martin at the bar of the Triple Play. It was Friday night. This week felt interminable and now Steve was trying to make it worse. The sad thing was that I wasn't sure that it could get any worse. I had been looking forward to a quiet evening because I have plans to go out with Autumn tomorrow (Powerhouse Players Club-Whoop! Whoop!), so I wasn't really in the mood for anymore shenanigans.

"Stop overreacting! You can be so dramatic when you want to," Steve sighed heavily and brushed some hair off my shoulder. He noticed that I had drained my glass and motioned to the bartender to bring us both another round. I was only drinking water, but it still felt nice to have him order me a drink. Steve's such a gentleman.

"Explain to me the situation just one more time," I begged him. I gave him my most pleading stare and he laughed in a good-natured way.

"Okay, okay," he patted my arm delicately. "Here's the story. I wasn't supposed to head back to school until the first week of September, but my itinerary has changed. I need to leave this weekend."

"Ohhh," I moaned. "You can't go. I need you."

"You don't need me," Steve said firmly.

"Yes, I do. I promise that I need you." I looked up at him and tried to put on my best smile.

"No, you really don't. You're going to be busy the rest of the weekend with Autumn. Then, you have all of Jessica's stuff next week. You won't have a spare second to breathe until next Monday and by then you'll have forgotten all about me."

"Hardly," I grunted.

"You will, you know it. Nathan will be here," he added that last bit on and gave me a sly smile. Of all my friends, Steve actually understood how I felt about Nathan. He thought it was kind of romantic that Nathan and I had maintained a friendship throughout all these years. He said that we gave the rest of the population hope. I was never quite certain what he meant by that, but it sounded polite enough, so I always took it as a compliment.

"Yeah, yeah, Nathan'll be here for two days and then what? Then, he's gone, too! Why must all the men in my life leave me?" I looked at him, searching for an answer.

"That's something I can't answer, Miss." He patted my hand again. I knew that he wanted to add something sarcastic onto the end, but I was relieved when he didn't. He was really restraining himself tonight.

"Aren't you going to miss me a little, Steve?" I tapped the top part of his hand in a rhythmic way.

"I'm going to miss you all the time. You're my pal. But it's not like I'm going to the moon. I'm just gonna go finish this law school thing and then I'll come back."

"You promise?" I asked quietly.

He put one finger under my chin and lifted it so that I was looking him in the eyes. "Of course, I promise. My dad owns that gigantic office building in the center of town. My future career is here. It's not like I could pick up and move, even if I wanted to."

That idea had honestly never occurred to me before. "Do you want to move, Steve?"

"No," Steve shrugged slightly, "I don't want to move. But you never know . . ." He allowed that last thought to trail off.

Steve wanted to move. I could tell. He'd never said anything about it before, and he might never mention it again, but I knew. I would always know that the reason he would come back to Charlotte wouldn't be because he wanted to; it would be because he felt obligated to be here.

"Steve, why do you have to finish law school? I mean, aren't you really enjoying this whole TV thing?"

He laughed and tipped his glass back slowly. He took a quick sip and looked at me with a funny expression on his face. "Yeah, Miss, I really like being on television, but I have to finish law school. I can't just quit now. Then it would've been a waste of time and money."

He was right, so I nodded thoughtfully. I could understand his need to go back to school. I was upset that he was leaving, but I wasn't totally irrational.

"I want to ask you to do something with me, but you have to promise to say yes first," he said unexpectedly. Steve was now sitting in his stool so he was looking directly at me. I turned in my chair slightly to mirror his posture. It wasn't the easiest thing to do in a tight skirt.

"I'm intrigued," I said and raised an eyebrow. I took a long drink of my water and looked at him coyly.

"Come on, Missy, you have to promise that you'll help me with this project first before I tell you about it."

"Hmmm . . . agreeing to something before I have the full details—that's not really my style, Stevie, and you know that."

"I know, I know, but it'll be as much for your benefit as it is for mine."

I pondered this for a second. Where was he going with all of this? My curiosity was piqued. Steve had a way of doing this to people. I've observed this sort of behavior before. He would lure someone into doing something for him. At first, whatever it was Steve wanted seemed like a great idea, but in the end, it always seemed to fall flat. I was hoping that this would not be one of those circumstances.

"Are you in trouble? Do you need my help with something? Because you know full well that between the two of us, you have all the legal knowledge. I would hardly be able to assist . . ." I began trying to reason through his proposition, but he cut me off.

"This has nothing to do with the law. You're right about becoming a lawyer. I'm not actually sure that it's something I want to do. I know that I want to finish the schooling, but working at my dad's practice might not be the job for me."

"So?" I asked.

"So," he said with a slow grin. "I want to pursue other ventures, but I need some help. Are you willing to help me?" The smile that he gave me next was totally unfair. He busted out his "I'm smoldering hot, totally unattainable, and also happens to be completely amazing" look and I just couldn't help myself.

"Yes, I'll help you," I agreed wholeheartedly. "Now, stop giving me that face," I added, playfully punching the side of his arm.

"Okay, now that you're on board, we can start planning. Here's what I'm thinking: You know how Ross is always on your case to start a blog?"

"Ugh," I groaned loudly. I spent a lot of time at the office. I worked weird hours, and I did a ton of news reporting, but Steve was right; Ross had been pressuring me lately to take my work home and write a blog. Needless to say, I wasn't dazzled by the idea.

"Don't moan, Missy. This is going to be a good thing. This is going to be a project that we can undertake together."

"I'm listening," I said and sighed. I gave him the "proceed" hand gesture and he continued explaining his brilliant idea to me.

"So, here's what I'm thinking. You and I should create a website together. The two of us should blog once a week and then we should also vlog once a week."

"Vlog?" I asked.

"Video blog—you know--tape ourselves ranting about something . . ."

"I knew what you meant. I just wanted some clarification."

"Okay," Steve shrugged.

"So, we'll blog and vlog. You'll appease your boss and alleviate any more future arguments that might arise about the topic, and I will still get to report the news."

"But what do we talk about? I mean, we'll be reporting from two different cities. Won't that be weird?"

"No, that's the beauty of it!" Steve clapped his hands together. He was getting really excited about this plan.

"I don't get it," I said quietly.

"Sure, you do. You're just not into it yet. Sit back. Have a real drink and let me explain it all to you." He didn't even give me a chance to respond. He motioned to the bartender to bring me a cranberry and vodka. That's not exactly my favorite drink, but I assumed that he was too worked up to remember such a minor detail.

"Okay, okay, I'll let you try to sell me on this project, but I'm not saying 'yes' yet, Steve Martin. Creating and running a website and a blog—that's a lot of work. Are you sure that you want to take all of that on and deal with your law classes, too?"

He didn't even pause. "Absolutely! I want to do this, and I want you to be my partner. We can do this together. We can take care of each other and help build our careers, side-by-side. Come on, Missy, please just promise that you'll listen for a little bit."

"I'll listen," I said grumpily just as the waiter arrived with my fresh drink. I took one look at the mixture and felt my stomach turn. I didn't want Steve to leave. On top of that, I didn't want to start some long-distance project with him. I just wanted him to stay here and hang out with me. I wanted him to continue working at WSTA and I wanted things to stay relatively normal.

But I knew I couldn't have any of that. Not only was Steve going to leave, but he was going to pressure me into doing this website thing. I just knew it. He could persuade me to do pretty much anything, so it felt like I was beaten before he even began.

I knew that I was sort of ignoring Steve right now, and even though I felt a tiny bit conflicted about it, I needed a moment to evaluate the situation. I scooted the glass away. I had no intention of drinking this alcoholic beverage. Not only did I not like the taste of it, but I wasn't in the mood for drinking tonight. I didn't feel like celebrating.

Steve was leaving. Adair was marrying Wesley. Jack was becoming a completely different person. I stared at the liquid concoction in front of me and thought about growing up. Did we have to make sacrifices in this world to get what we wanted? Did life always work that way? Couldn't we just say what we wanted and have it actually happen?

I guess maybe I knew better than that.

I gave Steve a long look and he stopped talking mid-sentence. "Are you okay, Missy?"

"Do you really want to leave me?" I asked and fought hard to swallow my tears.

"Oh, honey," Steve patted my back. "I don't want to leave you. I have to leave. There's a big difference--a huge difference."

"Yeah?" I asked quietly.

"Yeah," he echoed. "We're still going to see each other and when you agree to do this website with me, we'll still be working together. So, the only thing that will be different is that I won't be sitting beside you in some strange bar, ordering you drinks that you have no intention of drinking, and talking your ear off. That's the only thing that will change, honest."

I smiled and wiped out the tears that were threatening to spill from my eyes, quickly using the back of my hand. "You promise?" I said.

"Yes, I promise," he replied easily.

"Okay, then I promise that I'll be your partner in this project."

"Really?"

"Really, really," I responded.

"Oh, come on, Missy. You made that so easy on me!" He was joking now, and it felt good. It felt right. As much as I hated to admit it, Steve did have a good idea, and it would guarantee that we still managed to keep in touch with each other. I really couldn't argue with that.

He reached over stealthily and stole my vodka and cranberry. He tipped the glass back and drained the entire thing in one swallow. I whistled my appreciation.

"You're really excited about this, huh?"

"Absolutely!" He said and held his hand up for a high-five. I laughed brightly and hit his hand.

"You really want to work in television, don't you?" I said, hoping that my accusation wouldn't drain his energy.

Luckily, it didn't. "Yeah, I do, but please don't tell my dad." He gave me a conspiratorial wink and threw his arm around my shoulder.

Steve Martin: what was I ever going to do without this wise guy?

"So, you and Autumn are going to the strip club again tomorrow, right?" He changed the subject so quickly that I nearly couldn't keep up, but his gentle reminder made me smile from ear to ear.

"Yeah, tonight, I get to hang out with you, and then tomorrow, I get to ogle hot strippers. What more could I ask for?"

"Don't forget that Nathan's coming in next week!" Steve said loudly.

"Oh, I didn't forget. I'll get to see all my favorite guys within a week's time."

"You're one very lucky lady," Steve said and gave my shoulder a nudge.

"Yes, I am," I agreed and happily realized that I really meant it.

I have an outstanding group of friends. I couldn't be luckier. Sure, some of them would come and go, but when they were around, I vowed to make the most of the opportunity. I flagged down the bartender and asked him to refill my water. I needed to toast my new business partner!

Chapter Twelve

How Far Are You Willing to Take This?

"Okay, okay, just give me the information one more time." That was Nathan. We had been on the phone with each other for a good thirty minutes. Autumn was sitting on my bed, tapping her toe in an obnoxious way. She and I were supposed to have left for the Powerhouse Players about fifteen minutes ago, but I had received an unexpected call from Nathan that I couldn't purposely ignore.

"Alright," I said and sat down on the edge of the bed next to Autumn. She gave me an annoyed look, but scooted over so that I could sit comfortably. I smoothed my champagne-colored comforter and tried to focus my attention back on the call.

"Okay, Nate, write this down." I waited until I heard him ruffle some paper. "I live at 414 Fountain Park. The wedding starts at 1:45 and you will want to change before the ceremony, I imagine."

"Why would I want to do that?" He asked.

"Seriously?" I replied. "You'll have been in the car for seven hours. You may want to freshen up before you show up to this *formal* occasion."

"Easy there, girl--no need to get so testy. I'll shower before I go to the wedding. What else do I need to know?" he questioned, and I thought this over.

"Well, the wedding is at 1:45. It shouldn't last too long, and then the reception starts at 6:30."

"Hey, what am I supposed to do in between the wedding and the reception?" A little bit of hurt, or maybe it was annoyance, registered in his voice when he asked this question. I hadn't even contemplated it until Nathan opened his mouth. I thought quickly and gave the first response that came to mind.

"It's no problem, baby. You can just go to a bar and hang out with Autumn and the rest of the girls. Duke will be coming with Brooklyn, so you won't be alone." I looked at Autumn and gave her the thumbs up. She just shook her head and hopped up off the bed.

"Okay, okay," he said. I could hear Nate scratching his head on the other side of the phone. "So, I will meet you at the Fountain Park place before 1 and I will meet you at the reception around 7."

I pondered what he said. "I guess that's close enough," I finally decided.

"This should be fun," he said out of nowhere. "I haven't been back to Charlotte in a long time."

"I know," I said quickly. "Don't you have anyone else that you want to go see?" His family didn't live here anymore but he did still have a few friends living in the area, I thought.

"Naw," he said thoughtfully. "I really can't afford to fly down, so I'll have to drive. That really limits the time that I have there, so I need to make it count."

Autumn picked this point to clear her throat.

"Listen, Nate, I'm sorry to do this, but I have to go."

"Oh, do you have a hot date tonight?" He was teasing, but he still sounded a little offended. I think that this was a practiced voice.

"Not exactly," I said.

"Not exactly," he mimicked.

"Hey, you know, you really should get going. Don't you have a date with Terri tonight?" He had been seeing Terri for a few months. If I knew Nate, things were probably pretty serious by now, so I guessed that his Saturday night would be monopolized by his girlfriend.

"Nope," he replied. "Actually, I'm not seeing Terri tonight. We broke up last week."

"What? Why didn't you tell me?" I felt like he had held back very important information. I wasn't even considering the fact that I never tell him when my relationships come and go.

"It didn't seem like a big deal," he said, and I could imagine him shrugging his shoulders.

"Missy!" Autumn stamped her foot on the floor and pointed to the clock. I was running really late. We would have to leave in the next five minutes if we wanted to get a good seat at the club--and trust me--we wanted to get a good seat.

"Nathan, I have to go. Meet me at Fountain Park in front of my apartment at noon on Saturday. I will already be dressed, and I'll be making a special trip to meet you. You have to take a shower here and you can't be late."

"I swear I won't be late."

"See you soon," I said and hung up the phone before he had a chance to say good-bye.

I turned to Autumn. "Well, now I feel bad."

"You should," she responded. I had never heard Autumn sound like this before. I was slightly alarmed. I stood there and looked at her, but she was already in motion. She had grabbed her bag and was towing me out the front door before I knew what was happening.

As we hopped into a cab, she smoothed her hair and seemed to rearrange her expression. I waited expectantly for what she was about to say.

"Missy, why are you bringing Nathan to Adair's wedding?" She said that question in a polite enough way, and it was a valid statement, so I thought about it for a moment and then I answered.

"You see, the day I found out that Adair was engaged, I was telling Nathan . . ."

"Why did you do that?" Autumn interrupted.

"I just wanted to tell him the good news," I said with a blush on my face.

I thought back to that euphoric moment that I experienced on that day. I wanted Nathan to say that he loved me, too. I wanted everything to be perfect. I wanted . . . I wanted . . . I wanted . . .

"No, you didn't," Autumn spat. She saw through my lie.

I bowed my head and she continued.

"Why did you tell Nathan when you found out that Adair was engaged? If you wanted to share the good news, you could have called any of us. You were the first to know, and *we* would have actually cared."

I thought over her statement for a minute. I even thought about telling her the truth. But the truth was too painful. I couldn't tell her that I told Nathan that I still loved him. I couldn't tell her that he laughed at me. I couldn't tell her those things because I just felt so pathetic.

I began to sag a little in the seat and Autumn grabbed my arm and hoisted me up. "I'm sorry if I'm being a little brutal with your feelings, but you have got to pick a side on this Nathan issue. Do you love him? Do you hate him? Do you want us to play nice with him? Frankly, I can't keep up."

I knew what she meant. I don't know why I couldn't find a safe side within the Nathan argument.

"I want you to be nice to him," I mumbled.

"Okay," Autumn pinched my arm. "Now we're making progress. But back to my original question: Why is he coming with you to Adair's wedding?"

I looked up at her then. I didn't know exactly what she meant. I was waiting for clarification.

"What I mean is: Why him? You could ask out anybody. You have plenty of guy friends and there are certainly quite a few people who are more than friends that you could take. I'm sure that Steve Martin would have been happy to be your date for this. Why did you pick Nathan?"

I didn't know how to answer this. I didn't feel like I had chosen Nathan. I felt like he had wanted me, and it had been a long time since I was in that position with him. It felt nice that he was making plans around me. Plus, a big part of me wanted him around.

When Autumn realized that I wasn't going to answer, she changed her topic, slightly.

"Let me ask you this: If you are so eager to have Nathan back in your life, then what are we doing frequenting strip clubs every weekend?"

This was our third week in a row. Autumn and I had both attended Adair's bachelorette party at the Powerhouse Players Club, and then we went back again. Tonight was going to mark our third consecutive week.

"I don't know," I answered. "I just keep getting this rush every time I see that one guy . . . "

"Gabriel," she finished for me.

"Yeah," I sighed deeply. He was so good-looking; my insides actually hurt just thinking about him.

"Listen, kid," Autumn paused to look out the window, and then looked back at me. "I'll make you a deal. We'll go to the male revue tonight, but if you don't score with Gabriel tonight, then we'll take a break."

I thought it over for a minute. What did she mean by "score"?

"This offer is non-negotiable," Autumn added, and I gave her a perplexed look.

"Missy, we're grown adults. One of our best friends is getting married next week. We can't keep chasing after relationships that aren't meant to happen."

Just then, the cab pulled up in front of the Powerhouse Players Club. As I paid the driver and slid out the side door, I wondered exactly which relationship she was talking about: Mine and Nathan's or mine and Gabriel's.

It had certainly been a wild night. Because I was fairly certain that this was going to be my last hoorah at this particular venue, I decided to make the best of it. I actually flirted with the strippers, and I paid extra so that Roman would dance on Autumn for a full five minutes. This special attention put her in a great mood, and she managed to lighten up pretty quickly.

After Gabriel's first set, I found that I couldn't tear my eyes off him. I knew that he had noticed me--really noticed me-- during his last number. I think that he was starting to recognize my face. I guess that things like that happen when you go to the same club three weeks in a row.

When he climbed down off the stage, I wondered what he was up to. He was still wearing nothing but his combat boots and a G-string, so naturally, all eyes in the place were glued to his strong body. He was carefully weaving his way through the crowd. I could have sworn that he was coming in my direction, when a woman wearing a tiara--a bachelorette--hopped in front of him. She started swaying in time with the music and she grabbed his hand and deposited a wad of bills into it.

He reacted in the natural way; he picked her up over his shoulder and began to walk with her toward the V.I.P. section of the room. I had never been into the V.I.P. division. Frankly, I had my reservations about the place. I didn't really want to know what happened back there or what money could buy once you got in. It was reserved for all of the special lap dances, and at heart, I'm still a little naïve, so I liked to pretend that the only thing going on back there was dancing.

For some reason though, maybe because I knew that tonight was my last night, I followed Gabriel and the bachelorette with my eyes as they crossed into the V.I.P. area. Even though it was dark, even darker than the club, I could see into the room slightly. They had taken a spot right across from the entrance, so I could see most of what was going on.

"Look," I said and nudged Autumn. She turned to watch with me as Gabriel began doing a private routine for the woman.

"Where did he get a belt?" Autumn asked, just as I was thinking the same thing. She slurped the last of her amaretto sour and began to wave to the waiter. Back in the V.I.P. lounge, Gabriel was walking in front of the woman, cracking a belt on the ground like it was a leather whip.

"So, that's how he likes to play in the V.I.P. room." As I said it, Autumn giggled. We had just started to laugh when Gabriel turned around and saw us looking at him. He cracked the belt one more time and Autumn and I abruptly turned in our seats. We had been caught looking. Oops.

We tried to enjoy the show that was happening onstage, but it was no use. Autumn was really only into Roman, and some other stripper named Nero. But my mind was preoccupied by Gabriel. He had been back in that room an awfully long time. Just as I was about to dismiss myself to go to the bathroom, I felt a hand graze my shoulder. The hand was sweat soaked, and I didn't have to turn around to know who it belonged to.

He slid his hand down my shoulder and intertwined his fingers with my own.

"Come on," he whispered, as he pulled me up out of the chair. I quickly grabbed my purse and noticed the look of pure astonishment on Autumn's face as I allowed myself to be towed away.

I locked my grip even tighter on Gabriel's hand and let him lead me through the club. I thought that he was taking me back to the V.I.P. room, but then we swerved in a completely different direction. We came to a stop in front of the bar.

Standing there with him, I suddenly felt very self-conscious. I adjusted my dress and looked down at his bulging G-string. I felt myself gulp and my palms began to sweat profusely. I quickly let go of his hand. He ordered two beers from the bartender, and he handed one to me.

"Do you want to go . . .?" I started to say, and I motioned towards the V.I.P. area.

"Naw. I don't want to take you in there," he answered smoothly.

I felt a little ashamed and a little hurt.

Why didn't he want to take me in there?

He must have noticed the look on my face. "If we go in there, you have to pay me. And the things I want to do to you . . ." he paused and looked right into my eyes, "I want to do for free."

I felt myself gulp again. I felt like such a juvenile. I had no idea how to handle myself around this guy. Not only was he devastatingly attractive, but he was also oozing sexuality. It was his job. And, man, oh man, was he doing it well.

"Can you wait here for a few minutes?" He asked the question and I realized again that he was still close to my face. I tried to take a deep breath and I realized that I liked having him that close to me. I nodded and smiled broadly. He grabbed my right hand quickly and kissed it, and then he ran off towards the back of the stage.

A few minutes later, he emerged from the dressing room. He had not showered, but he looked cleaner. He had on a tight white T-shirt and a pair of light blue jeans. He looked so amazing that I felt awkward just standing around waiting for him.

He took his place back beside me and motioned for me to sit on a barstool.

"So, do you want another beer?" he asked.

"No, I'm good. Thanks," I answered. He nodded towards the barkeep and the man delivered a Bud Light in a matter of seconds. Gabriel took a long drink and then turned to me. Even offstage, his eyes still appeared to be black. They were so piercing.

"So, what's your name?" he asked.

"My name's Missy," I answered.

"I'm Jesse, Missy."

I raised my eyebrows at this little peek into his private life.

"Gabriel's my stage name. It always seems a little weird to me, but it's important that we protect our identities," he said with a shrug.

Kind of like a superhero.

"I can understand that," I nodded and took a drink of my beer.

"Did you like the show tonight?" He asked.

"Are you kidding?" I said this with a grin, and I was pleased because his face immediately broke out into a smile as well.

"Well, I supposed that since you and your friend there came back a few weeks now that we were doing something right."

"That's an understatement," I said, and he laughed at my honesty. In his last statement and especially in his laugh, I heard something that I hadn't imagined would be there before. He had a serious southern accent. Now, don't get me wrong-- most people in North Carolina had some sort of accent. But his was different. It was distinct. I knew instantly that he, like me, was an outsider.

"Jesse, I love your accent." I blushed even as I said. There were a lot of things that I wanted to compliment him on, but his accent was the one I had chosen.

He grinned in my direction, and I continued, "Where are you from?"

He leaned close to me and explained, "I live here now, but I'm from Texas. I grew up there, but then I joined the Marines. I moved here shortly after I was discharged."

My eyebrows shot up.

"I was injured in the line of duty," he said.

The look of surprise was still on my face. For the first time, I noticed that maybe he wasn't as young as I had originally calculated. Maybe there was more to this Jesse than just a pretty face and a tattooed back side.

Even though he was fully clothed now, I surveyed his body. I ran my mental image of him repeatedly. I even allowed my hands to run up and down his smooth arms. He didn't seem to mind.

"But wait if you don't mind my asking . . . I feel like I have seen a lot of your body, and I've never seen any wounds. How could you have been injured in the line of duty?"

He gave a short barking laugh, and he patted my hand. "First of all, you haven't seen ev'ry part of my body." His eyebrows arched meaningfully, and he continued, "Second, you can't really see the injuries when I'm up on stage. The lights white 'em out."

"Oh," I said and felt bashful again. I quickly removed my hands from his arms. But he swiftly grabbed my hand and placed it into his own. He didn't seem to mind the physical contact.

To change the subject and draw the focus away from my nerves, I asked him the first question that came to mind: "Why are you dressed?"

"What?" he asked and quickly swallowed his beer before it burst out of his lips.

I knew that I was making a tremendous fool of myself, but I kept going. "I mean," I said, "normally, you perform all night long. But tonight, here you are, all dressed and not performing. Don't you have to go back up onstage tonight?"

"Okay, okay, I see where you're goin'," he answered thoughtfully and took a minute to think before continuing. Then he said what I assumed was as honest as they came. "I saw you here a few weeks ago. I wanted to talk to you then, but I didn't want to embarrass ya in front of ya girls. Then, when ya'll came back last week, I was a fixin' to track you down after the show to see if ya wanted to hang out afterward. "

I thought back to last week.

"But..." he said, as if he were reading my mind, "you and your girl there," he motioned back over his shoulder, "left early. You didn't even stay for the final set."

He was right; Autumn and I had left abruptly. Hope had agreed to pick us up from the club, and she said that she wouldn't be willing to play chauffeur after 1 a.m. Note to self: Remind Hope later that she totally blew it for me. Well, maybe not totally . . .

He went on, "So this week, when I saw ya'll walk in the door, I knew that I couldn't miss my chance. I had to get ya alone and talk." He looked deeply into my eyes, and I felt a little flutter flip through my stomach. He was, in a word, breathtaking. I just kept looking at him, and the odd thing was that he didn't break the stare either. We both just sat and looked into each other's eyes for a few minutes.

It was the bartender who finally pulled us out of our reverie. "What else can I get you, Jesse?" He plopped in front of us and struck up a conversation. The two colleagues spoke to one another for a few minutes, and I nodded my head politely throughout. Pretty quickly, a server appeared at the end of the bar, and he began squawking for the barkeep's attention. I was relieved that he disappeared. I wanted Jesse all to myself.

As soon as the bartender strode away, Jesse ran his hand up and down the length of my arm. He asked, "Now, what do you do for a livin'?"

It was an hour after last call and Jesse and I were still perched at the bar. It hadn't exactly been a first date, but we had shared a lot of first date information. I knew quite a little bit about this exotic dancer, and likewise, he was starting to get a good clear picture of who I was. We had been very flirtatious throughout the evening, and part of me was wondering if we would amp things up at the end of the night. I'm not the kind to participate in one-night stands, so I make it a priority not to sleep with someone after a first date. But this wasn't technically a first date, and my hormones were going crazy. I was this close to suggesting the V.I.P. lounge again, when suddenly the stripper known as Nero appeared on my right side.

He was towing Autumn along behind him. I had actually forgotten that she was even here. She looked at me and giggled a little. For the first time in hours, I began to wonder what she had been up to.

"Jesse, it's time to go, man." Nero took Autumn's hand and gave her a kiss. Then he put her hand onto the back of my bar stool. "I've got to work tomorrow morning."

"Missy, this is Charlie," Jesse said and took a moment to introduce us. I returned the favor by introducing Autumn.

Even though Autumn was now waiting right behind me, and Charlie was clearly also ready to vacate, Jesse and I just sat still a moment longer. In a series of very smooth motions, Jesse reached behind the bar and produced both a napkin and a pen.

The bar napkin and the pen reminded me of Cowboy. The last time I wrote my number onto a bar napkin, the results had really devastated my life. Even though I had a good time with Cowboy, and I had genuinely liked him, I made a huge mistake by allowing myself to fall for him. I eyed Jesse now with those same critical thoughts in mind.

"I was wondering if you'd give me yer phone number. I'd like to give ya a call sometime," he said as he slid the paper in my direction.

His smile was so earnest, and the tone of his voice was so sincere, I appreciatively took the piece of paper. But even though I was trapped in this weird sort of melting zone, I hadn't totally lost my mind. I scribbled my name and number onto the nearby beverage napkin and started to hand it back to him, but I stopped before completion. I leaned into him very closely and whispered, "Jesse, listen--I don't give my number out to very many guys. I want to give it to you, but I won't do it if you won't call."

He examined me very closely for a moment and then without taking a breath he said, "Oh, I'll call. I'll definitely call you."

Less than a week later, my life was a whirlwind. Even though I was not the one getting married, I felt overwhelmed by the enormity of the whole ceremony. Everyone was hustling and bustling, except for Adair. She was in the eye of the storm. She was perfectly calm and collected. While her mother and all the bridesmaids were fretting over the final details, she was cool as a cucumber. I just think that she was genuinely happy to be getting married to Wesley.

The rehearsal and the dinner went by so quickly that I barely realized what was happening. The pastor that the couple had elected to perform the ceremony was a gentle man and he had baptized Adair when she was a baby. It was also very nice to see Jess' family. Her mother looked great, and her dad was all smiles. The Adair family was sincerely happy on this occasion.

After the rehearsal dinner, I had the joy of driving to the airport to pick up Benson. She had been able to scrape together a few funds after all, and she was flying in pretty late that night. I couldn't wait to spend a little time with her on the ride back from the airport. Even though I had offered my room for her visit, she had declined. And honestly, I was grateful. Now that Nathan was staying with me, I really didn't have room for another houseguest.

My job was to pick up Benson from the airport and then drop her off at Autumn's house. Autumn had plenty of room, so it actually made sense for Benson to stay there. I had to borrow Hope's car again to run this errand, but she understood the importance of me spending time with my friend.

Even though the ride back from the airport didn't take more than twenty minutes, Benson and I had a great time catching up. We had spoken briefly throughout the week, but we really hadn't touched on too many important topics.

Of course, I began the conversation by asking about Jack. Benson had seen her one more time in the last two weeks, and that was when she came to pick up her keyboard and her closet full of clothes. I got the feeling that Jess didn't really want to talk about Jack, and I couldn't blame her. I quickly changed the subject and was pleased to regale Jess with my tale about Jesse, the stripper.

"Only you," she laughed and shook her head.

"What?" I squawked.

"Only you would pick up a stripper one night and make him promise to call you later," Benson snickered and rolled down the window so that the night air would blow across her face.

"Well, if it makes any difference, he hasn't even called," I said this in a little bit of a huffy manner. I'm not going to lie. I was a little peeved that he promised he would call and didn't."

"I can't believe that," Jess said and I wasn't sure if she was being serious or mocking me. Either way, I decided to slough it off and I jumped back into more news.

"So, Nathan's coming in tomorrow," I started, but she gasped.

"*Nathan's* coming in tomorrow?" She repeated what I had just said, except that she appeared shocked and a bit dismayed.

"Yeah," I shrugged. "I thought that I told you." It was no large secret that Benson didn't like Nathan very much. First and foremost, she never forgave him for cheating on me in college. Second, he had been awfully nasty to her when we were in school, too. She had been dating one of his best friends and Nathan was always trying to make waves in that relationship.

"No, you didn't tell me," she said emphatically and turned in her seat sideways so that she was looking directly at me.

"Missy, what are you up to?" I could feel the accusation lurking in her voice. I kept driving and didn't respond.

"Just how far are you willing to take this thing?" She sounded a little bit angry, and I thought that it was odd that for the second time in a week, my girlfriends were giving me a hard time about Nathan.

"I don't know what you mean," I said as calmly as I could.

"You know exactly what I mean," she said flatly.

I kept my eyes focused on the road. "Benson, I'm sorry that I didn't tell you that Nathan is my date to the wedding, but it's the truth. I really thought that I'd mentioned it already. Either way, he'll be here tomorrow."

As I finished my sentence, I pulled off the highway and onto Autumn's street.

Benson shook her head, "I understand how you feel about him; really, I do. But I don't understand you. You have a perfectly good stripper wanting to take you out and you go and call Nathan--a guy who has broken your heart at least a dozen times. It doesn't make any sense!"

I laughed as I turned into Autumn's driveway. "A perfectly good stripper?" I echoed her sentiments.

"Yes!" She laughed too, but I could tell that she was still upset with me.

"He hasn't even called me, Jess," I said.

"But he will," she replied.

I put on the brake, turned the key back towards me, and eased my foot away from the pedal. I shifted in my seat so that I could look at Jessica.

"He may call, but he hasn't. Besides, Nathan and I are just going to the wedding tomorrow as friends. We made these plans months ago. It's no big deal."

"Nothing between you and Nathan will ever be 'no big deal,'" she sighed, raising her hands in the air to put virtual air quotes around the major phrase.

"I'm serious, dude."

"You're going to sleep with him," she said and punched me in the arm.

"No, I'm not." I felt my voice take on a high-pitched tone.

"Yes, you are. And then we will see just how big a deal it all is to you then."

"No, I'm not." I raised my chin defiantly.

"Yeah, okay," she guffawed.

"Harumph," I snorted and averted my eyes so that I was now looking out into the black night.

"Missy, let me tell you a story that I read just the other day." Benson cleared her throat and looked in my direction to see that I wasn't totally blowing her off. Even though I wanted to ignore her, it was seldom that I was graced by her company, so I made the effort to perk up my ears and turn my eyes her way.

"I was reading a book last week about Joan of Arc. As you know, she was young and valiant. As I'm sure you are also aware, she was burnt at the stake. She died for her cause. She is now considered a martyr and some people worship her like a saint."

"Okay?" I questioned. I have to admit; I had no idea where Benson was going with this story.

"The book that I was reading claimed that while Joan of Arc was burning on the pyre she was relaxed and calm. She took her punishment with grace and her veiled expression seemed to be her last act of defiance. She went to her grave confident that she was doing the right thing, even though she must have been experiencing excruciating agony."

"I don't get it," I started to interject, but Benson silenced me with a wave of her hand.

"You remind me a little of Saint Joan, Missy. Even though your relationship with Nathan burns you up inside, you can't just give it up. You hold your head high and take exactly whatever he decides to deliver your way next. You act like he is this mission that's worth fighting for and that you're willing to do anything to defend him."

"But here's the big difference, Miss. Nathan isn't a cause that's worth the trouble. You're not going to become a saint after fighting this battle. You're only going to have to suffer the repercussions. Unlike Joan of Arc, your purpose in this relationship isn't worthy, and this is not a noble sacrifice. It's just a painful one."

Ouch.

Just then, Autumn's light came on. We saw her silhouette appear on the front porch and I knew that it would be rude to keep her waiting.

I got out of the car and began helping Benson unload her travel cases.

"I'll see you at the wedding tomorrow, buddy," I said and gave Benson a quick hug.

She pulled back from me and held me at arm's length. "Missy," she said softly. "As your friend, can I just make one request?"

I nodded and she proceeded, "Before you sleep with Nathan tomorrow just think about how far you really want this relationship to go. Do you really want to invest time in him, even though he lives hundreds of miles away? Do you really want to fall in love with him again?"

I nodded at Jessica again, gave her another quick hug, and scooted her towards Autumn's front door.

The next night, after Adair's gorgeous ceremony and so many glasses of champagne that I lost count, I heard Benson's words echoing through my head.

As I unzipped my "Pool Blue" bridesmaid's gown and let it cascade to the ground, I couldn't stop myself from thinking: "How far do I want this to go? Do I really want to fall in love with him again?" Before my mind could formulate the answers, I was crawling into bed and wrapping my arms around Nathan.

End of Book Two

Mindy Killgrove is the author of the Kate Kellner Trilogy, the Missy Lawrence Trilogy, the Kanedy Productions Trilogy, and is the creator of the RILEY ROUNDTREE SOCIAL STORY LEARNING ADVENTURE SERIES. Killgrove is also a professional ghostwriter. She has penned one play, forty-one short stories, and thirty-six novels all while working as a freelance author.

She has a bachelor's degree from Heidelberg University and a master's degree from Bowling Green State University. She lives in Orlando, Florida with her adoring husband and three rambunctious, but beautiful children. When she's not writing or reading, she's exploring local theme parks, lounging on the beach, or aiming to bake the very best chocolate chip cookies in the world.

Explore more at www.mindykillgrove.com

The
Mindy Killgrove
Collection
Don't miss one of Mindy Killgrove's stories.
THE MISSY LAWRENCE TRILOGY
Meet Me at the Pond
Meet Me at Fountain Park
Meet Me at Blessed Creek
THE KATE KELLNER TRILOGY
Kate Kellner Throws a Wicked Changeup
Kate Kellner Throws a Filthy Drop Curve
Kate Kellner Throws a Perfect Game
KANEDY PRODUCTIONS PRESENTS TRILOGY
Royally Engaged
Majestically Married
The Princely Prize
EDUCATIONAL MATERIALS
If Teachers Could Talk...
CHILDREN'S BOOKS
The Riley Roundtree Social Story Learning Adventure Series